P9-DBM-280

ONCE UPON A *Holiday*

ONCE UPON A *Holiday*

BEVERLY JENKINS
ADRIANNE BYRD
KIMBERLY KAYE TERRY

ARABESQUE®

ISBN-13: 978-0-373-83191-3

ONCE UPON A HOLIDAY
© 2010 by Harlequin Books S.A.

The publisher acknowledges the copyright holders
of the individual works as follows:

HOLIDAY HEAT
Copyright © 2010 by Beverly Jenkins

CANDY CHRISTMAS
Copyright © 2010 by Adrianne Byrd

CHOCOLATE TRUFFLES
Copyright © 2010 by Kimberly Kaye Terry

Recycling programs
for this product may
not exist in your area.

www.kimanipress.com

Printed in U.S.A.

Dear Reader,

For this year's Arabesque holiday collection we decided to turn up the heat with some of the sexiest stories yet. Written by three authors known for their sizzling romances, *Once Upon a Holiday* includes fan favorites Beverly Jenkins, Adrianne Byrd and Kimberly Kaye Terry.

Beverly Jenkins's *Holiday Heat* tells the story of what happens when two hard-driving law enforcement agents—Eve Clark and Leyton Palmer—attend a masquerade ball that ends in a night of unbridled passion. But when the two can't seem to forget their anonymous encounter, the quest to rekindle that night becomes an obsession.

In Adrianne Byrd's *Candy Christmas* corporate rivals Montel Starks and Candy Lahane discover that their feud is more than just gamesmanship. To earn a coveted promotion, the two find that their competition ultimately leads to the bedroom, not the boardroom.

Ecstatic about her new promotion, Camille Jackson celebrates with a mind-blowing one-night stand in Kimberly Kaye Terry's *Chocolate Truffles*. Little does she know that her lover, Gideon Taber, will resurface in a most embarrassing way. But this time, they're no longer strangers and he has ideas about a more permanent relationship.

I hope you enjoy these super-sexy stories—something to keep you warm on those chilly winter nights.

Happy holidays,

Evette Porter
Editor

CONTENTS

A big thank-you goes out to Lt. Omar Davidson
of the Detroit Police and Fire Arson Squad,
and ATF Agent Fred Sharp for taking time
out of their busy day to answer my many questions.
Their help was priceless.

HOLIDAY HEAT
Beverly Jenkins

Chapter 1

Eve Clark looked around at all the goings-on in the large backyard of the home where she'd grown up. She smiled as she took in the legion of Detroit relatives that had gathered at her aunt and uncle's place that Saturday to celebrate her Aunt Rina's fifty-seventh birthday. Spread out across the yard were teenage cousins and their friends, little cousins playing with hula hoops and video games, while the uncles swapped lies and slapped dominoes. Some of the women, mostly Eve's aunts, were seated in lawn chairs underneath the big maple tree laughing and no doubt gossiping, while alternately yelling at grandkids and making sure the food on the picnic tables didn't run low. It was a typical Clark gathering, one of the few Eve had been able to attend because of the demands of her job as an ATF agent based in Chicago. In a few days she'd be back at work, but right now she was on vacation and enjoying just being a member of the family.

The birthday party, which was the day before Halloween,

was originally supposed to be held indoors. But because the weather was so beautiful for late October in Michigan, everything was moved outside to take advantage of the glorious day.

When seven-year-old Eve had lost her parents in a fire, Uncle Walt and Aunt Rina had stepped in to raise her. Even though they already had a daughter, Shelly, they still loved and nurtured Eve as if she was their own. Eve would be the first to admit that while growing up, her cousin Shelly had been the adventurous one and had gotten them into more scrapes than Aunt Rina could shake a finger at. But Eve's line of work had given her the edge in the adventure department now, even if a good portion of her days involved sitting at her desk doing paperwork.

Eve sighed as she saw her cousin Shelly making her way over to where she was sitting. She and Shelly were more like sisters than cousins. And for the past month Shelly had been calling and sending endless e-mails, trying to convince her to attend a big Halloween masquerade ball in Detroit. Eve had no desire to attend, but Shelly being Shelly, she'd refused to take no for an answer.

"Hey cuz," Shelly said, taking a seat in one of the empty lawn chairs. She put her plate of food on the table between them. "I've finished your costume and you are going to love it." Shelly was an award-winning Hollywood costume designer.

"But I'm not going, remember?"

Shelly shook her head, using her plastic fork to cut the edge of her ham. "How can a kick-ass woman like you be afraid of a Halloween party?"

"I'm not scared. I'm just not interested."

"It's going to be fun."

"Being hooked up with a stranger doesn't sound like fun to me, just strange."

"Where's your sense of adventure?"

"Back in my office in Chicago."

"Chicken."

Eve rolled her eyes.

Shelly took a sip of her Kool-Aid. "You need to put that ATF badge down for a night and get your freak on. Nobody will know it's you. That's the beauty of it."

"No."

"Suppose you get hooked up with a man who could make you forget all about saving the world."

"Yeah, right."

"The people who are invited are all quality, grown-folks, Eve. They've been vetted."

"I got that part, but I'm still passing."

"Why?"

"Because ATF agents don't get their freak on. I'm on the national task force, which means I'm on call 24/7. Suppose I catch a case in the middle of this? What am I supposed to do, grab my stuff and run out of the ball like Cinderella?"

"Suppose you don't get a call? I think you're just looking for excuses, Wonder Woman."

Eve smiled and looked away.

Shelly asked, "When was the last time you were with a man who wasn't in handcuffs in the backseat of a squad car?"

"None of your business," Eve tossed back, laughing softly.

"Uh-huh. You ought to try it. If you go to the masquerade ball you won't have to go looking for a man. The hosts will hook you up."

Eve still wasn't buying. Shelly pressed harder. "It's not every day that you get the chance to spend the night in a luxury suite complete with food and champagne free of charge. If the two of you just want to talk, that's okay."

"No."

"Come on," she pleaded. "Think of all the hours I spent slaving over this costume."

The persistent whine made Eve chuckle and remember all the other times her cousin had talked her into situations, some good, some bad, but none this outrageous. "So what's this costume look like?"

"It's a surprise."

Eve threw up her hands. "I know I'm not going now."

Shelly laughed. "No, it's one of the best costumes I've ever done. Everyone in my shop's excited. It's hot. It's classy. It's you, Eve. It'll have tongues falling on the ground all over the place. And besides, you know I'm going to hound you about going until you say yes, so save yourself the trouble, and just give in."

"You know I can kick your ass, right?"

Shelly grinned and stuck a celery stick in her mouth. "But you love me, so you won't."

She was right of course. Eve also knew that Shelly wasn't kidding about hounding her to the grave. It was one of the things she did best, besides costume design. Eve exhaled audibly. "Okay, I give up. But if I wind up shooting somebody, it'll be your fault."

"I love you, too. And by the way, I can't go."

"What!"

"I can't. Some producer didn't like the costumes created by another designer and so he wants me to see what I can do to fix them. Guess the director's having a meltdown. I'm flying back to L.A. in a few hours."

"So, I'm going to this madness alone?"

"Looks that way."

Eve never ceased to be amazed by her cousin's audacity, and today was no exception. "I'm going to kill you, you know that, right?"

Shelly simply smiled.

After the party had ended and the family had cleared off the table and moved everything back inside, people began to say their goodbyes. Since she'd arrived in Detroit a few days before, Eve had been staying at a hotel downtown because her aunt and uncle's house had been turned into a boardinghouse with so many out-of-town family guests. The room that had once belonged to her and Shelly now held five air mattresses, with four of the younger girls sharing two twin-size beds. Most of them would be heading home tomorrow.

"When are you going back to Chicago?" her aunt asked Eve as she and Uncle Walt walked her out to her rental car.

"Bright and early Monday morning. Shelly talked me into going to a masquerade party tomorrow night so I'll do that and then fly home." Shelly had already left for the airport, having put the box with the costume in the trunk of Eve's car. Her aunt gave her a long, loving hug.

"Been wonderful having you home. Next time you come, stay longer."

Eve tightly embraced the woman she cared for like no other. Her aunt had shared her terrible grief when Ginger—Eve's mom and Rina's older sister—had been killed. "I will."

They broke their hug. "And go to the party. No excuses. You're way too serious to be under forty. Have some fun."

Uncle Walt said, "Leave her alone."

Eve grinned and shared a strong hug with him, too. He kissed her on the forehead. "She's a crime fighter," he said proudly. "She's supposed to be serious."

"Thank you, Uncle Walt. You understand."

"That's because I used to fight crime, too." Uncle Walt was a retired police officer. There were a slew of cops and firefighters in the Clark family. Law enforcement seemed to be in their blood.

Her smiling aunt asked Eve, "Are you coming for Sunday dinner tomorrow?"

"If you're cooking, I'm eating."

"One o'clock."

"Yes, ma'am."

That said, she walked over to the car and got in. With a grin and a wave, she pulled off.

After Sunday dinner at her aunt's, Eve drove back to her hotel room. Although she'd told Shelly she'd attend the party tonight, she still wasn't sure. On the one hand, it had been a long time since she'd had any real fun, but who went to a party where you drew a number for the person you were going to spend the evening with? The ball was being given by a hotshot Hollywood producer who obviously had too much money and not enough to do with it if this was any indication.

She looked over at the large box lying on the bed. Her costume was inside, but she hadn't opened it yet. She placed her hands on the vanity table and stared back at her reflection in the big mirror hanging above. "Well, Clark, what's it going to be? At least open the box."

What she found inside made her cover her mouth with both embarrassment and awe. She picked up the costume in sheer disbelief. The black leather garment practically slithered out of the box and announced itself as the sexiest, most jaw-dropping catsuit she'd ever seen. But it wasn't just a catsuit. A band of soft gold lamé adorned the low-cut, V-neckline like the wings of a seagull in flight. Two odd-looking sleeves—she guessed they were sleeves—made of the same gold fabric were draped in rings from either side. A gold sash around the waist completed the outfit. Shelly hadn't lied about its effects. Any man crossing her path was going to keel over dead. "Shelly, Shelly, Shelly? What are we going to do with you? I can't wear this."

Holding the catsuit up against her body, she walked back over to the mirror. At age thirty-five, Eve had a body like seventies film icon Pam Grier, with the height and stature to represent. The catsuit would hug her frame like steam on glass.

Despite her reservations, she loved it. Every Halloween, Eve would dress up as a female superhero. One year she'd been Wonder Woman, then Super Girl. She'd even been Shera from the old eighties cartoon and had been ecstatic after finding out that the costume had come with plastic arm guards and a sword. Even back then she'd wanted to save the world. Shelly knew her entirely too well.

She found a pair of black leather short-heeled boots in the box that were as soft and well-made as the catsuit. There was also a black domino and a tiara-like headdress made of rigid fret-worked leather that looked like a series of stylized thunderbolts. Under the headdress was another smaller box and a folded note. Eve opened the note and read:

All Hail Great Warrior Goddess Oya!
Oya is the Warrior Goddess of the Yoruba people of Africa. She rules over tornadoes, wind, lightning, fire and magic. In the comics, she goes by the name of Storm and in the movies she's played by Halle Berry. Have fun. Love, Shelly

Eve's amusement showed in a shake of her head. "I can't wear this."

But the more she looked at the suit the more she kept saying, why not? Shelly's assessment of her bleak life had been close to the truth. Eve's last serious relationship had ended two years ago. He worked as an EMT for the city of Chicago and he'd resented the travel her job required, her male colleagues and her salary. Plenty of men admired her body and her looks, but she'd yet to find one secure enough to handle her strength and intelligence. Tonight would definitely be a walk on the wild side for her, but she couldn't pass up wearing something so gorgeous. She could always go back to saving the real world in the morning.

When she'd finished dressing, she took a look at herself in the mirror and grinned. The catsuit was sizzling. The black leather slid over her Junoesque proportions like butter. The seagull-like wingspan spread across her bustline in tandem with the golden swath around her waist set off her body like—bam! The oval-shaped sleeves that hung below her bare shoulders and the banded, low-cut neckline framed her toned biceps like two golden bracelets.

The small box under the note held a long silver wig with bangs. She put it on, styled it so that it looked good and put on her lightning bolt tiara. With the headdress positioned just so, the long, silver hair flowed behind her like an African waterfall. *No disrespect intended, but Ms. Berry, eat your heart out.*

To give herself just a touch more of the exotic, she added green contacts. In the early days of her career in law enforcement, Eve had done more undercover assignments than she cared to talk about. Because of her theater background in college, she had gone undercover disguised as everything from a crackhead to the haughty daughter of an African despot in an illegal weapons case. Her reflection told her that this might be some of her best work yet. She looked good. Damn good. She turned to check out the rear view. *Not bad.* She was a little wider than a decade ago, but thanks to her time in the gym, everything was still tight and where it should be.

She was still somewhat concerned about being paired up with a stranger for the evening. But she knew that if anything stupid jumped off, she had her training and the Glock in her small evening bag to back her up. She was required to carry her weapon with her at all times, even when posing as an African goddess.

The only thing left to do was to tie on the black velvet domino mask. It covered her eyes and was accented here and there with tiny sequins. Shelly had outdone herself. No wonder production companies were beating down her door. The girl had skills.

According to the engraved invitation, a car would be coming to transport her to the hotel where the party was being held. Taking one last look at herself, a smiling Eve wrapped the soft black cape Shelly had also provided around her shoulders and headed for the door.

Chapter 2

The hotel's large ballroom was decorated with black and orange streamers, elaborately carved pumpkins that were lit inside with candles and black cats. Hanging from the ceiling were animatronic witches, cackling and riding brooms as ghosts floated nearby. There were five food stations, two bars and a DJ playing 80s music. Mist from a fog machine rolled over the floor while the sounds of laughter and the din of conversation from the costumed guests competed with the volume of the music.

Through the eyes of his centurion-style helmet, Leyton Palmer assessed the gorgeous women milling about. Of course, with their faces masked, it was impossible to tell what they really looked like, but he was enjoying fantasizing about the French maids, she-devils, Playboy Bunnies and the five Tina Turners he spotted in the crowd. A dark-skinned Cleopatra sauntered by and gave him a saucy wink. He toasted her with his glass of soda and let her stroll on by. He appreciated the wink, but, unlike the rest of the revelers, he was working.

He'd had no idea he'd be attending this party until a meeting this morning with his captain. Leyton was a cop and an arson investigator, on the force fifteen years. Thanks to the tax breaks the state had been offering film companies, Michigan was fast on its way to becoming the Hollywood of the Midwest. Stars like Clint Eastwood, Drew Barrymore and Hilary Swank all had made movies in and around the city, and more projects were rumored to follow. In the meantime, the city fathers wanted to keep the big money folks safe. Having a discreet police presence at events like this helped that agenda. And with that in mind, a few gratis tickets had been distributed to the department. Leyton had drawn the short straw in his unit and now stood dressed like a Roman soldier, complete with armor, helmet and knee-high gladiator sandals. It was one of the few costumes the university theater department had that fit his six-foot-three frame. Having taken a few drama classes in high school and college, he was comfortable in the scanty armor. Apparently the women who kept strolling by him were comfortable with it as well, but he'd much rather be in his police car patrolling the streets for the fires that habitually plagued the city during Halloween.

And then, she walked in. First you saw the hair, flowing like silver moonlight. She handed her black cape to the attendant and strode into the room. She was wearing a sexy, low-cut black catsuit with strategically placed bands of gold. The leather suit rippled sensually in rhythm with her long confident stride, and Leyton almost dropped his drink. The music stopped. Gasps were heard and men's eyes all over the room popped from their sockets and rolled around on the floor.

Storm.

She had to be. He'd been devouring comic books since

learning to read. With that hair and that black leather suit, she couldn't be anyone else. Everyone stared transfixed. She paused to let them get a good look at her masked beauty, and look he did. He instinctively knew she wouldn't be paired up with the likes of him, but just the sight of her could keep a man in erotic fantasies for weeks. Tall, the way he liked, and that body—what could he say, but, *oh, my.* He gauged her to be a little less than six feet tall and she obviously took good care of herself. She gave off an air of power that said she was indeed as strong as the costumed character she pretended to be.

Still holding everyone riveted, she walked over to an unoccupied table and took a seat. The music started up again.

For the next half hour, Leyton positioned himself so that he could keep an eye on her. He'd seen her give the room's entrances and exits a quick but nonchalant sweep, and it piqued his curiosity, as did her equally discreet look up at the sprinkler system. He had no idea why she'd be interested in the ballroom's layout, unless under that sexy leather she was either law enforcement or there to cause harm. In the meantime, men in everything from donkey to penguin costumes, pimps and airplane pilots flocked to her like geese to corn, but not one seemed to make it past hello. He sipped his soda and smiled.

As she always did, Eve took a moment to check out the crowd, the entrances and exits, the locations of the overhead sprinklers and the fire extinguishers. She knew anything could jump off at a moment's notice, and she needed to be prepared just in case. But the men who kept coming over and slyly proposing all manner of inappropriateness were getting on her last nerve. After the third indecent proposal, she decided to act like the goddess she was supposed to be and not to put up with the rude and obnoxious behavior.

She eyed the short man standing in front of her now. He was in a Mario video game costume, of all things, and obviously didn't know that a goddess looked poorly upon having her breasts leered at.

"Who are you supposed to be? Storm?" Behind his mask, she could see his eyes were shiny with liquor.

"The goddess Oya. And you are?" she asked imperiously in the African-accented voice she'd used undercover.

"I'm Mario. How about we hook up later and I show you my magic coin."

"I'm sorry to hear you're only as large as a coin. There are implants for such deficiencies you know."

He froze.

She waited.

Even with the mask on, his fury was obvious. "Bitch!"

"You say that as if it's something bad. Go away before I turn you into a toadstool."

He stormed off, tripping over a chair, which completely undermined his outraged departure.

Scanning the crowd, she was distracted by the eyes of a man dressed as a Roman centurion. He smiled under his helmet and toasted her with his glass. She gave him a regal nod and wondered who she would have to threaten in order to get the hell out of there.

Leyton watched her dispatch Fred Flintstone, a mail carrier and an old man dressed as Super Fly before he decided to make his approach. Stopping by the bar, he got another soda for himself and one for her, and headed in her direction. In the soft, southwest accent he'd picked up from living in Texas for a decade, he said to her, "Tribute from the empire, my lady."

Eve turned, and for a moment got so lost in the dark eyes gauging her from inside the brass helmet, she couldn't form a reply.

"I was going to offer my protection, but you seemed to be doing well on your own."

She took the drink he offered. He was smooth. She had to give him that, so she smiled. "It's easy when you command lightning bolts, centurion. Sit, if it pleases you."

He sat, and Eve found herself intrigued. He was obviously educated and she was pleased by the role-play. Maybe the evening wasn't going to be a waste after all. She sipped and did a quick scan of him. Six foot three, and every brown inch, hard lean muscle. Not many men could pull off a black armor-covered kilt and sandals, but his biceps and thighs looked right at home. Because of the helmet, all she could see of his face were the dark eyes, sculpted cheekbones and the strong mouth. For a woman who'd been celibate for two years, it was more than enough.

"Personal questions are forbidden according to the hosts, so I can't ask what a beautiful woman like you is doing in a place like this. If it meets with your approval, I'll sit and enjoy the lady's company."

She nodded her approval and smiled inside.

For the next few minutes neither spoke. They spent the time sipping their sodas and observing the costumed crowd on the dance floor. They also kept eyeing each other and did so without much pretense.

The music stopped, and the DJ announced, "All right, we're going to hook you up with a partner for the evening. If you will bring the ticket you were given when you entered and put them in the hat, we'll get started."

Eve considered the men who'd approached her earlier and knew no way was she going to play along. She asked the centurion. "You have your ticket?"

He nodded.

"May I have it please?"

He handed it over, and she got up and walked to the DJ table.

The DJ was dressed up like Elvis. At her approach he grinned. "Hey, Storm. Looking good. Quite an entrance you made."

"Thank you. I've chosen the centurion. What do we need to secure a room?" At least the centurion had manners.

He appeared confused, "Well, you're supposed to wait like everybody else."

"Lady Oya is not *everybody else*. Where are the rooms?"

"Well, um. Hold on a minute."

While the crowd flowed around her to place their tickets in the blue hat for men and the pink one for women, Eve waited and watched as the DJ spoke with someone wearing a gorilla suit. The gorilla finally shrugged and handed the DJ a card-shaped door pass.

"Suite 2135." he said when he returned. "Enjoy yourself, your majesty."

"Thank you."

She walked back to where the centurion sat waiting. She handed him the card. "Our room key—2135—unless that displeases you?"

He stood and bowed. "I'm honored." His gaze held hers just long enough to almost make her lose her way again, then he gestured for her to precede him.

On the ride up in the elevator, even though he was standing a respectful distance away, Eve was very aware of his presence. The silence in the car only seemed to heighten the charged atmosphere and she wondered if she'd lost her mind. *Since when did she go around picking up strange men: since putting on the catsuit and taking on the goddess persona,* she thought to herself. *And since she didn't want to spend the evening with someone like that Mario guy,* she added. The real Eve should be back in her hotel room watching the NBA and packing for the flight home to Chicago. Instead she was headed up to a hotel suite to spend the evening with a man she didn't know from Adam's cat.

The suite they entered was spacious and luxurious. Not even the Halloween pumpkins, tons of lit candles, black cats and witches could take away from the sumptuous surroundings with cream-colored upholstery and windows that looked out over the river. She could see the night lights of the city of Windsor, Ontario, on the opposite shore. Eve made decent money working for the government, but it wasn't enough for a suite like this one, not even for a night.

Playing the centurion role, Leyton did his best to maintain his cool. The last thing he wanted was for her to feel threatened or uncomfortable. Watching her in the candlelit silence as she stood looking out at the river, he wondered again who she might be? Her regal bearing and African-accented voice were both on point. Was she an actress? Working girl? She didn't seem to him to be a member of the world's oldest profession; the way she'd dismissed the men in the ballroom proved that. In truth, he had no idea what she did in real life. But he hadn't seen a body like hers since Tamara Dobson and Pam Grier from the old seventies blaxploitation movies his mom liked to watch. Curiosity aside, even if they spent the time doing nothing but talking, he was looking forward to what he hoped would be an enjoyable and memorable evening. As an arson investigator, though, he could do without all the candles burning everywhere. For him they were an accident waiting to happen.

"Would you like some wine?' he asked softly. There were a number of unopened bottles sitting on the bar.

She turned from the window. "I would."

"Red or white?" he asked, drinking her in with his eyes.

"White, please."

After expertly removing the cork, he poured white for the

lady and red for himself. After walking over to her he handed her a glass and raised his own to toast. "To the empire."

She gave him a smile. "And to the Yoruba people."

He liked her wit.

Their eyes bored into each other as they sipped. She set her glass down on a nearby table and seemed to be waiting for him to make the next move.

"Shall we sit?"

"Only if we can snuff out some of these candles. All this fire makes me nervous."

He paused. Was she a mind reader? "I agree."

A few minutes later, all but a few of the candles were extinguished, and the air held faint traces of smoke. To compensate for the darkness, he turned on a few lamps. The dimly lit atmosphere remained intimate but was potentially less dangerous.

"Thank you," she said after taking a seat on the sofa.

He sat nearby in one of the upholstered armchairs. "My pleasure."

Silence crept over the room again until he finally said, "I've never shared an evening with a goddess before, so my apologies for not knowing what to say or do."

"This is uncharted territory for me, as well."

"Then let's see if we can find our way. What kind of music do you like?"

"World, preferably from the Mother continent."

"Any particular countries?"

"Mali. South Africa."

He was impressed. A lot of people didn't even know Mali was a country, let alone that the people there were known for their music.

"And what kind of music does the centurion prefer?" she asked.

He liked the way she said *centurion*. It had a soft, almost possessive sound to it. "Jazz. Old school. Lonnie Liston Smith. Miles. Sonny Criss."

For the next few minutes they talked about music, which led to a conversation about books, which led to movies.

"What's your favorite?" she asked.

"Gladiator."

"But of course," she laughed.

"And yours?"

"Clash of the Titans—the old one"

He chuckled. "Really."

"Yes. It's pretty cheesy, and the special effects are terrible, and they turned poor Andromeda into a blonde, but I still enjoy it."

"Andromeda? The constellation? What do you mean they turned her into a blonde?"

"Before she was made into a constellation after her death, the Andromeda of Greek mythology was an Ethiopian princess, not a blonde like in the movie. She was also the wife of Perseus who rode the winged horse Pegasus."

"Never knew that."

"Just a bit of goddess trivia," she said and raised her glass.

"More comfortable now?" he asked.

She paused for a moment. "I am. Thank you for wanting me to be so."

"You're welcome."

Eve decided she liked him. He was intelligent, well-read and considerate. He was also hot in that costume. Brawn and brains. For someone who'd been kicking and screaming about having to attend the party, she was having a good time.

There was a knock at the door. They stared quizzically at each other, then heard a male voice call, "Room service."

The centurion stood. "I'll take care of it."

She noted his confident stride and wondered if he'd ever

served in the military. As he'd said to her earlier, no personal questions were allowed, so she had no way of knowing who he was or what he did in his nine-to-five. Or even if he was married. Not wanting to deal with that possibility, she set it aside and reminded herself that tonight wasn't supposed to be about worrying.

With that in mind, she watched the waiter roll in the cart holding the food, accompanied by the centurion. The elaborate meal provided by the party's hosts was as grand as the suite: lobster tails, salad, sides and a variety of breads and desserts. To her delight, there was even Halloween candy corn in a fancy cut-glass bowl. She spied a bite-sized Snickers candy bar she planned on having later.

The table was positioned in front of the large windows overlooking the river, and once the waiter finished placing everything on the table, he quickly withdrew.

"This is very nice," she said looking at the beautiful setting. A pair of tall white tapers in silver candleholders served as the centerpiece for the table, and the twin flames added an intimate touch.

"Yes, it is."

"Shall we eat now?'

"A soldier dining with a lady should never sit with his back to the door, so…" He gestured in her direction.

She took the seat he offered, and when he came up behind her to help with her chair, his body brushed up against her. "Thank you."

He sat framed by the opened drapes and the night. Her eyes met his. There was an underlying current running between them that had begun the moment he first approached her downstairs. Although he hadn't exhibited any overt sign of desire, it was there. She could feel it as well as she could her own breathing.

Leyton felt it, too. When he'd drawn the short straw this

morning, he'd never imagined he'd be spending the evening with a woman so beautiful. He ran his eyes over the graceful sweep of her shoulders and the shadowy allure of her arms accented by the gold rings. The black velvet domino covering her face only added to her mystery.

She said quietly in her royal voice, "We should probably get started before everything gets cold."

They filled their plates, and as they ate, his focus kept straying towards her. He'd said it a hundred times in his mind, but good lord, she was gorgeous. The candlelight was flickering over her skin making him fantasize about how it might feel to brush his lips against the plane of her soft throat and to feel the lean strength of her arms under his hands. As befitting a goddess of Africa, her mouth was wide and ripe, and just looking at it made him want to taste it. Just thinking about her had him hard and aroused, so he thought it was probably a good idea to drag his mind to safer territory.

"What are you thinking, centurion?"

He looked up from his plate and for a beat tried to decide how to answer. "Truthfully? You don't want to know."

"I might."

He studied her. "No."

"Is it so terrible?"

"No. It's so male."

"I'm a big girl. Tell me."

"You sure now?"

She nodded.

"Okay." He put his fork down and let his eyes travel over her slowly before confessing in a rich voice, "I'm wondering how my lips would feel against your soft throat, and if your mouth will be as sweet as it looks when I kiss you."

Eve had to tighten her grip on her glass or drop it. "Such honesty."

"You asked, my lady."

His helmet-shrouded eyes filled her with a heat that made her core pulse with such intensity she had to draw in a deep breath to calm herself. He hadn't said *if* he kissed her but *when,* as if it were a foregone conclusion. She wondered when she'd lost control of this game they'd been playing because it seemed that she had. Having worked with men her entire adult life, she'd always been able to hold her own, but the man seated across the table had rocked her.

"My apologies if my frankness offends."

"Honesty is rarely offensive, centurion. Even bold honesty." Maintaining her role as the aloof Oya was becoming difficult. "Are you always so seductive?"

He shrugged. "Depends on the moment and the woman."

His conversation alone had her body open and pulsing. She couldn't imagine how she'd react to his lips and touch.

"Your thoughts?" he asked turning the tables on her.

She answered more smoothly than she felt. "Honestly?"

He nodded.

"How I might react to that kiss."

He gave her a soft smile. "You play the role well."

"Not as well as you, my centurion."

A few more long, silent moments passed, and Eve came to a decision. Rising to her feet, she walked the short distance to his chair and held out her hand. "Shall we put the mysteries to rest?"

In response he stood and, holding her eyes, slowly brought her fingers to his lips. The impact of the contact turned her knees to sand. He placed an arm against the small of her back and eased her body in against him. The heat of his torso and thighs burned through the leather to her skin.

"If you don't want this, please tell me now," he whispered, but he was already brushing his lips against her jaw and down her throat.

She couldn't have responded if she had wanted to.

Instead, she let him work his magic. The warmth of his lips, the wanderings of his warm, sure hands made her want more. When he placed a series of fleeting kisses against the trembling skin above her neckline, her eyes slid closed from the onrushing sensations.

Only then did he kiss her lips. The intensity deepened immediately. Their arms encircled each other, and they fed lingeringly yet hungrily. He was so good at it she thought she could kiss him until the end of time, and again she wanted more.

So he gave her more, and when he pulled aside the top of her suit to plant kisses on the crowns of the twin beauties it hid, she moaned.

"I'm going to worship you, my lady," he promised thickly. "Take you to heaven and then worship you again…."

His mouth and hands on her breasts were dazzling. Were it not for his strong arm caressing her back, she'd be a puddle on the floor. All her inhibitions seemed to burn away. She wanted his touch everywhere. Caught in a maelstrom of desire, she shamelessly offered up her breasts and he paid her a sweet, torrid tribute.

He raised his head and looked down into her eyes. Holding his gaze, she reached under her arm and slid the zipper down. He leaned in and kissed the skin she brought into view. By the time she'd guided him to her waist, she could no longer think. His masterful loving left her so mindless she could only stand there and ripple from the top of her tiara to the heels of her boots. He pulled the suit down past her waist, and one of Chicago's senior-most ATF agents stood in the center of the softly lit hotel suite wearing nothing but her mask, her catsuit halfway off and a black thong decorated with tiny rhinestones.

Leyton almost came there and then. Drawing in a deep breath, he ran passion-laced eyes over the erotic picture her tall, lean body presented. If she wasn't really an African goddess, she should be. Beauty called to him every place he looked. The ripe breasts, the strong expanse of her thighs highlighted by a provocative thong made him harder than he'd ever been with a woman before. He slid a finger over her parted lips and down the valley between her breasts, pausing a moment to toy with the hot nipples still hard and damp from his loving. The touch continued down the firm torso to tease the small whorl of her navel. Holding her humid eyes, he brushed his hand over the thin strip of silk, then slid his fingers into the warm triangle covering the place a man most wanted to be. Her lids closed, and she widened her stance so he could delve deeper. Pleased by that, he leaned in and kissed her mouth. "You're very hot, my lady." Not waiting for or needing an answer, he gave each of her nipples a sultry lick, and when she moaned in response, his finger between her thighs moved aside the miniscule panel and found slick damp flesh. "You're very wet, too...."

The combination of his actions and words sent Eve over the edge, and she came, shuddering and buckling. It had been so long since she'd had a man, she should have been embarrassed, orgasming so quickly. But the waves of heat emanating from his scandalous touch were too glorious for her to care.

Leyton wanted to watch her come again and again. Her body seemed made for his hands. Lord he was hard and if he didn't get some relief soon... "Let's go to the bedroom."

Hazy and breathless, Eve dragged the catsuit up her body and forced her shaky legs to follow.

In order to keep their identities hidden, he didn't turn on any of the lamps. The moonlight coming in through the open drapes gave off just enough illumination to lighten the shadows, but not enough to see clearly. The darkness allowed him to remove his helmet with the certainty that she couldn't see his face any better than he could see hers. After removing his costume and wrapping himself up, he joined her on the shadowy bed.

No sight was needed. With their hands and mouths they began again. Leyton wondered how he'd ever get enough of the feel of her skin under his lips or the sounds of her gasps of pleasure. At sunrise this fairy tale would end, so he set out to savor her because the memory would have to last a lifetime. With that in mind, he worshipped her slowly, scandalously and completely. He dallied at her breasts until her nipples were hard and damp again. The heat between her thighs drew him like a thirsty man to an oasis, and he touched and plucked and teased her there until her long legs parted and her satiny hips rose in silent need.

"Are you ready, Your Highness?"

"Yes. Please…"

It was an order he was happy to obey, so he slid himself into paradise. The sensations were so powerful he had to fight off the orgasm that threatened to explode there and then. His body wanted to take her like there'd be no tomorrow in order to get the relief it had been craving since the first kiss, but his mind wanted to linger over the feel of her tight flesh around his hardness, and the way she began to move in response to his slow rhythmic strokes. He ran his palm over her breasts and played while she crooned. He grazed a finger over her parted lips and she flicked her tongue against it. When she reached down between their joined bodies and wrapped a hot hand around the base of his shaft, he growled with pleasure and increased his thrusts and rhythm. He heard her whisper, "Come for me, centurion."

The sultry invitation was too much. The orgasm broke through his defenses, and he began stroking her madly. A moment later, he felt her shatter beneath him, and her shout of release joined his. Their world became a firestorm of lust and sensation. Holding on to her hips, Leyton pumped and thrust and poured out his soul until he had nothing left. As they lay tangled together in the aftermath, their harsh breathing was the only sound in the otherwise silent room.

Eve had indeed been taken to heaven. He definitely knew his way around a woman's body, and she was truly grateful for it. The two orgasms she'd had continued to echo, and all she wanted to do was lie with him like this for the rest of her life. When he withdrew from her body, her soft wordless protest brought on a soft chuckle and a finger that circled her straining nipple.

He kissed her softly. "You make a soldier not want to return to duty."

"And you make a goddess want to abdicate her throne."

His fingers on her nipples were reigniting her fires. Wondering how she'd ever get through the rest of her life knowing he was in the world, but not knowing his name, she pushed the thought away and reminded herself again that this was just a one-night stand. No identities, no commitments. Just good, hot loving.

And for the rest of the night, they gave each other plenty of it.

At four o'clock in the morning, sated and so full of pleasure she couldn't move, Eve grabbed hold of what little discipline she had left and sat up on the edge of the bed. In a soft voice filled with regret, she told him, "I have to go."

He traced a slow finger down her spine. "I understand. So do I."

She glanced back over her shoulder at him. "I wish I didn't."

"Me, too.

She searched his shadowed face. "Thank you for a wonderful time."

"You're welcome"

Leyton wanted to ask for her name, but knew that was out

of line. "Give me one last kiss, then you go and get yourself together. I'll leave after you're gone."

Eve didn't want to leave but life called. Being late for her flight back to Chicago wasn't an option.

They shared a final parting kiss that was filled with longing, loss and regret. When it was over, she drew her fingers slowly down his strong cheek. "Good bye, my centurion."

"Be well, my lady."

Eve gathered up her clothing and padded through the shadows over to the bathroom.

Sitting on the bed in the dark, Leyton saw the bathroom light go on and for just a moment, caught sight of her nude back and hips before she disappeared behind the closed door. He still didn't know her name, but from that brief glimpse he knew that she had a butterfly tattooed at the base of her spine. It was the only clue he had, and it gave him hope that he'd find her again—somehow, even if it took the rest of his life.

Chapter 3

Dead on her feet, Eve got herself back to the hotel just in time to transform back into her real self and run down to meet the six o'clock airport shuttle that was due to arrive in ten minutes. As she waited, memories of the centurion and his lovemaking continued to reverberate inside. Telling herself she was back in the real world and that the fantasy was over didn't help. All she could think about was him. She floated back to their last kiss, but her reverie was interrupted by the arrival of the airport shuttle. She set it aside and waited to board the shuttle van when her cell phone began to buzz. Exasperated, she pulled it out of the pocket of her brown suede jacket and looked at the number on the caller ID. It was her office. "Yeah, Hank."

"Hey, Foxy." Hank Ingram headed up the Chicago office, and he'd been calling her Foxy Brown since the day they'd met. She liked him a lot. "Where are you?" he asked.

"At the hotel waiting on the shuttle."

"Good. Get out of line and report to the local office there."

"What?"

"Big fire there last night. Since you're on the ground, it's yours."

"Hank," she whined.

"I love you, too." He gave her the name and number of the person she was to contact. "Call me later and give me an update."

"Okay. I'll be staying with my aunt and uncle. Be in touch."

"Ciao."

Eve closed her phone and sighed aloud. *Damn.*

Driving home, Leyton was blue. He had Miles on. It was a little past dawn, and the sky was still gray—a Miles kind of morning. As the horn fed his soul he wondered where she was. Home in Detroit somewhere, or at the airport getting ready for a flight out. He could still taste her lips, hear her voice and feel the warmth of her skin under the slide of his hands. Who is she? The memories of her would be haunting him for some time to come. She'd been regal, commanding and totally uninhibited in bed. Not the kind of woman a man would easily forget. According to the briefing on the party, the attendees had come from all over the world. Finding her again would be like finding the proverbial needle in a haystack. During his law enforcement career, he'd found murderers, arsonists and every other kind of bad guy the city could offer up, so surely he could find a woman with a butterfly tattooed on her back. *Right,* he told himself sarcastically. There were millions of butterflies on the backs of women all over the world. What were the chances of him running into her again? Suppose she was from Africa, or France or some other foreign country? But he didn't care. He'd find her.

Keeping one eye on the light morning traffic, he fished his phone out of the glove compartment. It and his weapon had been locked inside while he he'd been at the party playing centurion. He hit the speed dial to connect himself with dispatch. Joyce Ingalls, the head clerk, answered. "Hey, Joyce."

"Where've you been?"

"Morning to you, too."

"Get yourself over to the new Morgan's complex."

"Why?"

"Sucker burned to the ground last night. We've been blowing up your phone since two a.m."

"What?"

"Just go. Everybody's already on the scene."

"Thanks." *Damn.*

He reached across the seat, grabbed his emergency light and slapped it on top of the car. With the blue light flashing, he turned the vehicle back the way he'd come and roared off in an easterly direction.

He smelled the smoke six blocks away. It wasn't the thick, acrid smoke of a fully engulfed fire but the fainter type associated with mopping up. The side streets leading to the complex were littered with hoses and uniformed firefighters moving with the slow, measured steps of having been in a long fight. Fire trucks flashing lights lined the way. The shields on the sides identified them as from station houses all over the city. Only something big would require such a strong show of force.

He flashed his badge at a uniformed cop and was allowed to drive into the parking lot. What was left of the multimillion-dollar shopping complex was a smoking hulk of charred brick and not much else. Firefighters in full gear were on the roof wielding axes. He parked and got out. "Glad you could join us, big brother."

His brother Keith's smiling brown face was black with smoke and sweat. He was in full gear also and had his ax and helmet in hand. He and a couple of his crew appeared to be on their way back to their engine.

"You okay?"

"Just the usual burns and bruises. Mom said you went to a costume party."

Leyton ran his eyes over the small army of police and firemen swarming the scene. He was looking for his crew. "Don't ask. You seen any of my people?"

"Yeah. Saw Chief Sawyer over with the mayor. Neighbors said the place went up like a match."

"Great. I'll see you later. Let Mom know I'm here."

"Will do. Take care of yourself."

Seeing his brother alive and well gave Leyton one less worry, but hearing that the building had gone up fast and hard meant he was in for a long day.

Wearing her shades, an ATF jacket, baseball cap and T-shirt, Eve was introduced by one of the local ATF agents to the other people in the room. This was a meeting of the task force being put together to investigate last night's fire. "Glad to be on board," she said and took a seat in one of the empty chairs.

They were in a conference room in the city's federal building. Local police and fire, a couple of FBI agents, Eve and the other agent from ATF, a young kid named McBride, were represented. McBride's office had requested national task force help because the locals were undermanned. Two of the five members were in Ontario working with the Canadian Mounties on an illegal weapons sting; another member was recovering from gunshot wounds suffered in a confrontation last week, and another was in Kansas City burying her mother.

That left McBride in charge. He'd been with ATF less than six months.

The Detroit fire department was running the meeting, which was fine with Eve. The last thing she wanted was to come in and start throwing federal weight around. Usually, partnering didn't go well when that happened. This was the city's turf; she and her people were there to assist.

"Okay, let's get started." In charge was one of the city's fire chiefs, a man named Stan Sawyer. He also headed up the arson squad.

According to him, the place that burned down last night was a multimillion-dollar development that represented part of the city's revitalization efforts. It was to have been the first new shopping complex built within the city limits in twenty years. The ribbon cutting had taken place less than a month ago.

"The initial canvass of witnesses said the place went up in minutes and was fully engulfed a short time later."

To Eve that sounded suspiciously like arson, and the chief seemed to concur. "With fires still to investigate from this weekend's Angels night activities, we're spread a little thin, so I'm going to appoint Chief Investigator Palmer as the point person, and I'm hoping Agent Clark will agree to assist."

"No problem," Eve said. "Is he here?"

"No, but he should be shortly. He's at the scene."

She nodded and hoped she and Palmer got along. Even though it was the twenty-first century, some men still found it hard to work with a woman.

The chief continued, "In the meantime, the mayor's office is anxious to get this resolved. Having a prominent development like this go up in smoke gives the city just one more unneeded black eye. Any questions?"

There were a few, and the chief answered them as best he could considering he was working with preliminary information. "Everything we have for now on the building's value, its owners, developers and vendors are in the packets in front of you."

Eve flipped through some of the pages. A man entered the conference room. He was tall, brown-skinned and wearing a long, beat-up leather coat. Only when he walked past her did she see the battered cowboy boots on his feet, and note that he smelled like smoke. He nodded at the chief. "Sorry I'm late." He took a seat and looked around the room. "I know everyone here except the ATF in the back."

Eve answered. "Clark. National task force."

"Thanks in advance."

"You're welcome."

Eve judged him to be about six foot two, muscular but lean, short hair, with a clean-shaven face. His build brought to mind the centurion, but chastising herself because this was neither the time nor place, she refocused on the here and now.

The chief was saying, "Captain Palmer, I've asked Agent Clark to partner with you."

"That's good." He turned her way as if seeking her opinion.

"I'm okay with it," she responded, shades masking her eyes. He held her gaze for a beat of a moment longer than she thought necessary before turning back around. She hoped he wasn't planning on hitting on her. Fending off the wannabe charmers always brought out the rhymes-with-*rich* in her, especially when operating on no sleep, like now.

By the end of the meeting, everyone had their assignments and was ready to roll. She and Palmer exited together.

He asked, "You want to take a look at the scene?"

"Yeah. Be a good way for me to get up to speed."

"Okay. Car's across the street in the lot."

On the ride to the site, Eve looked out at the changes that had taken place in her beloved hometown. There was so much of it gone now, and what remained appeared tired yet still hopeful.

"Where you from?" Palmer asked.

"Right here. Eastside."

He looked surprised. "Really?"

"Born and raised."

"It's home for me, too. Westside, though. What high school?"

"Cass."

"Ah, one of those brainiac girls."

She shrugged. "I did okay." Eve decided they'd chitchatted long enough. "Tell me about the scene."

Leyton gave her a long look. He guessed she'd made all the nice she intended to make and was ready to get to work. "Heavy scent of gasoline. Real heavy."

"Point of origin found yet?"

"Not yet. Place is still too hot. Once the engineers say the place is shored up and safe, we should be able to get in and look around."

"We're talking tomorrow morning."

"At the earliest."

He watched her open up the file given out at the meeting and glance at one of the sheets inside.

"Anyone talked to the corporate people?"

"No. I've an appointment with a district VP later. You're welcome to ride along."

"Thanks."

"No problem. He's a black guy named Crenshaw... supposedly the man behind the project. Probably not too happy this morning."

"Probably not."

Leyton wanted to ask her if the shades were prescription but decided to hold on to the question for now. She gave the impression of being *prickly,* a word his late grandfather sometimes used to describe a woman. Her height made him think of the goddess, though. Had it really been less than six hours since they parted? He shook off the thoughts. Although the height was right, he doubted Ms. Prickly ATF would be caught dead in a black leather catsuit.

When they reached the scene of the fire, Eve surveyed what was left of the buildings. At the briefing by the chief, the complex had been described as a high-end mini mall. A big name supermarket chain, a major retailer and a hardware giant had come together to offer Detroiters a shopping experience usually reserved for the surrounding suburbs, and someone had burned it to the ground.

Walking up to the charred remains, she could smell the faint scent of gasoline. Some of the brick walls on the huge hardware store remained upright, but much of the roof was gone. The other two buildings, although not as high, were in similar condition. She really wanted to get inside and start looking for the fire's origination point. Determining that might shed more light on whether the incident had been accidental in nature or deliberate.

"City had a lot of hope for this place," Palmer told her as they ducked under the yellow police tape cordoning off the area. "And now?" he shrugged as if no further words were necessary.

Eve agreed. It hurt her to watch her hometown being beat down in the media on what seemed like a daily basis. If she noticed the bashing in Chicago, it had to be up close and personal for the citizens of Detroit. They deserved better.

They stood in front of the block-long rubble and looked around. There was still water from the hoses everywhere. At scenes like this one, fire investigators always wore sturdy boots. Not only because of the water, but because of what might be in the water. Eve's well-worn hiking boots also kept her feet safe from broken glass, nails, splintered bricks and shards of wood. Mingled in with the debris outside of the supermarket were the remnants of burnt tin cans and the melted remains of plastic milk bottles and two-liter beverage containers. She was sometimes amazed at how capricious a fire could be when it came to what survived. She remembered a house in Ohio the year before that had blown up and burned down because of the meth lab in the basement. There'd been no loss of life, but the fire had wiped out everything inside except an old-fashioned cameo the owner said had once belonged to her great-grandmother. The flames hadn't touched it.

But she doubted she'd find great-grandma's cameo this time. All she'd find here was the burnt-out husk of one the city's dreams and she was determined to get to the bottom of it.

"You know," he told her, "the conspiracy theorists are convinced that the rest of the world has it in for the city of Detroit and are doing all they can to keep us from rising. When I look at something like this, I can almost agree."

She understood.

They tracked down one of the structural engineers to get a report on the progress he and his team were making.

"Hey, Leyton."

"How's it going, Charlie? This is ATF agent Clark from Chicago. She's helping us out."

He shook her hand. "Charlie Bates. Nice to meet you."

"Same here.

Charlie looked to be near retirement age. His dark face sported gray eyebrows the same color as the hair peeking out of from under the edges of his yellow hard hat.

"So where are we, Mr. Bates?" she asked.

"Should have the place shored up and safe to enter by the morning. Budget cuts have us shorthanded, but we're doing what we can with what we've got. It's a big complex, so it's going to take us awhile."

Both investigators understood.

"Prelim police report say no loss of life," Charlie said. "That been verified?"

"Far as we know," Leyton answered. "The only person working that night was a guard and he was the one who called 911."

"Okay. Just don't want to find any surprises. Nice meeting you, Agent Clark."

Eve nodded. "Thanks for your work."

"No problem. Leyton, tell that pretty mama of yours I'm still waiting."

Leyton chuckled. Charlie's crush on his mother went back to high school. "I'll let her know."

With a wave, Charlie left to return to his duties, and Leyton and Eve headed for the car.

Chapter 4

As they left the scene and merged into the traffic on Jefferson, Leyton looked over at the woman riding shotgun. "I need to get something to eat. Hungry?"

"I could use something."

"Preference?"

"Doesn't matter as long as we can get it quick. What time's the appointment with the VP?"

"One. He's in Southfield. How long have you been in Chicago?"

"Ten years."

"You must like it then."

She shrugged. "It's okay. Different from here, though."

"In what way?"

"Infrastructure works, the city works. Politicos go to jail just like here, though."

He pulled into one of the city's famous Coney Island places and parked. "What can I get you?"

"I can pay my way. I'll come in."

"I can afford to treat you to a Coney dog, Clark."

"Thanks, but no thanks."

She got out of the car.

He sighed and got out, too.

Inside, they gave the kid behind the counter their order, then took a seat to wait for their food. Leyton had worked with a bunch of women over the years, and nine out of ten had been models of professionalism. But Clark—he was trying to figure her out. She was the personification of icy. It was as if she'd erected a wall around herself and had no intentions of letting anyone in, even to offer her a hot dog. He supposed the attitude was rooted in her being a woman in what used to be a man's world. But he was just trying to be pleasant, nothing more. He'd worked with Detroit's ATF agents in the past, and they'd usually partnered up well. They'd also been able to share a beer or a meal after the job and had gotten to know each other fairly well. This one didn't appear to want to share anything, and she definitely didn't have a get-to-know-me kind of vibe.

Their food arrived. "Do you want to take a minute and eat here, or eat on the ride to Southfield?"

She checked her watch. "It's nearly noon. We should probably eat on the way. I know Southfield's not that far, but I'm anal about being late for an interview."

"Up to you." After his night with the goddess, and having to hit the ground running this morning on the fire, he'd really wanted to sit, eat and catch his breath. But apparently she'd gotten a full night's sleep. He'd have to remember not to give her a choice next time. He stood and gestured toward the exit.

Leaving the Coney Island when they did turned out to be a good thing. An accident on the northbound Lodge Expressway squeezed traffic down to a single lane crawl. Southfield was one of Detroit's closer suburbs and normally a quick trip. Not today. The drive took nearly an hour and they arrived at the Morgan supermarket chain's corporate office five minutes before the appointed time. Not that the promptness mattered. According to the secretary who greeted them, the man they wanted to see was in a meeting and would be available shortly.

Eve and Leyton shared a look, then took seats in the waiting area.

Marvin Crenshaw came out to greet them thirty minutes later. He was short, had a shaved head and was wearing an expensive black suit that looked imported. His snow-white shirt had fancy embroidered cuffs. He didn't offer an apology for making them wait. "Have they found my car?"

Eve raised an eyebrow and looked to Palmer who asked, "Your car, sir?"

"Yes, I was carjacked the night of the grand opening. A brand new BMW. Had it less than two days."

"Sorry to hear that but there was nothing in the briefing about a stolen vehicle."

"Well, call someone—if there's anyone in the police department competent enough to answer the phone. No wonder the city's crumbling around your ears, bunch of fools in charge."

Leyton put up a hand. "Wait, wait, wait. We're not here to listen to this—just to interview you about the fire. I'm sure the officers assigned to your case are doing the best they can to locate your property."

"And I'm not. It's been over a month now and nobody will return my secretary's phone calls."

Eve felt his pain. "Can we talk in your office?"

"What about my car?"

"Can you tell us where you were at approximately 11:00 p.m. last night?"

"Why?"

"Routine questioning."

"I didn't set the fire."

"No one's accusing you, but for our investigation we need to know where you were and what time you were made aware."

"Oh, all right. Come in. This better not take long, though. I have to leave for a corporate meeting in Lansing in twenty minutes."

The interview lasted long enough for Leyton to come to the conclusion that Marvin Crenshaw was a whiny little jerk. He kept trying to make the conversation all about him and the stolen vehicle, and Clark kept swatting him down like a bug. She did it professionally and emotionlessly, but she let him know who was in charge. Leyton interjected a question or two, but mostly he just sat back and watched her work.

"So, okay, Mr. Crenshaw," Eve said, "let me make sure I have everything correct. You say you were with friends last night having dinner and drinks, and you got the call about the fire about midnight?"

"Correct."

"Can I have the name of one of the friends so we can corroborate your statement? It's routine."

He gave her the name: Lavita Brown.

"And to your knowledge no one in the company or in its employ has received any threats connected to the mall."

"Correct."

"What about the building contractors or the vendors?"

When he didn't reply right away, Eve looked up from the notes she'd been making and met his eyes. "Yes or no, sir."

"Uh, no," he stammered. "I didn't have any contact with the contractors. That was handled by our architects and their people."

"I understand," she assured him with a faint smile.

He looked at his watch. "I really need to go. If you have any more questions, just call my secretary."

"We're almost done," she said, effectively overriding his attempt to hasten their exit. "According to my briefing, this new development was your baby. You were the executive who spearheaded the whole project."

"I did. But it's clear they obviously don't deserve it."

"They, who?" she echoed questioningly.

"The citizens of Detroit. You try and be a *good brother* and help out and all you get is carjacked. Are we through?"

Eve studied him. She wondered if he'd been this bitter before being jacked. "For now, sir. Yes. Thank you for your time. If we need to talk to you again, we'll be in touch."

"All I want is my car."

"I'm sure the detectives are working as hard as they can. Have a nice day."

Once she and Palmer were back in the car, she turned his way and asked, "What do you think?"

"I think he's an ass."

She hid her smile. "Besides that?"

"I noticed the hesitation when you asked about the developer."

"Me, too. Wonder what that was about?"

"I think maybe we should find out." He looked through his notes until he came across the developer's name, then pulled out his phone and dialed the number provided.

It was a short call and when it ended he explained. "His secretary says he called in sick yesterday. Flu. She thinks he may be in later this week. I told her to have him call me, but since I'm the suspicious type, let me make another call."

"To whom?"

"To a friend over at the courthouse."

When the friend answered, he asked, "Can you give me a quick and dirty on Phillip Brandywine and Brandywine

Construction? Highlight anything that jumps out at you—warrants, liens, child support."

He talked for a second or two longer, then closed his phone. "They'll get back to us soon as they can."

Pleased that the ball was rolling, Eve asked, "So, where to next?"

"I want to run down a few of the resident pyros, see if they know anything about last night."

"These are arsonists you're talking about, right?"

"Yep. Serial arsonists. Some do it for profit, some just for the high they get watching things burn."

"Okay. I'm game."

Before he started up the car, though, he said, "Crenshaw was a jerk but you handled him well."

"Not that I need your approval, but thanks."

Leyton meant it as a compliment, but evidently she didn't need any of those either. "You're a tough lady, you know that?"

"Can't be ATF and not have balls, Palmer. The job expects it."

"That why you wear the shades and no makeup?"

"Do you ask male agents why they wear shades and no makeup?"

He blinked. "Think I'll start the car now."

"Good idea."

Driving out of the parking lot, all he could think to himself was, *wow*.

While they made the short drive back to Detroit, Eve had to admit that Palmer had hit the nail on the head. The shades, lack of makeup and the way she pulled back her hair were her attempts to render herself less sexual. With her curves shielded by the big windbreakers she favored, most people were forced to deal with her on a professional level. Of course, some men being men saw her as a woman anyway and took her refusals to say yes to their offers of sex as a challenge to their male egos. She looked over at Palmer. So far, he hadn't come at her with any of that and that was good.

Leyton was feeling incredibly stupid. He knew he shouldn't have asked her that question, but it came from him wanting to figure her out. At this point, a smarter man would probably opt to leave her alone and just focus on the job at hand. But he'd always been interested in people's stories because it helped him understand who they were and how they ticked. He was intrigued by the prickly Agent Clark. When you looked past the facade, it was easy to see that she was a good-looking woman, which probably had a lot to do with her no-nonsense attitude. Tall, stacked and probably gorgeous when she ditched the shades, she was one the finest law enforcement agents he'd ever seen. Nowhere near as gorgeous as his goddess, though, and once again the memories of her floated back, and once again he forced himself not to think about her.

Leyton and Eve spent the rest of the afternoon combing the shadier neighborhoods of the city searching for his firebugs. He wanted to talk to two in particular: an old-timer named Sally and a younger man who went by the nickname of Blazer.

They found Blazer on the west side, sitting on his aunt's front steps feeding two black squirrels. When Leyton and Eve got out of the car, the thin dark-skinned man stood, and the squirrels scampered off. Only when they came closer did Eve notice his haunting green eyes.

"Blazer," Leyton said in greeting.

"Marshal. Who's the babe?"

Eve answered for herself. "Clark. ATF."

"*Federales*. Welcome."

"Thanks."

"So what brings you to the Ponderosa?" he asked Leyton.

"That fire last night."

"Read about it in the paper. Wasn't me. I was home with my mama watching *Gunsmoke*."

"Good to know."

"I'm also reporting regularly to my parole officer, and seeing the shrink once a month."

"How's that going?"

He shrugged. "She's in a bad marriage. I'm trying to help her through it."

Leyton shook his head. "Give me your theory on the fire."

"Paper said it was gasoline. Only an amateur splashes around a bunch of gasoline and throws in a match. At least have some style, you know? I'm surprised whoever it was didn't blow themselves up."

"We checked all the hospitals. No walk-in burn victims last night."

"Well, that's something."

"Will you keep your ears open for us?"

"Anything for you and the lady marshal. But you have to promise that if I do get the itch and my fire jones comes down, she'll be the arresting officer."

"You got it," Eve told him.

"Good."

He watched them until they drove away.

"Quite the character," she said once they were in transit again.

"Math genius. Got a PhD in Fractal Geometry at sixteen. In jail at seventeen for setting fires at one of the campuses back East. When he got out, he came back here. A year later, we sent him to jail for doing a warehouse. He got out again in 2005. We're sure he's set at least three fires since then. Just haven't been able to prove it."

"You think he was involved last night?"

"No. Like he said, splashing around a lot of gasoline isn't his style. His accelerants are usually laid out pretty precisely."

"Because of the fractals background."

"Yep."

Eve pondered that for a moment. Some serial arsonists had unique signatures and took a sick kind of pride in their work. Palmer would know his perps better than she would, so she was willing to go with his assessment of Blazer not being responsible for last night's fire. The sun had gone down, and due to daylight savings time it would be dark soon. "What about this other person—Sally?"

"Yeah, we're en route to his place now."

"What's his story?"

"Profit pyro only. The days leading up to Halloween are his money-makers."

"Taking advantage of the whole Devil's Night-Angel's Night thing, I'm assuming."

He nodded. "People across the country think all Detroiters do on Halloween is burn down the city. What the media doesn't say is that this madness began when absentee landlords started paying people like Sally to set the fires. No sense in fixing up your property when you can torch it and make a profit instead."

"I know. I've explained that to non-Detroiters, too. Usually gives them a whole new perspective on what's really going on. When I was growing up here, Devil's Night was for mischief— knocking over trash cans, soaping car windows. These fires are relatively new."

"Yeah. The city changed the name to Angel's Night as a nod to all the volunteers who keep an eye on the abandoned homes in their neighborhoods and spend the nights leading up to Halloween riding around in their cars looking for trouble spots."

"I hear they've made a difference."

"Absolutely. Be a lost war without them."

He gave Eve the impression of being passionate about his work and his city. He was also a good-looking man, she noted. Not that it mattered to the job. She glanced at his strong hands on the steering wheel. No ring. With the long leather coat and cowboy boots he looked like a throwback to the old West. She bet the women he worked with were happy to see him walk into work every morning. Even though he was handsome, he was no match for her centurion, though. Then again, no man in her future ever would be. Refocusing herself, she asked, "Where's this Sally live?"

He slowed to a stop in front of a two-family flat. The windows were boarded up with plywood. "Apparently not here anymore," he responded wryly. He got on the phone. Dispatch told him that Sally Riggins was locked up for violating parole and was currently housed in Dickerson, one of the county lockups. He thanked the clerk and ended the call. After relating the info to his partner he added, "So much for that."

"How long has he been in custody?"

"Five days, which means he wasn't involved." He ran his hand over his weary eyes. "How 'bout we call it a day? Not much more we can do until we get inside in the morning."

She agreed. "You can drop me back at the fed house. My car's in the lot."

"I'd ask you if you wanted to grab some dinner but you've put enough holes in my hide for one day, so I'm taking myself home."

"You look pretty tough to me, Palmer. You can take it."

He heard the amusement in her voice so he took it in good spirit. "We'll see."

He drove her to the parking lot and waited while she walked over and got into her car. The nondescript, dark blue Ford called little attention to itself, a plus in a rough-and-tumble place like Detroit. The thoughts brought Crenshaw's carjacking to mind and Leyton made a mental note to check the files in the morning. But if the detectives had no leads, he held out little hope of finding it. By now, a fancy car like that had more than likely disappeared down the rabbit hole into the city's underground world of chop shops or been driven out of state for an illegal sale. As Crenshaw stated, he'd been trying to help, but apparently no good deed went unpunished.

Clark drove past him. She gave him a nod and headed off. Leyton put in a Miles CD and did the same.

Eve's aunt and uncle were out at the movies when she got to the house, but there was food waiting for her on the stove and plenty of hot water in the tank for the long shower she took after her meal. After that, it was a short walk to the bed in the bedroom she and her cousin Shelly once shared. Back then her still growing body had almost fit the twin bed. But now, at her height, it didn't fit at all, and she wondered if she'd be on the case long enough to have to make a decision about buying a bigger bed for the room. Putting that off for now, she lay in the darkness and let her weariness take hold. What a day. Twenty-four hours ago, she'd been in full costume and getting ready for the night of her life with a man whose presence had quietly stalked her all day. Only now did she allow herself to think back to his kisses and the hot lust that had filled them both. She replayed the hard slide of him entering her and how good it had felt. The remembrance of how he'd toyed with her breasts and his fingers between her thighs soon had her nipples hard and her body craving more. There wouldn't be more, though. He'd returned to his world just as she'd stepped back into her own. In a way, it left her sad, but the memory of their night together would be something she'd have forever and that had to be consolation enough.

Leyton lay in bed, and for the first time that day gave his mind permission to dwell on last night's interlude. Where was she? It was a question he'd asked himself a hundred times or more over the course of the day, or so it seemed. Who was she? Yet another unanswered question. It left him frustrated. He would have liked to have been with her longer—not just in bed. He got the impression that they might have connected on a personal level as well as the physical had time not been a factor.

So there he lay, reliving the weight of her soft breasts against his palms, the taste of her kiss and the soft sounds of pleasure she'd given when his manhood slowly entered her warmth. The lusty memories made him hard, and that left him frustrated as well, so he decided to try sleep. It took awhile.

Chapter 5

The morning's briefing was scheduled for eight in the conference room where they'd met yesterday. Wearing her shades and dressed in ATF gear, Eve arrived at seven-thirty. Only a few people were inside. Palmer was one. He was standing at the white chalkboard and drawing a large rectangle that she guessed represented the Morgan Grocery complex. At her entrance he looked up and stopped. "Morning, Clark."

She liked his smile. "Morning, Captain."

"Coffee in the back if you want it."

"Thanks."

For a moment he didn't move and neither did she. Something unspoken flowed between them before he broke the connection and returned to his drawing. She mentally shook off whatever it had been and grabbed her coffee. After greeting the other people in the room, she took a seat on one of the folding chairs. Slowly sipping the steaming brew, she watched Palmer work. He was sectioning off the rectangle into four compartments and numbering them one to four. Today he was wearing an army green T-shirt under a short black leather jacket that was as beat-up as the long coat he'd worn yesterday. The jeans framing his hips and thighs had seen better days, too, but she liked the view. The face wasn't half bad either with its strong lines and nice lips. She'd dressed for warmth. Her gray turtleneck was topped by a burgundy hoodie with ATF emblazoned across the front. Layered over that was a heavy insulated parka. They were going to be working in a burned-out, unheated building that was open to the elements. Only a few days before at her aunt's birthday party, the weather had been warm and reminiscent of early September, but today the temperature was struggling to reach forty; November had arrived and it was alive and kicking.

The meeting began promptly at eight with reports from the teams. Each had been given specific assignments ranging from questioning witnesses to taking pictures of the site, to making arrangements with federal and state crime labs to handle any evidence that might be found. McBride, the young ATF agent, gave his report on the logistics and the canines that would be a part of the day's team. Earlier, during Eve's commute from the east side and his from suburbia, they'd had a brief phone conversation on how their agency might assist the investigation. The feds had more resources and money at their disposal than the locals to pay for necessary backup items such as canine support and forensics, and because the Morgan complex was a commercial enterprise and dealt in consumer goods that had crossed state lines, the fire fell well within ATF's jurisdiction, thus qualifying the investigation for federal assistance.

Once the reports were heard and photos of the site passed around, Palmer drew everyone's attention to his drawing on the board. He designated which teams would take each segment, and when everyone was clear as to their roles, he had two things to add. "For now, this fire is on the books as suspicious. If after the investigation it proves to be arson, the parent company of Morgan Foods will be offering a fifteen-thousand-dollar reward for information leading to an arrest and conviction."

Eve nodded approvingly.

"Secondly, the engineering crews have shored up the buildings and they've run lights inside. It's going to be cold, but that'll be no excuse for hurried or shoddy work. I'd like for us to have an official determination as soon as possible. Any questions?"

No one had any, so they gathered up their gear and filed out of the room to begin the day.

On the drive, Eve found herself sneaking looks at him. Although he'd initially impressed her as being laid-back, he had a commanding way about him as well. At the meeting, he'd been in control without acting as if he wanted everyone else to know it. She'd worked cases in the past where the inflated egos of some of the lead investigators made it hard to get the job done. Not so this time. He hadn't belittled anyone's efforts or treated them as if they were working *for him*. All he seemed concerned with was getting the work done as efficiently and as thoroughly as possible, and she appreciated that. "Did we get anything back on the developer?" she asked.

"Yes, the preliminary report says Brandywine Construction is legit, no red flags. We still need to talk to him about any threats he may have received."

Eve agreed. "Did you look into Crenshaw's car?"

"Talked to the detectives this morning, and so far they have nothing, except that he was pretty abusive to the uniforms that showed up after he was jacked."

"How did I already know that?"

"Yeah, and, according to the report, he was reeking of urine when they arrived at the scene."

"Urine?" She puzzled over that for a moment, then turned to him in surprise. "He wet himself?"

"Apparently the carjackers scared him so bad, he wet his pants."

"That probably only added to how pissed he was. Pun intended."

He turned her way. "So, you do have a sense of humor?"

"Why would you think I wouldn't?"

"You're so stern and stoic."

"Thanks."

He smiled. "There's a lot more to you than you let people see, isn't there?"

She shrugged. "I suppose, but all the job wants are results."

"True, but why the big bad shield?"

"Makes for less drama."

"Meaning?"

"There aren't that many women in the agency. Most do a kick-ass job and most have had to deal with drama coming up. Whether it's the men who want to hit on you, or the ones who think you're incompetent because you don't carry a penis in your pants. Luckily, things have gotten better. But you learn not to let your guard down."

"Just in case?"

"Yeah. Just in case."

"Makes sense. Thanks for explaining."

"Thanks for asking and thanks for not giving me any of the above."

"You're welcome. So if I ask are you're married, would you be offended?"

"Not as long as I can ask you the same thing."

"I'm divorced. You?"

"Single all my life. How long were you married?"

"About five years. Just long enough for Angie to figure out she should've married someone else."

"What do you mean?"

"You know what the job is like—long hours, getting called in the middle of the night. Missing anniversaries, birthdays, because some joker set a warehouse on fire. She got tired of me not coming home when I said I would."

"Any kids?"

"One. A daughter. Kia. She's eight."

"Do you get to see her?"

"Yep. Angie's good about making sure Kia and I stay connected. Her mom and I are much better apart than we ever were together. She's remarried. Name's Oliver. He's a pretty good guy."

"Most men don't usually sing the praises of their ex or the new husband."

"I'm not most men."

"I'm starting to see that."

"Good." He looked her way and for a beat of a moment silence filled the car, and she felt the tingle of attraction slide through her blood.

"So, why're you single?" he asked.

"Take your list of why you and your ex split, and add the men I meet not being able to handle me being me. Can't seem to hook up with anyone who wants the brain that comes with the body. My last relationship crashed because he couldn't deal with what I do and because I wouldn't quit and get a more female job."

"Female job?"

"His words. Wanted a more traditional woman, I guess. Dinner on the table. Shirts ironed and ready, that kind of thing."

"Not you."

"Nope, so that was that."

"Sorry."

"It's okay. I'm fine."

They pulled into the parking lot of the site. He cut the engine. "We're here."

"Yeah, we are."

They sat silently for a moment, discreetly checking each other out. Finally, he said, "Thanks for the conversation."

"You're welcome."

Inside the shadowy remains of what had once been the supermarket portion of the mall, Eve was careful where she walked. The rest of the techs, investigators and canine teams were doing the same. The floor was littered with scorched metal, bricks and charred cans. Heat-warped beams that had once been a part of the ceiling now formed a grim and blackened obstacle course. Fire had signature smells. House fires smelled of burnt food, fabrics and wood. Commercial buildings—burnt electronics and plastics. This site had both. The foul scent of torched food and wiring mingled with plastics, fibers and wood. Because of the variety of materials in the store, the fire had burned big and hot, but rarely did one burn so hot that it obliterated the flash point, and this one was no exception. It had begun at the back of the building.

Outside, Eve stood in the cold and watched the techs measuring burn patterns while others chipped off pieces of the blackened bricks to send to the lab for tests. The faint scent of gasoline still had been detectable inside but was particularly strong where she and Palmer were standing. "What's your take, Captain?"

"I think Blazer was right. The way the gasoline was thrown around I'm surprised the perp made it out alive. The initial flame up had to be enormous."

Eve looked down at the twisted, melted remnants of the security camera lying amidst the debris on the ground a few feet away. If it had any taped evidence, they'd never know. "So, an amateur maybe?"

"I'd say yes."

They were interrupted by one of the canine handlers who had a clipboard with some paperwork the captain needed to initial. Once that was accomplished, the uniformed female officer and her big gray German shepherd named Lucy moved on.

Eve asked, "You checked the area hospitals, right?"

"Yeah."

"How about we widen the parameters and take Michigan, Ohio and Indiana?"

"Sure. Can't hurt."

She pulled out her phone and made some calls. When she was done, she said to him. "They'll get back to us if they turn up anything."

"Thanks." He looked at his watch. "My, how fast four and a half hours fly by when you're having fun. We've done all we need for now. Let's let them finish up and we head back to file the paperwork. I want to get the word out on the reward as soon as I can."

"Sounds good."

The wind whipping off the Detroit River made an already raw day a subfreezing ordeal. By the time they got back into the car, Eve was so cold from being out in the elements she didn't think she'd thaw out again until spring. Inside her boots, her feet felt like blocks of ice. "Oh! Turn up the heat."

He chuckled, "It's on full blast. Give it a minute. Thought you were from Chicago."

"I am, but cold is cold. And don't pretend you're not freezing. I can see you shivering."

He stripped off his gloves and blew on his hands. "Who, me?"

She rolled her eyes.

"Are you ever going to take off those shades?"

"If I do, I'll have to kill you."

He grinned and drove off the site. Upon merging into traffic, he said to her. "I need to make a quick stop before we head back. That okay with you?"

"As long as it's inside and we get something to eat afterwards, I'm good."

"Okay."

They didn't drive far, but she was a little caught off guard when he pulled into the parking lot of a school.

"My daughter Kia goes here," he said, explaining. "Our fire department got a grant to buy smoke detectors, and they finally came in. The principal's going to give them away to families that can't afford their own. I got her school's share in the trunk."

"That's a great idea."

"Just trying to keep my daughter's friends safe."

Once he parked, he took the box out of his crowded trunk, and she walked with him into the building.

The principal was a woman named Randall. Eve guessed she was in her mid-forties. Tall, willowy, light-skinned. By her body language and smile, it was obvious that she found Palmer even more pleasing than the donated smoke detectors. He introduced Eve. After a cursory hello, Randall pretty much ignored her from that point on and went back to beaming at Palmer.

"Mind if I see Kia for a minute?" he asked Ms. Randall.

"Oh, of course not. I'll call down. Just have a seat." Then as if suddenly remembering Eve, "You too, Agent Dawson," she said.

"It's Clark, Ms. Randall."

She waved off the blunder. "I'm sorry. Terrible with names."

Eve decided to stand. "I'm fine. Thank you."

While the principal made a call to his daughter's room, Palmer and Eve shared a silent look that affected Eve much like it had back at the briefing earlier. A part of her wanted to drop the shield and let him in, but other parts were more skeptical. And she wasn't sure which side held her vote. He was certainly gorgeous and seemed to accept her for who she was, and that, more than anything else, helped tip the scales in his favor.

A few minutes later, a little girl, sporting dreadlocks and who looked a lot like Palmer, entered the office. Upon seeing him, her face widened into a grin, and she squealed, "Daddy!"

He stood. She ran to him and he hugged her up. The happy scene touched Eve's heart. She remembered running to her late dad in much the same way and being swept up into strong arms. It was one of the clearest memories she had of him, and she wondered if Kia knew how lucky she was.

"Did you bring the smoke detectors?" Kia asked him.

"Yep."

She hugged him around the neck. "You're awesome."

He put her back on her feet, and when he did, she seemed to notice Eve for the first time. "Who's she?"

"This is Agent Clark. ATF."

"Nice to meet you, Kia," Eve said.

"Nice to meet you, too. You look real fierce in those sunglasses and your gear."

Eve grinned. "Thanks."

Kia said to Palmer, "Daddy, next Halloween I don't want to be Mae Jemison again. I want to be ATF."

He looked over at Eve and laughed. "Okay."

Eve smiled. "I'll send your dad a hat. How's that?"

"That would be really nice."

Everyone seemed to be having a great time except for Principal Randall. She had a smile plastered on her face, but there were no smiles in the dark look she shot Eve before turning to Kia. "Kia, you should get back to class now."

"Okay," she replied, still checking out Eve.

Her dad said, "Give me another hug before you go."

They shared a short, intense hug, and it was easy for Eve to see how much they loved each other.

"You coming to get me Saturday so we can go to the Science Museum?"

"Gonna do my best."

"Okay. Nice meeting you, Agent Clark."

"Same here, Kia. I won't forget the hat."

"Thank you."

A second later she was gone, and although Ms. Randall tried to get Palmer to stay a bit longer by asking about the big fire at Morgan Foods that was all over the local news and in the papers, he politely declined to comment and said goodbye.

Once they were in the car and rolling again, she said, "I like your daughter. Anybody who wants to be ATF for Halloween is all right with me."

"She's something. She'll probably make me buy her shades like yours just as soon as she gets in the car on Saturday."

"I'm impressed she was dressed like Mae Jemison."

He shook his head in amusement. "The Charles H. Wright African-American museum had Mae Jemison's space suit on display. Kia made me take her downtown to see it so many times I had to get us a family membership. Angie and Oliver use it when I can't take her. The Wright and the Science Museum next door are her favorite places. If they'd let her move in, she would."

"It's easy to see you two have a good relationship."

"I'd give my life for her. You and your dad get along?"

Eve turned away to watch the city roll by. "Lost him and my mom to arson when I was seven."

"I'm sorry," he said softly.

"Thanks. That's something you don't ever get over, I think. Probably the reason I'm in law enforcement."

"Where'd you start out?"

"San Diego. Moved there after college. It was a combined force so I was a street cop first, then got certified to ride an engine. When ATF needed some women to do undercover, I applied. My dad was a firefighter, too."

"So was mine."

"Here in the city?"

"No. Dallas. He and my mom divorced when my brother and I were small. She moved us here when I was four."

"Who's the oldest?"

"I am by three years. He's a firefighter, too."

"Runs in the family, huh?"

"Guess so."

"Lots of cops and firefighters in my family, too."

"Based here?"

"Some yes."

"Give me names. Maybe I'll know one."

So she did, and when she got to her cousin Victor, he turned to her with surprise. "I know Vic Reed. He's in the same engine house as my brother. That's your cousin?"

"Yep."

"Wow. Small world."

"Yes it is." She didn't know why that made her smile inside, but it did. He knew her family and his family knew hers.

"Do you have any siblings?"

"Nope. Only child, but my uncle and aunt who raised me have a daughter. She's a year older so we may as well be sisters." Thinking about Shelly made her remember that she hadn't had a chance to call and tell her how the Halloween party turned out. As if cued, the centurion floated across her mind and she pushed him away.

"Was the arsonist who set the fire ever found?"

"No."

"Damn."

"Yeah."

Leyton could feel his heart opening to this complicated woman and not just because he felt sorry for her loss, but because of how damn impressive he found her to be—beauty, brawn and brains. Cop. Firefighter. Undercover. A man would have to be crazy to be turned off by such a powerful combination, but apparently at least one man in her past had been. "So, where do you want to eat?"

"Doesn't matter."

"I'm a Coney fiend, so how about the place we went to yesterday? We sit inside and eat this time, though."

"Why?"

"Just to power down a minute."

"Okay."

She held his gaze for a moment longer than necessary before looking away, and he wondered if she was feeling whatever this was, too. It was subtle and new, but it was there, sprouting like the first green seedling of spring, and he had no idea what to do with it. "You ready?"

She nodded and they got out.

Because their stop at the Coney Island yesterday had been so brief, Eve hadn't paid much attention to the clientele, but this time as she and Palmer got their orders and claimed a small table by the window, she did. "Is this a cop joint?" she asked as she bit into one of the best corned beef sandwiches she'd had in ages. Uniforms and plainclothes personnel filled the small interior. The music was old-school Motown.

"Yeah. The owner's a former county sheriff. When she retired ten years ago, she opened this place.

"Corned beef is fabulous."

He smiled at her from his seat on the other side of the table. "What else do you like?"

"Sports. Blueberries. You."

He stilled. "Really?"

She wiped her mouth with a napkin and then shrugged. "Yeah, I do. No drama does a girl good."

"So how am I supposed to take that?"

Again, she shrugged. "No idea. Just thought I'd be up front."

Leyton studied her.

"What?" she asked, smiling over her sandwich.

He shook his head. "I wasn't expecting that."

"Good. Sometimes the unexpected works best." That said she slipped off her shades, set them on the table and met his eyes.

Leyton was struck dumb. From the curve of her perfectly arched brows to the full sweep of her lips, she was stunning. "Wow."

Amusement curved her lips, and she put the dark glasses back on. "Now, you know."

Yeah, he did and understood. No woman with her face should be slogging through burned-out buildings looking for flash points or chasing perps. She'd probably been beating off her male colleagues with sticks for years. Beauty like hers was more commonly showcased on the covers of magazines or on the arm of some celebrity. *Damn!* He had no idea what he'd done to deserve having two drop-dead gorgeous women show up in his life the way they had that week, but he'd take it, no questions asked. "So, do you kill me now?"

She chuckled. "Your Coney's getting cold."

Grinning, Leyton went back to his food.

Chapter 6

On the ride back downtown, Eve wondered if she'd done the right thing by revealing herself to Palmer the way she had, but she instantly tossed out the second thoughts. It wasn't as if they were in high school. They were both grown and unattached. Her night with the centurion had reminded her just how long it had been since she'd enjoyed male companionship, and it wasn't just because of the off-the-chain sex. They'd had a nice evening. His helmeted face shimmered across her mind's eye. As much as she wanted to, she doubted she'd ever know his true identity or see him again. And because of that, he would always remain her private fantasy, but she had to live in the real world, and Leyton Palmer represented that. When he had walked into the meeting the first day wearing his cowboy boots and long leather coat, she hadn't expected to be attracted to him but she was. The old Eve would never have opened up to a man she'd known a total of two days, so the only thing she could attribute it to was the interlude with the centurion. Dressed up as the goddess Oya, she'd taken a walk on the wild side and now her alter ego seemed to be whispering to her to let go and enjoy life. Although Eve was a risk-taker in her profession, she was a lot more cautious when it came to her private life. With her losing record, it was justified. There was no guarantee Palmer would be any different, but the Oya inside was willing to explore the possibility that he could be.

"I'm used to working out a couple days a week," she said to him. "Do you have a weight room in your shop?"

"Yeah. Basement level, near the locker rooms. You lift?"

"Yes, I do. You?"

He nodded. "I prefer mornings, though."

"Evenings for me. It helps burn off the stress. Can I get in there tonight, you think?"

"Sure. Do you need a spotter?"

"I do."

"Then I'm your man."

"Thanks." It was always better to have someone with you just in case the weight slipped. Eve had been in gyms where the guys spotting for her had been so focused on her curves, the weight bar could have dropped down onto her throat and they would have been too mesmerized to notice. Palmer didn't give her that impression. "My gear's in a bag in my trunk."

"How about we swing by and pick it up after we file our paperwork? I've room in my office where you can use your laptop, if you don't mind the clutter."

"Sounds good."

"And by the way. I like you, too."

She laughed softly and enjoyed the light dancing in his brown eyes. "Good to know."

When he turned his attention back to driving, Eve turned hers to the city moving by, and the Oya inside smiled.

By the time they filed their reports and got her gear out of the trunk of her car, the sun had set. It had been a long couple of days. She couldn't wait to work up a sweat by challenging herself both mentally and physically. Palmer showed her the way to the ladies' locker room and she went inside to change.

When Leyton entered the weight room, he spied a few familiar faces amongst the men and women working out and nodded a silent greeting. Because of the time of day, the place wasn't very crowded. He looked around for Clark, and for a moment didn't see her but then saw her stretched out on a weight bench across the room. For a moment he stood and watched her as she went through a series of slow reps. From the size of the weights on each end of the bar and the ease with which she was pumping, he assumed she was in the process of warming up and in no immediate need of a spotter. The other men in the room were doing their best not to stare at the beauty effortlessly pressing 150 pounds, but they were having a hard time, and so was he. She was wearing a pair of loose gray sweats, black sneaks and a gray midriff-length sports bra. It was standard female attire in gyms everywhere, but on her it didn't look standard at all. He found himself admiring the strong flex of her arms and the tight cut of her abdomen as the bar continued rising and falling. He couldn't ever remember wanting to make love to a woman on a weight bench before, but he did then.

Deciding he needed to get moving before she caught him drooling, he walked over just as her phone rang. She sat up, grabbed the towel lying beside the bench and quickly wiped her face. Phone to her ear, she acknowledged his approach with a nod and began responding to the person on the other end of the call. "When was this?" she asked.

She glanced up at him and her expression made him sense something had happened.

"Okay," she said into the phone. "We'll be there soon as we can." She ended the call.

"What's up?"

"That was McBride. A man in Grand Rapids was just

admitted to a local hospital with shock and fourth-degree burns on his hands, legs and feet. And get this. His name— Phillip Brandywine."

Leyton froze. "The developer?"

"Apparently so, and the person who rode in the ambulance with him was Marvin Crenshaw."

Leyton stared.

"That's too much of a coincidence for me, so you up for a road trip?"

"Oh, yes."

"Meet you upstairs in ten minutes."

She hastily walked off in the direction of the locker room and he followed. He was so focused on the question of how Brandywine and Crenshaw might be connected, he almost missed the winning answer to another burning mystery. Glancing up, he saw that on Clark's back, in the bare space between the bottom edge of her bra and the top of her sweats, floated a familiar-looking butterfly. He stopped, blinked and stared hard. Heart pumping and wide-eyed, he fought to make sense of that even as he quickly gauged her height and the way she moved before she disappeared through the locker room door. The last time he'd seen that butterfly the woman it belonged to had been walking away from him in much the same manner. *Oh, my God!* His knees went weak. It was her! Never in his life had he imagined finding her right under his nose. He wanted to shout hallelujah. He was grinning like an idiot because he couldn't help himself. She was going to have a fit when he revealed himself, he just knew it. And the thought of the look on her face made him laugh so joyously he drew stares, but didn't care. The centurion had found his lady!

On the drive to Grand Rapids through the dark, the pleased Leyton kept his eyes on the road and his mind on the goddess riding shotgun. It was still hard to be believe that he'd found her, but in his gut he knew he wasn't wrong. Hard-assed ATF Agent Eve Clark was in reality the warrior goddess Oya, and it was taking all he had not to let her know that he knew. The knowledge had him smiling so broadly he was glad his features were hidden by the shadows.

"McBride said Brandywine was supposedly burning leaves and used too much gasoline," she said.

"Who uses gasoline on leaves? Burning leaves has been illegal for years."

"I know, and I suppose there are people dumb enough to still be doing something like that, but the Crenshaw connection makes me wonder."

"Did McBride know when the accident happened?"

"Crenshaw told the doctors today, but the doc told McBride that from the looks of Brandywine's condition when the EMTs brought him in, it might have been a few days ago."

"Which would place it within the timeline of our fire."

"Exactly. Hopefully this won't turn out to be a wild goose chase."

"Nice night to be driving either way."

Eve agreed. It was a nice night. The moon was fat and full, and there wasn't a lot of traffic. "I've never been to Grand Rapids."

"I was up here last summer for some training. Surprised to find out it's the second-largest city in the state."

"Never knew that," she admitted. With the jazz playing softly in the background, it was easy to believe that they were just a couple out for a late-night drive and not two arson investigators hoping for an interview with a potential suspect. Eve looked his way and reminded herself that they were working. "Obviously Crenshaw knows the developer, so why did he play dumb with us when we asked about their relationship?"

"He did seem to stumble, but maybe he was telling the truth about not knowing anything about threats."

"Well, I want to know what he was lying about."

"Which is why we're out here in the middle of the night."

Eve looked over his way. The dark interior hid his features. "If we have to spend the night, I'm authorized to pay for a couple of rooms."

"Good to know. If we can't question Brandywine until the morning, we'll need a place to catch a few winks."

Eve wondered what it might be like to spend the night with him. Would he be a generous lover? Before speculating further, she chastised herself and pushed the thought aside. He might be intriguing and fine, but no way were they going to sleep together this early in the game. The last time she threw caution to the wind she was left wanting a man she had no hope of ever seeing again. She allowed herself a few quiet moments to think of her centurion and the fantastic night they'd shared before she let the bittersweet memories go and stepped back into reality.

At the hospital, they weren't allowed to question Brandywine. He was sedated. The floor nurse did allow a quick peek through the windows of his room in the ICU, and all the monitors and drips he was hooked up to showed how serious his injuries were.

After the solemn appraisal, the nurse told them, "I don't think he's going to be able to give you any kind of statement for a while. He's pretty messed up."

"Were there any witnesses that you know of?" Eve asked.

"We weren't told about any, but his wife's down the hall in the family waiting room. Maybe she knows something."

Eve and Leyton thanked her and walked the short distance to the room the nurse indicated. Once inside, they saw a lone woman reading a magazine. She looked up at their entrance, offered a small smile and went back to her reading.

"Mrs. Brandywine?" Leyton asked quietly.

She looked up again, and it was easy to see the slight confusion in her tired eyes. "Yes?"

Leyton made the introductions.

Their titles made her stiffen sharply, but she pulled it together. Looking between him and Eve, she asked, "Why are you here?"

He explained, and as she listened her lips tightened. Eve noted how well-dressed she was. The gray twinset appeared to be cashmere. There was a single strand of pearls around her neck. She looked more suited for a Sunday afternoon sorority meeting than keeping vigil for her critically burned husband.

Leyton asked, "So, can you tell us about how he was injured?"

Before she could respond, Marvin Crenshaw walked in. Upon seeing Leyton and Eve, he stopped and asked, "What are you two doing here?" He sounded perturbed.

Eve answered. "We're here about Mr. Brandywine's injuries."

"He was burning leaves. I was there. Barbara, you don't have to tell them anything."

Her chin came up, and the anger in her eyes matched her clipped tone. "Suppose I want to."

"Don't say anything," he ordered as if accustomed to telling her what to do.

Leyton countered with, "Mrs. Brandywine, if you know something that will help us in this case, even if it's criminal, it's better you tell us now."

Barbara met Crenshaw's hostile stare and then looked down into her lap.

Leyton asked, "Mrs. Brandywine, how long have you known Mr. Crenshaw?"

"He's my brother," she revealed in a disgusted tone. "My baby brother."

That information took both investigators by surprise.

Crenshaw said evenly, "And as your brother I'm advising you not to say anything else."

"Why?" she tossed back bitterly. "If my Phillip dies, you'll just put the blame on him. Why shouldn't I tell them that you were the one who talked him into setting that fire?"

"Shut the hell up!" he yelled.

She jumped to her feet. "For once in my life, I will not! You planned it, you bought the gasoline, but you didn't have the guts to do it yourself! You bastard!"

And then she was across the room hitting him and swearing and crying as if her grief and anger were all she knew. Leyton immediately grabbed her and pulled her away even as she tried to free herself from his hold. "I'll kill you if he dies! Kill you!"

Nurses and hospital guards poured into the room in response to all the screaming, and while Mrs. Brandywine continued to wail and threaten, Eve saw Crenshaw bolt out the door. "Palmer! Call for backup!" And she sped out after him.

"Stop! Federal agent! Stop!"

But he kept running. An orderly pushing a mop bucket turned into Crenshaw's path and was sent flying. "Stop him!" she yelled.

Nurses were sticking their heads out of doors but, upon seeing the action, ducked back inside.

Flying, Eve had her weapon drawn but knew better than to open fire in a hospital, so she kept running. He blasted through a set of doors and was out of sight until she busted through and found herself on the fire stairs. She could hear his feet pounding down the stairs below.

"Dammit! Stop!"

But he kept going, and so did she.

The small hospital only had three floors, so moments later they were outside and she was chasing him under the artificial lights in front of the building. He was heading for the parking lot. Eve looked around to make sure no citizens were in sight, then raised her weapon. "Stop or I'll shoot."

He didn't slow, so she squeezed off a shot over his head. "Crenshaw, you are under arrest."

"Go to hell, bitch!"

That made her mad, so she kicked up her pace and gained on him. They were in the parking lot. Off in the distance she heard approaching sirens. Backup maybe, but she didn't have the luxury of waiting to see. It was her and Crenshaw. Still running, he tore around a line of cars. She knew that if he got into his vehicle, he might manage to get away, so she increased her speed again and gained enough ground to hear his harsh breathing and to see the panic on his face when he turned and saw her just a few feet behind. For a woman with Eve's height that few feet meant zip, so she launched herself. She tackled him, and he hit the pavement hard enough that he screamed with pain. Trained to ignore the impact's toll on herself, she heaved him up, threw him forcibly against a car and held him there while she snatched out her cuffs and snapped them shut around his wrists. She took in a series of deep breaths to regain her wind, then, after giving him his rights, grabbed his arm and marched him back toward the building.

Palmer appeared, gun drawn, face grim, but upon seeing her, relaxed and holstered his weapon.

"Party's over," she said to him.

Smiling, he bowed with a flourish of his hand, and she shoved the cuffed and limping Crenshaw forward.

Later, Leyton stood in the hospital lounge that the local law enforcement had turned into a mini command post and watched Clark giving her statement to the district FBI agent. Wow. What a woman. With Crenshaw now in custody, the feds would be handling the case from that point on, including prosecution. He looked down at his watch. It was just past midnight. A lot had happened since finding out Clark and his lady Oya were one in the same. What a woman, he thought to himself again. She'd taken off after Crenshaw like she'd been shot out of a cannon. He'd stayed behind momentarily to place Mrs. Brandywine in the care of the hospital's security unit before running out to join the chase—totally unnecessary. Not only had she run Crenshaw down, she had taken him down. Looking over at her now, all he could think about was taking her somewhere and making hard hot love until neither of them could walk. However, he had his own paperwork to complete, so he buried the fantasy, took a deep breath and began to work on the form on his clipboard.

He was just about finished when she walked up. Without looking up, he asked, "Are you done?"

"Yeah. Did Brandywine's wife make a statement?"

"Yep. Apparently, our Mr. Crenshaw has a gambling problem. Her husband's construction company is on the rocks because of the economy so Crenshaw came up with the brilliant idea of burning the mall down. He figured when the Brandywines' insurance check came through, they'd split the money and no one would be the wiser. And get this—he picked Detroit because in his mind, arson is commonplace."

"So that whole song and dance about trying to be a good brother and helping out the city was just BS."

"Pretty much."

"So he was there the night of the fire."

"Yes, but the wife said her brother chickened out at the last minute, which is how the husband wound up with fourth-degree burns. My man Blazer was right. Amateurs." He went back to the paperwork.

"The Bureau will handle transporting Crenshaw back to Detroit."

"Good, because we need to talk," he said still writing.

"What about?"

"You and me, my lady." He could feel her go still in response but continued to write nonchalantly.

She asked quietly, "What did you just call me?"

For the first time, Leyton looked up, still acting as calmly as if they were discussing the weather, he said just as quietly, "My lady."

Her eyes widened.

He kept his grin hidden. "Let me take this over to the local sheriff, and then we can go." The look on her face was priceless. "And those two rooms you were going to get? We'll probably only need one."

And he walked away.

Eve stood there with her mouth on the floor. Why had he called her that? Only one man had ever addressed her that way. Surely Palmer didn't know about the costume party. Did he? And if he did, how? Had he talked to Shelly? But then she remembered that *she* hadn't talked to Shelly, so that couldn't be it. Maybe she'd been driven so crazy by the centurion that she was jumping to conclusions. And what did he mean saying only get one room? Was he planning on driving back with Crenshaw and the FBI agent? She was so confused her head was spinning. When she came back to herself he was standing in front of her, and she swore there was mischief dancing in his eyes.

He asked, "Ready to ride?"

"Palmer, I'm confused."

"That's why every goddess should have a centurion around to explain things."

She froze and stared. "What!"

His answering chuckle didn't help her mood but cemented the fact that somehow or another he knew about the costume party. "Who told you?" she asked angrily, fighting to keep her voice down.

"Nobody had to tell me. I was there and so were you." He

then slipped into the soft Southern voice of her centurion. "Remember?"

Eve felt dizzy. For the first time in her life, she thought she might faint, but since there was no fainting allowed in ATF, she grabbed hold of herself, turned on her heel and strode off.

Leyton shook his head and followed.

Outside, he found her standing by the car and said, "Thanks for not breaking the window, hot wiring the engine and driving off."

"Didn't have enough time," she confessed, eyeing him.

He gave her a half smile. "Been missing you, girl," he said emotionally.

Those four words made all of Eve's warring emotions melt into a puddle. She had no defense against the truth she heard in his tone. "How long have you known?"

"Just since tonight. I noticed the butterfly on your back in the weight room. It matched the one I saw Sunday night when you slipped into the bathroom to get dressed."

"So, you haven't been playing me since we started working together?"

"No darlin', never. Seeing that butterfly at the gym almost dropped me to my knees."

Eve looked out into the night.

"So, can we go somewhere and talk?"

After a long moment of silence, she turned to him. "Yeah."

Chapter 7

Eve had never considered how she'd respond should she ever meet the centurion again, so now that she had, she was at a loss as to how to handle it. On one level, she was ecstatic, of course. But on another level, she was admittedly wary. What would he want from her? Was it just more sex? She thought too highly of herself to be just a booty call. In her mind, the two of them had made a real connection that night, but did he feel the same way? Granted, he'd said he'd missed her, and the sincerity in his voice couldn't be denied, but where did they stand really?

She'd already called ahead to a hotel to book a room, and when they found it, she went inside to get the key while he waited outside in the car. The old Eve wanted to sign for two rooms, but the Oya part of her was ready to pick up where they'd left off on Sunday. The memories of what they'd shared overrode her cautious instincts, so she took the key to room 214 and went back outside to rejoin him. She justified the decision to herself by agreeing with his suggestion that they needed to talk.

"We're in 214," she told him after she got back in the car.

He held her eyes for a moment and then drove around to the parking lot.

The suite was large. The national chain catered to the business class and had a small kitchen complete with pots, pans and dishes. There was a bedroom downstairs and another upstairs. A nice sized fireplace anchored the main area and she saw a couple of logs stacked beside it.

"Nice place," he said, dropping his overnight bag onto the floor. "I'll take the bedroom down here if you want to take the one upstairs.

"That's fine."

She noted that he was watching her and seemed as uncertain as she. That made her wonder what he might be thinking and where they'd be when it came time to drive back to Detroit later that morning. "I'm going to put my bag upstairs," she said.

"Okay."

She felt his eyes on her as she climbed the stairs, but she didn't look back.

When she came back down he was in the kitchen going through the phone book.

"I'm trying to find someone who'll deliver. I'm starving."

She was, too. The last food she remembered was the corned beef sandwich she'd had for lunch. She took a seat on one of the kitchen stools while he called around.

He finally found a pizza place that promised delivery in thirty minutes, so they put in their order and he put his phone away.

"Do you want to wait in here or on the couch?"

"Couch." It had been a long day—from the investigation

of the fire, to driving here, to chasing Crenshaw through the parking lot. She wanted a long soak in a hot tub.

"How about a fire?" he asked. "Logs come with the price of the room. We might as well use them."

She shrugged her shoulders. "Sure."

So while he hunched down in front of the fireplace and lit the prefab logs with the long matches provided, she walked over and doused a few of the lights. He swung around and looked at her for a few silent seconds.

"Can't enjoy the fire with all the lights on," she said.

The dimmed lights made for an intimate setting, and only after she took her seat did she wonder if that was a good thing or not. Once he got the fire started it didn't matter. She enjoyed the flickering shadows that filled the room.

He sat in one of the arm chairs next to the fire, and in the silence that followed they spent a lot of time looking at each other, but no words were exchanged. It was as if neither of them knew how to begin.

Finally, she asked, "How'd you wind up being a centurion at the party? Did you know the organizers?"

"No. I was working. Mayor wanted the department to keep an eye on things. You?"

"Talked into going by my cousin. She's a Hollywood costume designer."

"She make the suit?"

Eve nodded.

"Great job."

"I thought so, too."

He chuckled softly and said again, "Great job." He met her eyes. "When you walked in, you were the hottest thing I'd ever seen."

His face and voice in the firelight were doing things to Eve's senses she wasn't sure she was supposed to be acknowledging this early in their conversation, but her growing attraction to him didn't seem to care. All it wanted to do was remember his kisses, the way his hands had expertly roamed her body and the way he'd filled her. It also reminded her how sad she had felt leaving the hotel that night. "Never thought I'd see you again," she told him in a voice as quiet as the flames.

"Same here," he added. "I kept telling myself not to think about you, but it hasn't worked real well."

"Here either."

A smile played at the edges of his lips. "So, what do we do?"

"I don't know, but I'm not going to be a booty call."

"Me, either."

She laughed. Couldn't help it.

"What's so funny?" he countered with mock offense. "Men don't want to be treated like a piece of meat, either."

"Yeah, right. Name one."

He shook his head in amusement. "You're cold."

The flickering shadows showed her smile.

Leyton doubted she knew how much he'd enjoyed her company these past few days. He'd worked with a lot of women in his career, but never one so fierce or so beautiful. She was the type of lady he wanted to wake up to every morning and come home to every night—a woman who understood why he had to put in such long hours on the job, or had to leave their bed in the middle of the night because of a fire. She got it because she lived it, too, and something inside him wanted them to live that life together. He was pretty sure he was in love with her, which didn't make any sense because he was not the I-met-you-let's-get-married kind of guy. He was usually cautious about starting a relationship because some women just didn't understand the demands that working in law enforcement could place on a couple. But that wouldn't be an issue if the partner worked in the same field. "So, do you believe we can work on something that's more than a booty call?"

She met his gaze and for a moment didn't respond. He couldn't tell whether she was trying to think of a reply or just thinking about what he'd asked.

Finally, she said, "I do."

He smiled and his heart soared. "I do, too."

Her answering smile made him ask, "Then do you think I can come sit next to you?'

She chuckled. "Yes, you may."

He came over and sat down, and when he put his arm around her, Eve felt like a teenager. Being next to him felt so natural she snuggled closer and rested her head against his shoulder. "Better?"

He gave her a squeeze. "Much."

Savoring the quiet moment and the presence and nearness of each other, they sat in front of the blazing fire. With a finger he gently lifted her chin and gazed down into her eyes. Awestruck at finding each other again filled them both, and when the kiss came, it was heaven.

They wanted to go slow but the need had been building since their separation on Sunday, and it touched off a desire to make up for lost time. They were plunged into a greedy kissing frenzy. His lips moved over her cheeks, her jaw and her eyes, while hers sought his mouth, his throat and the lobe of his ear. Hands moved frenetically touching each other as if it might be the last time, and soon they were breathing like two runners in a race. And then it became a race to see who could get out of their clothes faster. Still kissing frantically, they snatched open buttons, dragged off shirts and undid zippers. Eve only managed to get her jeans part way down her hips before she was stopped by the searing sensations of his wicked fingers between her legs. He pulled her thong down her hips and heated her with his touch. She tried to counter by planting tiny bites along the strong cords of his neck, but his fingers were impaling her and moving with such raw rhythm her body bowed up and she groaned in heated response.

"I'm going to love you until you can't walk…" he promised gruffly.

The words made her throb and tighten in response to the glorious play of his hand. Through the haze surrounding her, she set her hand against the hardness jutting against his unzipped jeans and took hold. His head fell back. Her eyes glittered with passion and satisfaction at what her rhythmic possession was doing to him, and she kept it up until he growled and stopped her hand. A loud knock on the door broke the moment. A young male voice called loudly. "You ordered a pizza!"

They both cursed.

Leyton slid his fingers across her damp vent and kissed her. "I'll take care of the pizza. Meet me in the shower in two minutes."

Eve had no idea how she made it up the stairs, but she did.

The shower was the most decadent one she'd ever had. While the water poured over them, he kissed his way from the wet globes of her breasts to the nook of her navel, and then on his knees slowly treated the already swollen and pulsing gates of her soul to a shameless act of devotion. He fed greedily, thoroughly. She spread her legs wide and when his mouth took in that small kernel of flesh that made her woman, the orgasm broke her down, and she twisted and cried and came. She grabbed his shoulders for support, but he continued dallying, coaxing until she let out another strangled scream of surrender. If not for his strong hands on her waist, she would have gladly melted to the shower floor and drowned. Instead, her grinning centurion soundlessly invited her to turn and face the shower's back wall. With his hands and his lips he prepared her again. He ran a worshipping hand down her spine and caressed the butterfly that had brought her back to him. Brushing his lips across the back of her neck, he teased his fingers over the spot he'd just prepared so lustily a moment ago, and then slid his strong hardness into her welcoming softness. She purred from the bliss. Holding her by the waist, he began to move in and out—teasing, coaxing first slowly and surely, then quickening the pace. She caught fire again. It was so good and so incredibly erotic, her orgasm exploded. The delicious contractions of her tight sheath pushed him over the edge, too, causing him to shudder and stroke and yell out his release until they both collapsed under the hot pounding spray.

Standing in the steam filled bathroom, he dried her while giving her long, lazy kisses. His free hand was wandering slowly over her warm damp skin, and they both knew they hadn't had enough, but she let him continue his languid task while she basked with closed eyes, and while echoes of the orgasm pulsed softly between her thighs. "Till you can't walk…" he whispered from behind her with his lips against the dewy edge of her neck. He reached around and filled his hands with her velvet weight and gently plucked and toyed with her nipples until she leaned back against him and moaned.

"Come with me," he invited, but first, he turned her to him and dropped his mouth to her breasts. Once her nipples were tight and pleading, he took her gently by the hand and led her into the bedroom.

The moment her back touched the sheets, he silently followed her down, and they began again. He treated her to more centurion magic—seducing her, enticing her and whispering to her to let him make love to her like only he could. And she had no defense. No man had ever touched her so tenderly or so scandalously. She was more uninhibited with him than she'd been with any other, and she was the one on her knees and feeding on him. He groaned breathlessly in response to her wanton devotions and then she slid up his body, taking his swollen shaft into her and smiling down at him with sparkling eyes.

"You like this, don't you?' he asked.

She began to move. Leaning down, she whispered against his ear, "Every woman likes it with a man who does it right."

"Then ride on, goddess," he invited as they kissed.

And ride she did.

For the rest of the night and into the morning they made love—sitting, standing, in the shower again. Eve vaguely remembered being led from the shower and laid on a blanket downstairs in front of the fire. There in the dark, he made orgasms pour out of her like the river Nile and only then did they crawl into bed.

Spooned against him and with his arm holding her close, she chuckled, "Good thing this place had two beds," she chuckled.

He brushed his lips against her bare shoulder. "I couldn't walk back upstairs if somebody paid me a million dollars."

"That bad, huh?"

He ran a hand over her hips. "No, your majesty, that good."

She grinned.

He asked, "So, would a centurion be rising above his station to ask a goddess about a long-term relationship?"

Eve turned to face him, and just as she opened her mouth to answer, her phone rang and the ringtone played the distinctive bass throbbing music from the TV show *Cops*.

"Don't answer that."

"Have to, it's the office." Lord knew she wished she could ignore it like he wanted her to, but she had to answer.

Leyton lay in the bed looking at her beautiful back with its distinctive butterfly. He could tell by her cryptic responses that whatever was going on was important, and probably important enough to bring their interlude to an end. He was right.

She closed the phone and looked back at him. "I have to go."

"Chicago?"

Her response was quiet. "Can't tell you."

Sighing, he sat up. "How soon?"

"According to the call, an hour ago. I need to be out of here ASAP."

"At least let me run you to the airport."

She shook her head. "Can't even let you know what airline I'm flying. I'm going to get a quick shower and call a cab."

"Are you going under?"

She met his eyes just long enough for him to see her sadness before she left him and hurried up the steps to the shower. Alone, he pounded the bed.

Upstairs, Eve showered quickly. Leaving him this way was breaking her heart, but she had no choice. The job came first, and yes, she was going undercover with no idea when she'd surface and see him again. That was the most painful part, just when they'd found each other again, the government needed her and its need overrode her own. She dried off and dressed herself in the set of nondescript jeans and top she always carried in her suitcase just in case and grabbed her coat.

When she got back downstairs, he was making coffee in the kitchen. He'd pulled on a pair of black sweats and a DFD tee and all she could think about was being in his arms again.

He asked, "Are you going to answer my question?"

She knew what question he meant, but she didn't really

have time for this now. "Let me do this first, okay? When I'm done, I'll be in touch."

He nodded.

"I'm sorry, Leyton."

"So am I, baby."

She knew that if she went into his arms she'd start bawling. But since there was no bawling in the ATF, she said, "Take care."

He shrugged. "Sure."

She sensed she'd hurt him, but she was already hurting enough for the both of them. A horn blew outside. "That's my cab. Be well, my centurion."

"You, too, my lady."

They shared a gaze filled with sadness and regret, and then she hurried out of the door.

When his coffee was ready, Leyton took a seat before the now-dying fire and slowly sipped in the silence.

An hour later, Eve was on a flight to L.A. and Leyton was driving home to Detroit.

Chapter 8

In the weeks that followed, Leyton threw himself back into work. Phillip Brandywine recovered enough to agree to testify against his brother-in-law, Marvin Crenshaw, in exchange for a lighter sentence. But Leyton didn't think the developer would ever do any real time due to the extensive rehabilitation he was facing as a result of the fire. Crenshaw hadn't been able to make bail so he was angrily sitting in the county lockup awaiting his day in court.

It was now December. Leyton got up from his desk and walked over to the window to look out at the city in winter. Puffs of steam from the city boilers rose from the manhole covers in the snow-lined streets as people bundled up in hats and gloves pulled their collars high, quickly making their way to their destinations. He hadn't heard a word from Eve. He kept replaying their last moments together, seeing and hearing her seem to duck the question he'd asked. What would she have said had the phone not interrupted them? Yes? No? He had no way of knowing, and at the time he hadn't been able to tell because of the poker face she'd been wearing. What he did know was that he now understood how his ex felt about the abrupt nature of the job. Until then, he'd always been the one hurrying away, never the one left behind, and the realization was an eye-opener. He'd never known this feeling of loss or considered that it would be mixed with disappointment, worry and a bit of resentment. He wasn't sure he liked being on this end of things.

However, Ms. ATF's lack of an answer didn't change the fact that he thought about her every morning when he opened his eyes and every night before he went to sleep. If she was undercover, he hoped she'd be safe, and if she hadn't gotten in touch because she chose not to—he didn't want to think about that. He wished her the best.

Eve was half way across the country seated at a desk in a huge used tire warehouse in Santa Barbara, California. She was working undercover as an office temp hired as an administrative assistant to the boss, James Quinn. Quinn was under investigation for money laundering, dealing in illegal weapons and tax evasion. She'd been working the job now six weeks to the day, and so far the various agencies in the government task force had amassed almost enough evidence to convict him and everyone else in his five-man organization. Although being undercover in an office was way better than being on the street playing a hooker or a crackhead, she hoped that the operation would be wrapped up soon so she could fly home. Leyton had been on her mind since the moment they'd parted. In hindsight, she supposed she could have taken two minutes to answer his question instead of leaving it up in the air the way she had. But she'd been so focused on transforming herself back into Agent Clark that she'd had to set aside Eve Clark the woman, and as a result him, too. If she had given in to the happiness of saying yes, or to the sadness she felt getting into the cab and leaving him behind, the transformation would have taken longer, and she hadn't had that luxury. She'd had to hit the ground running, turn herself into Tamika Wells, prim, soft-spoken and efficient, get on the job, and help the government get the goods on Quinn and the rest of the bad guys. In her private moments, she ached for Leyton and hoped when the investigation finished he would understand, take her in his arms, and let her say, yes.

But in the meantime she had a job to do, so she went back to the letter Tamika was typing for the boss on the computer screen.

Three days later, the day after Christmas, the government swooped down on James Quinn and his illegal operation like Godzilla on Tokyo. When the dust finally settled, Eve was on a flight to Chicago and home.

After an indulgent bubble bath and a good night's sleep, she got up the next morning and tried to decide what to do about Leyton. Should she contact him? She knew she wanted to but wasn't sure he'd still be interested after all this time. She mulled it over for the rest of the day and in the end, decided she would. The question then became how? Thinking it over for a while she came up with a plan.

One of the fire department's mail clerks stuck her head in Leyton's office. "Captain Palmer, FedEx left this for you."

Leyton took the small package and thanked her.

After her departure, he used a box cutter to slit the tape and opened the top panels. The inside was filled with scented black tissue paper and inside was the black velvet domino Eve had worn the night they met. His heart started to pound as he slowly lifted it free and the memories it evoked filled his mind. *Is this her way of saying goodbye?* There was a note enclosed, so he set the mask down and read:

The Warrior Goddess Oya humbly requests the centurion's presence New Year's Eve.
Suite 2135—10 p.m.

He picked up the mask again, eyed its sensual beauty and grinned like the happy man he was.

By Eve's calculations it would take her three months to pay off the credit card bill for the suite she'd reserved, but as she walked around and viewed the way the table was set and the intimate atmosphere created by the hotel staff, she decided it would be well worth the budget busting, but only if Leyton showed up. There was no guarantee he would, so she was a bit apprehensive as the time on the clock approached ten.

She'd reserved this particular suite because it was same one they'd been in on Halloween, the night they met, and in spite of her hard-boiled demeanor, Eve was sentimental. In the weeks they'd been apart, she'd spent an inordinate amount of time thinking back to how much of a good guy he was and how magical he was in bed. It was the former that stood out, however, and the part of Leyton that she valued the most. She could be herself with him—good, bad or ugly. Even though he hadn't seen those parts yet, she was certain he could handle it. She knew he wouldn't turn out to be perfect either, but that was the beauty of a relationship, at least in her mind. Taking the good with the bad and attempting to make lemonade out of whatever lemons they each brought to the table. Not that she'd ever experienced any of that in her past dealings with men, but having watched her aunt and uncle growing up, she knew that that kind of give-and-take would be necessary.

But in order for her to sip that lemonade, he had to make an appearance. So to keep herself from pacing, and yes, worrying, she snagged a meatball from the buffet laid out on the table in the suite and took a seat.

At ten minutes past ten, the phone in the suite rang. Eve picked up.

"Evening, your majesty."

Eve melted into a puddle at the sound of his Texas drawl. "Hello, centurion."

"I was at a fire, but I'm on my way now. Didn't want you to worry about whether I was going to show up or not." He paused for a moment to add softly, "Good hearing from you."

"Same here."

"I'm just turning into the parking garage. Be right up."

The call ended, and the great warrior goddess, wearing her black leather catsuit and long platinum wig, kicked up her heels with glee.

Moments later there was a knock on the door. Drawing in a deep breath, Eve went to answer it. A quick peek through the hole showed him standing on the other side, so she opened it.

For a moment neither spoke. They were too overcome by the memories.

"Your centurion reporting for duty, my lady."

She feasted her eyes on the sight of him, and her nipples tightened in response to the heat in his eyes. "Welcome." It had been too long since she'd seen him last. Way too long. "My answer is yes. In fact, I think we should just cut to the chase and think about making this permanent."

"Really?"

"I do, but if that scares you or makes you want to run, I'll understand. There's the elevator."

He shook his head and walked by her and inside. She closed the door and turned to face him.

He was standing with his arms folded.

"What?"

"You've been gone for almost eight weeks. You get me up here, you're wearing that suit and all you want to do is talk and give orders. Come here and let me give that mouth of yours something else to do," he fussed with mock severity.

She tried hard to keep from smiling but failed. "It's what we goddesses do."

His own smile peeked out. "I know, but come here anyway."

So she went to him and let him take her in his arms. It felt good.

"Much better," he said brushing his lips over hers. "I think we should make this long-term, too, but for now, I want to spend the next little while getting you out of this suit, and then you can talk all you want—if you can."

"Is that a challenge?"

"It would be if you had a chance of winning." He was already sliding her zipper down. "I give you twenty minutes, tops, before you're screaming loud enough to be heard in Canada." He punctuated his words by placing hot kisses on her throat and the tops of her breasts above the neckline of her catsuit.

She crooned in response. "You're on."

He slid the front of the suit down to free her breasts, and before he leaned down to help himself, he promised, "You are so going to lose."

And Eve did lose—again, and again and again. In between, they did manage to remember to toast in the New Year with flutes of champagne and even to eat a bit of the food, but for the most part, they just made love.

Finally when they settled down to sleep, Eve caught a glimpse of her catsuit lying in a puddle on the floor of the bedroom and made a mental note to make sure Shelly freed up her calendar so she could be maid of honor at the wedding. After all, this was her fault. With that decision made, Eve cuddled back against the man she planned to spend the rest of her life with, and as he pulled her closer, she closed her eyes, the happiest woman in the world.

* * * * *

To Didier: we'll always have Paris

CANDY CHRISTMAS
Adrianne Byrd

Chapter 1

A giddy Georgine Duran raced through the Christmas-decorated office of Nu4us in her black Prada heels and tight pencil skirt. "He's coming. He's coming," she informed the ladies in their cubicles.

Practically all of the women whipped out their compact mirrors, added swaths of lipstick and checked to make sure that their various hairdos were picture perfect. Some even added a spritz of perfume. A split second later, the *ding* of the elevator bay had them all scrambling to put their mirrors and makeup away and cast their eyes toward the elevator doors as they opened, in time to see their morning attraction.

Montel Starks lifted his head and strolled into the office dressed in a sharp slate gray suit that fitted his model-size six-three frame to an absolutely perfect tee. The man effortlessly oozed suave sophistication. Heads swirled, hearts fluttered and panties grew moist as he glided past the company's supermajority female staff. There was something for everyone.

Whether you liked a broad chest, powerful legs or a sexy ass, Montel had you covered. Without a doubt, he put the "h" in handsome and the "s" in sexy. With his chiseled jaw line, Tyson Beckford eyes and LL Cool J lips framed in a shadowy beard, Montel was the very definition of fine.

"Morning, ladies," Montel greeted.

"*Morning, Montel,*" the women chorused back, cheesing their best smile.

His beautiful lips lifted a bit to reveal a white smile that lit up his entire face. He even tossed a wink to a few lucky women who looked ready to swoon out of their chairs. In Nu4us, Montel Starks was, hands down, a bona fide rock star, and the female employees were his number one fans.

"Don't you look lovely this morning, Georgine," he said, stopping in front of his assistant's desk. "New outfit?"

Georgine blushed and fluttered a hand to the top of her sweater. "What? This old thing?" Her gaze caught the price tag hanging from her wrist, and she quickly dropped her hand to her lap. "Um, Mr. Carter scheduled a meeting this morning at ten so I took the liberty of rearranging your nine-thirty for three o'clock."

"I'm sure Ms. Baxter was thrilled about that," he joked.

Georgine turned up her nose. She couldn't stand the über-rich femme fatale who tied up her phone line at least six times a day. "*Mrs.* Baxter threw her usual fit because she can't see you when she wants. But I told her to either take the three o'clock or wait until after the Christmas holidays. Needless to say she took the three o'clock opening." Georgine discreetly pulled the tag off her sleeve and then handed him his morning messages. "If you ask me, *Mrs.* Baxter is interested in more than just business."

Montel's smile stretched wider. "I'm sure I don't know what you mean." He winked.

"Uh-huh."

"Any idea what the ten o'clock meeting is about?" He absently shuffled his morning messages around, trying to pretend that he wasn't anxious to hear who made top sales executive of the year and would most likely get the promotion to VP of sales.

"Well, it is that time of year," Georgine said, seeing through his act. "It could be the big announcement."

He winked and then glanced around the office. "Any word how our main competition has fared yet?"

"Not yet. That camp is keeping their cards close to the vest... but if you ask me—" She leaned forward and whispered, "I think you're finally going to knock Lahane off the throne."

Montel shrugged even though his smile grew wider. "I don't know. Lahane has been number one for the past seven years."

"Yeah. But that was before *you* joined the company. Now there's some real competition and frankly my money is riding on you."

"Don't tell me there's a pool on this."

"Are you kidding? There's a pool on everything in this office."

"I'll keep that in mind." He laughed. "But for the record, I wouldn't be so quick to count Lahane out. The woman is a tiger."

Candace Lahane breezed through the doors of Nu4us looking like a million bucks in a pleated, houndstooth Victoria coat, large Gucci shades and a pair of Christian Louboutins that hadn't hit the shelves yet. It had long been her philosophy to be number one in both business *and* style.

"Good morning, Ms. Lahane," Wendi, the front desk receptionist, greeted her with a timid smile and a half nod.

Candace ignored the woman and continued with the conversation that was buzzing in her Bluetooth. "No. Mr.

Scarborough, I'm all over it. I'll have my assistant, Mia, send those proposals over to you within the hour by courier. Trust me, you're going to be thrilled with the final product." She stepped into the elevator and pressed the button for the top floor. Just before the door closed, a team of men in blue suits crowded in behind her. *"Good Morning, Ms. Lahane,"* they greeted her in synchronized precision.

She pressed the mute button on her Bluetooth and flashed them all her expensive smile. "Good morning, gentlemen," she said in her best feminine purr.

Each one of them beamed smiles back at her like eager puppies, starving for her attention. She enjoyed her power over the opposite sex. It was an art form that she'd spent years perfecting and putting to good use her entire career. And why not? If men insisted on thinking with the wrong head, why not use it to one's advantage?

The elevator's bell dinged a second before the door slid open. "You fellas have a good day," she said sweetly and then sauntered out of the small compartment with a little extra swing to her hips.

"You too, Ms. Lahane."

Candace caught the few eye rolls and head shaking from a few dozen women in their cubicles. Haters—and hypocrites—each and every one of them. She'd seen how they all fawned and swooned over that self-absorbed, conceited playboy Montel Starks. They, along with half his client list, made fools of themselves hanging on his every word and blushing like know-nothing teenagers whenever he dropped platitudes or phony compliments. She, on the other hand, saw straight through him whenever he turned his so-called charm on her. The eye-winking, the slow, deliberate way he licked his lips or how he would purposely invade a woman's personal space so that his masculine-scented cologne permeated your senses so that he could try and seduce his way into whatever he wanted.

She knew that playbook.

Hell, she wrote it.

"Morning, Mia," she said, breezing past her desk. "Call the courier. I need you to send that final proposal over to Mr. Scarborough's office pronto." She tapped her earpiece. "Mr. Scarborough? Yes. I've arranged everything. We can reconnect in one hour."

"You're the best," Scarborough said.

"That's what you're paying for," she volleyed back and then disconnected the call.

Behind her, Mia marched in with a smile and Candace's morning order of a tall half-skinny, half-one percent, extra hot split quad shot—two shots espresso, two shots regular latte with whipped cream. "Here you go. I already called the courier service when I first came in this morning. They should be here any minute now."

"Great." Candace whipped off her shades, sat her briefcase down and peeled out of her coat before accepting her latte. "Have we tracked down Walter Anderson yet?"

"Still on it." Mia grimaced. "I swear that the man is worse than Carmen Santiago."

"That may be, but we need to find him. Landing an account with his company—any account will be like a cherry on top for that VP position." Candace took her first sip of coffee and sighed as her morning caffeine fix immediately started to settle her nerves.

"Speaking of which," Mia said. "I had to rearrange your calendar today. Mr. Carter called a ten o'clock meeting."

Candace's mind raced. "Any clue what it's about?"

"None." Mia glanced over her shoulder to double-check that they were alone in Candace's posh corner office and still elected to lower her voice. "I did hear some speculation in the break room that Mr. Carter has made a decision on the VP position and he wants to announce it early before the Christmas break."

"Really?" Candace leaned back in her executive leather chair with a sly grin. "Have you crunched our numbers?"

Mia looked downright giddy. "1.8 *billion*. Five percent higher than last year's total. We're a shoe-in."

Despite the good news, Candace shook her head. "Don't count our chickens before they're hatched. Any clue how *he's* doin'?" She didn't say his name because she'd made it a rule never to utter that slick devil's name in her office, the one who had all the women in the office losing their minds.

Mr. Hot Shot. Mr. Know-It-All. *And* Mr. Pain-in-the-Ass. Well, at least in Candace's ass. From the moment he'd walked through the doors of Nu4us, it seemed that everyone at the company could talk of little else. In a way, it was sort of understandable. In his short time at the company, he'd completely shaken up the game. Landing and closing big advertising accounts with what seemed like little or no effort at all. Now he was nipping at her heels and threatening everything she'd worked for.

After seven years of being on top at Nu4us, the VP position should've been a no-brainer. Instead, Mr. Carter, who'd seemed just as hoodwinked as his female employees, spent boys night out at ball games, cigar bars and gentlemen clubs with He-Who-Must-Not-Be-Named on the regular.

"I don't have any solid number," Mia said. "But I know that sneaky assistant of his has been nosing around lately trying to find out our numbers."

"Oh, really?" Candace took another healthy gulp of her coffee. "That means that he thinks he actually has a shot of winning this." She shook her head. "Bastard."

A knock had both women jerking their head toward the open door. A young lanky-framed brother removed the earplugs to his iPod from his ears. "I'm here to pick up a package?"

"Right." Mia strolled out of the office to retrieve the package for Scarborough, leaving Candace to churn this latest information inside her head and, more importantly, to try to guess what was going on in Montel Stark's head, because in the end only one of them could be on top.

Chapter 2

Montel strolled into the conference room along with a few other ad executives. All of them slapping him on the back and congratulating him on his presumed promotion.

"Man, you got this in the bank," Doug, a fifteen-year employee, boasted. "Believe me when I say that you're our hero."

A murmur of agreement encircled Montel as a few more pounds hit his back.

Montel held up his hands and tried to feign humility, but in truth his ego was swelling so much it could barely fit into the room. His history with Lahane wasn't as long or as aggressive as his colleagues, but she definitely brought out his competitive side like no other.

Before meeting and, consequently, bumping heads with the woman whose whispered nickname was Hard Candy, Montel had always thought that women who looked like Lahane got their money from either posing in front of a camera or by hooking their claws into aging billionaires during their annual trophy-wife hunt. Sure, it was a bit sexist, and maybe he shouldn't have told her that at a cocktail party, but that had always been his experience.

Frankly, nothing in his life had prepared him for meeting a woman like Lahane. The Harvard grad was quite possibly the smartest person he'd ever met. He'd witnessed on several occasions her ability to talk about virtually any subject and recall facts and figures off the top of her head. And except for the guys she squashed in competition, men absolutely adored her.

With good reason.

He and Candy had a secret. They had actually met two years before he came to work for Nu4us—in Bora-Bora, in fact. He'd never forget her itsy-bitsy silver dress that had had him thinking about putting a ring on it.

Gerald, a short, thick-waisted brother who'd had the misfortune of coming in a distant second in sales for the past seven years, puffed out his chest and added his gruff two cents into the mix. "I plan to snap a picture on my iPhone and make Christmas cards when Carter makes the announcement."

The guys laughed.

Gerald continued, "It's time that bitch was knocked off her high horse and Montel is just the man to do it."

The crowd laughed. Montel frowned.

It was unfortunate that Candace chose that moment to prop up against the conference room's door. "Think so, Gerald?"

The group of gossiping men jumped and swiveled their necks toward the door. The festive celebratory atmosphere evaporated despite the fact that Candace was smiling. "Sounds to me like you *boys* can't handle a woman playing in your little sandboxes." Her eyes swept toward Montel. "Pity."

Montel started to clarify that Gerald wasn't speaking for him, but then Mr. Carter waltzed up behind Candace.

"Good morning, gentlemen…and Ms. Lahane."

Candace tilted her head and then entered the conference room with her head high and her hips swinging. Angry or not, every eye followed her as she made her way to the other end of the long conference table.

Montel's gaze roamed from her hips to her perfectly round ass that had a nice jiggle when she walked. He sucked in a quiet breath and even mouthed, "Goddamn" before she sat down. The hard-on he'd had from the moment he'd laid eyes on her stretched a few more inches and challenged the seams of his pants. It must've been true for all of them because he and the rest of his colleagues scrambled for chairs before their dicks saluted her—including Mr. Carter.

"Looks like we're all here," Mr. Carter said, straightening his tie and clearing his throat. "How is everyone doing this morning?"

Everyone responded with an out of sync chorus of "good" and "fine."

"Great." Carter plopped open a leather folder. "Well, I'm only going to take a few minutes of your time. We usually announce our top ad executive around this time every year. And as you also know, Sloan McAvoy will be leaving at the end of the year, so I'd decided that this year's top executive will be assuming his position."

A lot of head-bobbing and sideward glances followed Carter's opening statement. Candace calmly drew a deep breath and folded her arms under her breasts. The injustice of this position being awarded on the basis of just this year's performance pricked her skin. It seemed to her a seven-year proven track record would have been the way to go, but whatever.

"The accounting department crunched the numbers— several times—and to my great surprise we have a first," Carter said, clapping his hands together.

"A first what?" Candace asked, not sure that she was following him.

Carter's face lit up. "Our first *tie*."

Candace and Montel leaned forward and blinked stupidly at him. "A tie?"

"Amazing, isn't it? Both Candace Lahane and our new guy, Montel Stark, had generated 1.8 billion in ad revenue for the company. Absolutely amazing in this economy." He led everyone into a round of applause, but a current of disbelief rippled around the table as well.

Montel and Candace's gazes flew to one another. Neither of them looked as if they were ready to swallow that bitter pill. In fact, Candace's hands itched to wrap around the smug bastard's neck and squeeze it until he passed out or someone called the cops.

"So what exactly does that mean?" Candace asked, returning her attention to the head of the table. She hoped to hell that he wasn't about to suggest that she and Montel share the VP position. That would just lead to the next world war.

"It means that we're going to have sort of a face-off," Carter announced proudly. "Between you and Montel here."

Montel looked skeptical. "I'm not following you."

Carter continued to look proud about this scheme he was cooking up. "We usually run these from November to November. But given the stakes I'm going to a one-month only competition between the two of you. So whichever one of you lands the biggest account in December will win the salesperson of the year *and* land the VP position."

Whatever smile Candace had sported when she'd walked into the conference room was definitely gone by the time she rushed out.

"This is some bullshit!" she declared, breezing past Mia and storming into her office.

Mia grabbed her notepad, jumped out of her seat and followed her boss into her office. "How did it go?"

"Close the door."

Mia doubled back and closed the office door. "Was it that bad? Did Mon—"

"Don't!"

"I mean…did *he* beat us?" she fretted.

"No." Candace dropped into her chair and drew in several deep breaths, but it really wasn't helping. Maybe if she pinched herself hard enough, she'd wake up from this nightmare. Desperate, she actually grabbed the back of her left hand and pinched. "Ow."

Mia frowned and stepped back. "Are you all right? Do I need to call someone for you?"

"No. But I could really use a drink."

"It's not even noon yet."

"So? Who made up that bullshit rule?"

Mia eased into one of the vacant chairs across from her desk. "Maybe you should just tell me what happened."

"That *man* is what happened," she exploded. "The good ole boy system is alive and well on Madison Avenue. Every one of those assholes knows that I deserve that VP position. But they keep inventing new ways to move that damn goal post farther and farther away from me."

"Wait. You won the best sales, but they still gave it to Mon—"

"Ah. Ah. Ah." Candace waved her finger back and forth. "Don't you dare say that man's name!"

"Sorry."

"They didn't give either one of us the position…*yet*." Candace couldn't stand sitting anymore so she hopped up from her chair and started pacing back and forth in from of the window. "I have the good mind to quit."

"What?"

"Start my own agency. Yeah. Hell, my clients love me. They'll follow me wherever I go." That last part was spoken with a little less conviction. There was never any such guarantee in this business. Over the years she had witnessed many friends and colleagues take that leap of faith only to crash and burn in the brave world of start-up ad boutiques. The truth of the matter was that a small *anything* was usually swallowed up by a bigger fish.

"Ms. Lahane, I'm still confused about what's going on," Mia said.

"It's a tie," Candace said, rolling her eyes. "Can you believe it?"

"A tie?"

Candace quickly gave her assistant a recap of her morning meeting and then felt herself get all heated again. "You know, I should just let them go ahead and give it to that asshole. That's what they want to do anyway. I mean…what am I supposed to do in December? It's our weakest month as far as snagging new accounts. All the bigwigs are going to be God knows where during the holidays."

Suddenly, Mia's mouth stretched into a wide smile.

Candace stopped pacing. "What?"

Mia started fanning herself with her notebook. "I think I'm about to earn a big bonus," she sing-songed.

"Oh?" Candace's brows leapt upward. "I'll be the judge of that. Whatcha got?"

"The address for Walter Anderson's company Christmas party. Word is that he'll be in attendance. I figured that you might be up for crashing a party."

Candace's heart raced, but she kept it cool for a few more seconds. "You're kidding me."

Mia shook her head. "Let's just say I pulled a lot of strings and agreed to a couple of dates I'm going to regret."

Candace squealed and raced over and embraced her

assistant. Together they bounced up and down as if they'd just won the lottery. Then Candace got a hold of herself and stepped back. "You're right. You absolutely are going to get that big bonus. Book me on a flight to Paris A-S-A-P."

"I'm on it." Mia pivoted and rushed back to the door but then gasped when she jerked it open and nearly crashed into the massive chest on the other side. "Mr. Starks!"

"Mia, what have I told you about mentioning that man's—" Candace glanced up "—name."

"Ouch," Montel said, pressing a hand to his chest. "I think I might be offended." He glanced off in the distance as if thinking about it. "Yes…I'm pretty sure I'm offended."

"Then sadly, you've mistaken this as the office of Who-Gives-a-Damn," said Candace.

Montel's head flew back with a hearty laugh. "Careful. I just might fall in love with that wonderful sense of humor of yours."

Candace rolled her eyes. "Mia, could you please take care of that thing for me?"

"Right away." Mia tried to squeeze past Montel. "Excuse me."

He finally stepped aside and allowed her to pass. "Do you have a few minutes?" he asked Candace.

"No," Candace said, returning to her desk.

"No matter. This will just take a few minutes." He invited himself into the office and shut the door. "I just wanted to apologize about that bit you heard just before the meeting this morning."

She rolled her eyes again. What on earth had she done in a previous life to deserve this man torturing her so much? "Forget about it. I know you guys like to get together and gossip."

"That's just it," he said. "I know it looks bad, but I don't agree with what some of the men were saying."

"Yeah. My favorite part was when you stood up for me," she said sarcastically. "Such chivalry nearly swept me off my feet." She turned toward her computer. "Now if you don't mind, I need to get back to work."

"I really didn't get a chance to say anything to Gerald. You spoke up, remember?" He strolled closer to her desk. When she didn't respond, he added. "Anyway, I just wanted you to know that I don't think that you're a bitch, Candy."

Her gaze jumped up at him. "It's *Candace*. And frankly, I don't care whether you or your playground friends think I'm a bitch." She cocked her head. "Now—are we through here?"

Montel laughed.

Candace leaned back in her chair and folded her arms. "What's so funny?"

"You. You're really a piece of work," he said, unbuttoning his jacket and taking a seat.

"Don't get comfortable,' she said testily.

"See?" He gestured toward her. "That's what I mean. You've been cold toward me for a while. I'm not quite sure that I deserve it."

"We can either start with you being born or when you invited yourself into my office. You pick." Candace leveled her gaze with his. It was a dangerous thing to do, given that his dark, sensual eyes had a way of drawing in his prey. Not to mention that every other minute, he habitually ran his tongue across his full lips—making them glisten and call out her name.

"Can't we all just get along?" Montel suggested. "After all, one of us is going to be the other's boss pretty soon. It only seems logical that we clear whatever…misunderstanding there is between us."

"Misunderstanding?" Candace cocked her head. "I thought I was making it *very* clear that I don't like you."

"Liar." Montel's brows stretched upward while his smile

stretched wider. "In fact, I'm willing to bet that you're still in love with me."

Candace's mouth clamped down tight as she shivered in her seat.

"Ah. Cat got your tongue?" he inquired, standing. "Have I finally hit on the truth of the matter?" Montel started walking around the desk.

Alarm bells rang in her head. "What are you doing?" She eyed him suspiciously.

"I'm just curious," he said, propping a hip on her desk, and then he leaned so close she was sure he could smell the spearmint gum tucked in the back of her cheek. "How much longer are you going to keep this act up?"

Candace's eyes drifted close as her breath seemed to stall in her chest.

"You still like how I do this?"

She turned her head but didn't pull away, which allowed for Montel's hand to cup and caress the side of her face.

Taking full advantage of her collapsing defenses, Montel leaned forward and pressed his full lips against her perfectly glossed lips. Her soft moan made him hard and ready for whatever.

Candace's mind hit the mute button on those alarm bells that were trying to ruin the moment. Right now she just wanted to bask in the feel of Montel's soft lips. One thing that was as true now as it was the night they had met was that this fine devil could kiss like nobody's business.

Montel's confidence kicked up a notch when he saw the raw desire flickering in her cinnamon-brown eyes. For the past year, he had loved giving the sexy no-nonsense businesswoman a run for her money. Their occasional verbal sparring was fun and, at times like these, it turned him on. He'd sensed that it was the same for her, and now he had proof. He also knew that Candy would rather die than admit it.

He pulled her up from her chair and directed her to stand in between his legs. That was an even bigger mistake because it left him free to roam his hands over her thick curves and settle them on each ass cheek. "Damn. You still feel so good," he murmured against her lips.

"I bet you still feel good in other places, too."

Before she could even process what he was saying, Candace found herself turned around and her breasts pressed against the cold floor-to-ceiling window, with her skirt up over her waist and Montel easing in between her legs from the back. She gasped aloud, her warm breath steaming up the window.

"Shh," he warned. "Unless you want Mia coming in here and seeing who this pussy still belongs to."

Candace bit her lower lip and kept her voice down to soft moans and whispers.

Montel dove his head into her curtain of vanilla-and-coconut scented hair and stretched a hand down in between the soft V of curls between her legs so that he could drum his fingertips against her throbbing clit.

"Tell me how much you hate me now," he dared. "Tell me how much you hate what I'm doing to you right now."

Candace gulped, swallowed and gasped. No way could she manage to get such a huge lie through her lips when she was seconds away from coating his dick with a gallon of honey.

Montel's mocking laughter was a bit humiliating but the tiny waves of pleasure that rippled up from the walls of her pussy to the tips of her nipples made it all worthwhile.

"Ah. Ah."

"What, baby? You want to say something?" His hips and drumming fingers picked up speed.

From the corner of Candace's droopy eyes, she locked gazes with a stunned window washer. He was just one office over, but was taking in the scene as if he'd just been given an early Christmas gift.

"Ah. Ah."

Montel covered her mouth with his free hand and whispered. "That's it. You better come before Mia waltzes in here. She's only going to leave us alone for five minutes."

Candace slammed her eyes shut and rammed her ass back on Montel's dick with as much zeal and gusto as she could muster. "C'mon, baby. C'mon."

Four strokes, two drums later and Montel was swallowing her cry of release in a soul-stirring kiss that reflected the true passion that still existed between the two of them. Montel pulled his lips away from hers and smiled. "If this is how you hate me, then I'm curious to see how you act when you finally realize that you still love me."

Chapter 3

Mia kept casting nervous glances toward the closed door as she printed out Candace's Delta airline tickets and itinerary. One didn't have to be a rocket scientist to know that it wasn't a good idea to leave those two alone for long. A few other office girls waltzed by, mouthing, "Is he still in there?" to which she would just nod and fret.

As office pools went, there was growing speculation that there was something more to the top two ad executives' visceral dislike for one another. "Something" meaning sexual. Mia had done her damnedest to convince everyone that nothing could be further from the truth, but the more she denied it, the more people believed the opposite.

Then it came time for her to put her money where her mouth was. The bet was simply whether Candace and Montel would sleep together by the end of the year. One hundred bucks. It seemed like an easy bet at the time, but lately she wasn't too sure. And now that every assistant and receptionist had jumped into the pool, she stood to lose or win a small fortune. Now that they were cruising into the final month—the homestretch—she was as nervous as cat on a hot tin roof.

Mia snatched the itinerary from the printer's tray and bolted toward Candace's door to conduct an immediate emergency intervention. "Ms. Lahane, I have…" She froze at seeing Candace and Montel leaning so close that either they were about to kiss or had just finished kissing—or something.

Montel sprung away from Candace's desk as if the sucker had just caught fire. "I guess that's my cue to leave," he said.

Candace simply leaned back in her chair and slowly crossed her legs. "Guess so, since English seems to be a challenge for you."

"Cute." Casually, he strolled from around her desk and headed for the door. "We'll continue this conversation at another time." He smiled and winked at Mia. "She's all yours."

Candace rolled her eyes, but her heart didn't stop racing until he'd finally walked out of her office. "Smug bastard," she mumbled under her breath as she withdrew a small mirror from her purse and checked her appearance. "Thanks for coming in—though next time don't leave him in here longer than two minutes."

Slowly, Mia started to relax. "Sooo…nothing happened?"

Candace's face twisted. "What do you mean?"

Mia realized that it was an inappropriate question, but she drove ahead anyway. "I mean, it just looked like, um—"

"Oh, please! Never in a million years." Candace waved her off, but then looked around. "What's with the heater? It's burning up in here."

Uh-oh. "I'll, um, get maintenance to check on it." Mia approached her desk. "I've booked you on a six-fifteen flight out of JFK Airport. I called your housekeeper and asked for her to pack a bag for you. When your driver picks you up this afternoon, he'll have your bag."

"Walter Anderson," Candace said, smiling again. "I'm definitely going to have to bring my A game for this one." The president of Anderson Vytex, Anderson, had long been considered a flamboyant and eccentric billionaire who owned everything from casinos to clothing lines. For six months every advertising agency in New York had been dying to land his lucrative account ever since he'd split with Elige.

Everyone.

"You'll do great. I have faith in you," she said encouragingly and quickly made her way out of the office. Back at her desk, everyone in her line of vision gave her an inquiring look, to which she just gave them a small shake of her head. There were looks of both relief and disappointment directed her way, but she kept it moving and headed toward the bathroom.

When she came out of the stall to wash her hands, her best friend, Vicki, was leaning against the sink. "What? Did they send you in here to get the 4-1-1?" Mia pumped soap into her hands and turned on the water.

Vicki smiled and pushed a lock of her blond hair behind her ear. "You know the drill, so spill it."

"There's nothing to tell. When I walked in, they weren't doing anything lurid, if that's what you want to know."

"Lurid?" Vicki rolled the word around. "That might be a little strong. How about something a little more subtle?"

"No," she said shaking her. "No. Nothing at all. They weren't doing anything, really."

Ever the detective, Vicki cocked her head. "Now why do I get the feeling that you're not telling me something?"

"Because you're paranoid." Mia shut off the water and then reached for the paper towels. "Candace was relieved that I interrupted them and now she's preparing for an important meeting in Paris tomorrow."

"Paris? She's spending the holidays there?"

"Better." Mia lit up and glanced around to make sure that they were alone. "I found him."

Vicki inched closer. "Found who?"

"Walter Anderson."

"Anderson Vytex's Walter Anderson?" Vicki asked in awe. "How in the hell did you find him? The man is like a ghost."

"I know. I really caught a lucky break. She's heading out on a six-fifteen flight this afternoon. She lands this account and that promotion belongs to us."

"Damn. That sounds like a reason to celebrate. You want to hit Olivia for happy hour?"

"Hell, yeah. I'm going to need it." They laughed and headed out of the bathroom.

After the door clicked closed, Georgine lowered her feet back down onto the tiled floor in the last stall in the bathroom and tried to process everything that she'd just heard. Candace Lahane was flying to Paris to meet with Walter Anderson. She and Montel had been trying for months to locate that man.

She quickly rushed out of the stall, washed her hands and then sprinted across the office to find her boss. "Montel, thank God you're in here."

"There you are, Georgine." Montel glanced up from his stack of papers on his desk. "I need you to get Jessie Glover on the line. It's time to get him off the fence and sign his restaurant chain. That's a ten million dollar account right there. And then we'll see about tracking down Richard Leakes. Every dollar is going to count in the next two weeks."

"Forget Glover and Leakes," Georgine said. "You're going to Paris."

Montel frowned. "I am?"

"Yes." She turned around and closed the door.

"And why am I going to Paris?" He leaned back and watched as she approached his desk almost like a giddy teenager.

"You're going to meet Walter Anderson."

Montel's eyebrows jumped. "You found him?" He sprung up from his chair and unceremoniously swung her around. "You're a lifesaver! Do you know what this means? That promotion is as good as ours!"

"Wait. Wait. Put me down," she said, feeling a bit breathless.

"What? What's the problem?" He picked up a strange vibe and braced himself for the bad news that always accompanied good news.

"*I* haven't tracked down Walter Anderson. Candace has."

The wind definitely went out of Montel's sails. Candace landing the lucrative account meant the death knell. If Candace landed the VP position, no doubt her first order of business would be to kick him out of the door.

"Hear me out," Georgine said. "You've always said that nothing matters until the client signs on the bottom line." She held up her hands. "Well, Candace hasn't signed him *yet*."

Slowly, Montel's smile returned. "Shrewd thinking."

"Thank you." She folded her arms, rather proud of herself.

His lips quirked up into a smile. "What time is my flight?"

"Six-fifteen."

Usually traffic from Manhattan to the JFK Airport was long and tortuous. Add to the mix Christmas travelers and tourists and you have chaos. Candace also wrestled with the issue that she didn't really have an official meeting with Walter Anderson but would have to do a sort of ambush presentation in the middle of his company's Christmas party and hope for the best. It was something she hadn't done since she'd first entered into advertising, and frankly, it really had her adrenaline pumping. Of course, the cherry on top would be seeing Montel Starks's face when he learned that she had landed the eccentric billionaire's account.

The image made her laugh in the back of the luxury car. When the driver glanced back at her through the rearview mirror, she collected herself and slid on her Gucci shades. Outside her window she watched snow flurries descend and cover her beloved New York. Christmas wasn't Christmas without the white fluffy stuff. And the white fluffy stuff always reminded her of Christmases long past. Year after year, her single mother had managed to pull off miracles and there would always be gifts under a lopsided plastic tree for her three children.

Christmas was the only time there had been any peace in their cramped apartment in Brooklyn. The rest of the year they had fought like cats and dogs over everything—whose turn it was to do what chore; whose fault it was that their father had left to start a new family in the neighboring borough of Queens. Nevertheless, her mother had soldiered on through it all. Candace had never seen her cry or get emotional about her dad leaving. She just got up every day and did what she had to do to put food on the table. She was a strong woman—but had never showed any interest in finding love again.

Candace drew in a deep breath while her brain abruptly shifted gears to her own love life—her own single-minded focus on her career. Sure, there were times loneliness would creep up on her, but for the most part she viewed men as a complication that she couldn't afford. Besides, what was the point? Men and women didn't stay together anyway. Her parents were a testimony to that. And if that wasn't enough, every single one of her girlfriends was either divorced, playing wifey or pretending to be single and satisfied.

Men leave.

That was just a fact of life. She pulled at the thin chain around her neck and played with it all the way to the airport. She told herself not to think about Montel—but of course she sat smiling, replaying that little quickie in her office. What had she been thinking? What if Mia *had* walked in? "You got to pull yourself together better than that," she told herself, but then went right back to smiling.

When Candace was dropped off, she had forty minutes to get through security and race to the opposite end of the airport. So of course she was running toward her gate and yelling at the top of her lungs. "Hold the plane! Hold the plane!"

The ticket agent at the door glanced down and tapped his watch.

"Thank you. Thank you," she said, handing over her ticket.

The smiling man scanned her ticket and gestured her through. "Enjoy your flight."

Candace raced down the ramp and was greeted by the two airline stewardesses. When she stepped onto the plane, she finally exhaled a relieved breath. People were still trying to shove bags into the overhead compartments in coach. She headed toward the front of the plane as she tried to read the aisle numbers in first class. When she finally reached her seat, she received the shock of her life.

"*Candy,* you made it," Montel said, smiling. "I was *just* beginning to worry that you weren't going to make it."

Chapter 4

"What the hell are you doing here?" Candace snapped as she snatched off her shades.

Montel only laughed at the silly question. "What does one normally do on an airplane?"

Candace glowered.

"Well, besides *that*." He jiggled his brows.

"I wasn't thinking…" She glanced around and saw the door being closed. "Why are you on *this* flight?"

"Do you need any help with your bag, ma'am?" a handsome passenger said from behind her.

She smiled, but before she could answer, Montel had popped out of his seat. "I got that for her," he said, snatching her leather carry-on bag from her hand and then shoving it into the overhead bin.

Candace had to move back, but then accidentally stepped on the handsome stranger's foot, and they both went tumbling backward into a vacant seat behind her.

"Whoa," Mr. Old Spice said when she landed in his lap. "Are you all right, ma'am?"

Candace wiggled around a bit too much while struggling to get back onto her feet, and the result was her feeling something that she didn't necessarily want to feel. "Oops. Oh, my goodness."

Montel reached over and pulled her out of the stranger's lap. "Are you finished flirting now?" He shook his head and turned back to his seat.

Candace frowned and rubbed her arm. The man had almost yanked it out of its socket. She glanced back at Mr. Old Spice as he climbed out of the seat and started making his way back down the aisle. "Thanks again for your help."

"Not a problem." He smiled but then glanced nervously over at Montel. "I didn't mean to get you in trouble with your boyfriend."

"He's not my—"

"Ma'am, if you could take your seat," the flight attendant said. "We're getting ready to take off."

"Yes, *honey*," Montel patted the chair next to him. "Have a seat."

Candace glared at him as she dropped into her seat. "I'm still waiting to hear what you're doing on this flight." She settled her purse and laptop bag underneath her seat.

"Business. What else?" Montel shrugged and then picked up a magazine from the seat pocket in front of him.

"You're meeting a client?" she asked skeptically.

"Something like that." He turned his dazzling smile on her. "Why? Do you have something else in mind that you'd like to do?"

Candace ignored his come-on and started grilling him. "You said that you were worried about me. You knew I would be on this flight. How?"

"Let's just say I have my ways." He winked.

"You've been spying on me," she accused.

"Absolutely. The name is Starks. Montel Starks."

"Whatever, Agent 007."

"I was thinking something more like Agent 69."

Candace rolled her eyes. "Figures."

"Besides, I hear that Paris is lovely this time of year. After I conclude my business, what do you say you and I find a nice little room somewhere and have another one of those scorching international affairs that are all the rage. Bora-Bora part *deux*."

Candace frowned and shivered as if the mere thought gave her the heebie-jeebies.

Montel rocked his head back as a deep rumble of laughter shook his entire frame. "So now you're just going to sit there and front? All right. I'm gonna let you have that. *Candy*. But know this—" he leaned so close that his fresh breath and seductive cologne started to lull her into a trance "—what happened in your office was just a sample of what I intend to do with you on this trip. You still want me. You're sitting there glaring, but your body is definitely calling my name."

Candace fluttered her long lashes, and she launched into her best Southern belle voice. "Oh, my. What a mighty big ego you have, sir."

"You know that's not the only thing big on me, darling."

"Oh, God." Her eyes rolled. "Do women *really* fall for that cheesy-ass line?"

"You tell me."

Her eyes snapped back up. "I was drunk."

"And you're a lousy liar," he volleyed back and then whispered, "I'll let you in on a little secret on how a man can tell whether a woman wants him."

"This should be interesting," Candace said, folding her arms.

Montel lifted a finger and then tapped it against the

side of her neck. Candace sucked in a breath at the touch of his hand.

"This vein right here is connected to your heart muscles and whenever your heart starts racing, this little baby right here starts pulsing like crazy. And this sucker hasn't stopped jumping since you sat down."

Candace swallowed but refused to give up ground. "You know what else gets my heart racing? Anger. Now remove your hand."

Montel laughed but did as he was ordered. "As you wish."

During their little spat neither one of them noticed that the plane had already taken off until a small "ding" alerted them that they were now free to walk about the cabin.

"I need some air." Candace hopped up from her seat and made a beeline to the bathroom. Montel's annoying laugh trailed behind her as she continued to roll her eyes. "Pompous ass."

Once in the tiny bathroom, she drew in a couple of deep breaths and tried to steady her nerves. "I must've pissed somebody off in a past life." Candace shook her head and then stared at her reflection in the small mirror. Curious, she leaned forward and stretched her neck up to check out this damn vein Montel was referring to, but she couldn't see a damn thing. "He probably just made it up."

One thing he didn't make up was that there was definitely something still between them. If that little quickie in her office didn't prove it, then the fact that naked images of him kept flashing in her mind had to mean something. She had been ignoring it for a while, but it was clearly getting harder to do. Even now, it had been a good five minutes since he'd touched her and her skin was still tingling. "Pull yourself together, girl. And keep your legs closed."

Just as she said those words, that damn naked image of

Montel all hot and sweaty flashed across her mind again. Her knees weakened on the spot. "I don't like him. I don't like him."

Knock. Knock. "Ma'am, are you almost done in there?"

"Damn." Candace preferred to remain in the bathroom over the entire Atlantic Ocean than return to her seat.

Knock. Knock. "Ma'am—?"

"I'm coming. I'm coming." She drew in a deep breath and unlocked the door. "Sorry about that," she said to an elderly, cherubic-looking gentleman who could've easily passed as a department store Santa Claus.

"No. Sorry I had to rush you out but I'm at an age when the bladder says you have to go—it usually means pronto." His laugh even sounded like a "ho, ho, ho" as he squeezed past Candace.

She smiled and wondered if the older gentleman was actually going to be able to fit into the small compartment. When she heard a small "click," she glanced back and saw the man had indeed managed to pull off the impossible.

"There you are," Montel said, pulling off a pair of Bose headphones. "I was beginning to think that you were sucked out of the plane or something."

Candace didn't dignify that statement with a reply and instead opted to pull out her laptop to get some much-needed work done. Maybe if she just ignored Montel, he'd pick up on the hint and leave her alone.

"Ah. The silent treatment." He laughed and shook his head. "I'm disappointed in you."

Candace clenched her teeth, determined to ignore his unsolicited commentary.

"I've always pegged you as a fighter. Someone that wasn't afraid of anything—or anyone."

That little gem got under her skin. "Am I supposed to be afraid of *you* and this weird psychobabbling you're doing?"

Montel tossed up his hands. "I'm just calling it like I see it, *Candy*."

"Allow me to call it like I see it too, *Monty*. You're an asshole. This whole suave James Bond bullshit is just that—bullshit. And frankly, I don't have time for it. I've put up with men like you my whole career. You think you can have anything and do anything you want just because you're handsome and *mildly* charming. Well, I got news for you. I'm not going to just melt out of my panties and lay back so that you can screw me out of everything I've worked damn hard to get. Got it?"

Monty's smile never faltered. "I think I got a hard-on. Does that count?"

"Grr. You're impossible."

Montel tapped the center of his neck. "Buh-bump. Buh-bump." He winked at her. "No need to fight the inevitable. You and me."

Candace snapped her laptop closed. "I've got to get out of here." She jumped back out of her seat and grabbed her things.

"You can run, but you can't hide." Montel laughed and plopped his headphones back over his ears. "Buh-bump. Buh-bump."

"Keep dreaming." Candy went in search of a vacant seat on the plane. It was either that or risk catching a case on the friendly skies. "Excuse me. Is anyone sitting here?"

The Santa Claus-looking gentleman glanced up and smiled at her. "No. No. Please, have a seat." He moved a newspaper out of the way.

"Thank you so much. You have no idea how much I really appreciate this."

"Don't mention it." He smiled. "Did you and your boyfriend have a little fight?"

"Please," she said, rolling her eyes. "That man is *not* my boyfriend."

"Pity. You two make a beautiful couple," he said cheerily.

Frowning, Candace glanced back over her shoulder.

Montel smiled and thumped his finger against his neck.

"Good Lord, give me strength."

Montel eased back into his seat, shaking his head at Candy's antics. She could run, but she sure as hell couldn't hide. He was going to make damn sure of it. Who knew that this was how it would all play out when they met two years ago...

Christmas 2008...

Bora-Bora was a blast. Montel was living it up with his best friends and business colleagues, Robert and Fred. They were gambling and drinking more than what seemed humanly possible when the finest woman any of them had ever seen was at the craps table with a raucous crowd gathered around her. She wore a short, shimmering silver dress that showcased a pair of legs that had him and his partners drooling. It was clear that she was on a hot streak, so Montel approached the craps table anxious to ride the wave. When he managed to work his way next to her, her beauty took his breath away.

He stacked an impressive amount of high dollar chips on the "pass line" and caught her gaze to let her know that he was putting his faith in her hands. She quickly glanced over at him, smiled and then rolled the dice. The dice settled on a two and a five and a cheer went up.

Montel doubled his money. He left his pile of chips on the table to let it ride. His new good-luck charm rolled a couple more sevens, winning him a massive amount of money before he cashed out. The very next roll, she threw snake eyes and crapped out. But the connection had been made. Between dice throws, her eyes kept creeping over to him.

A few minutes later, Candy ditched her sister, Christine, and headed to the casino's hot club, Lava. Montel and Candace were in their own world, grinding on the dance floor and giving each other a peek of what they were working with. Montel definitely liked what he saw and was mentally peeling Candy's clothes off.

After a few more drinks, he and Candy were laughing and stumbling into his bungalow on stilts that hovered over the water. There was a nice cool breeze drifting in from the private deck that overlooked the lagoon, but neither he nor Candy were interested in the view.

"I don't normally do this," she said, slipping her arms around his neck and then nibbling on his lower lip.

"Mmm-hmm." Montel's arms went around her waist while his hands dipped lower to squeeze her thick ass. Baby was a brick house from head to toe.

"I don't," she insisted, shifting her lips to his lower jaw. "I'm usually this...very professional and...very conservative businesswoman who busts men's balls all day." She giggled.

Montel had a hard time picturing her as she was describing herself. So far tonight, she had been a wild, fun-loving, uninhibited woman with a killer body and a delicious mouth. "Is that right?"

"Mmm-hmm." She tugged his shirt up from the waist of his jeans and then smiled approvingly at the hard ridges of his six-pack. "My. My. My."

While she oogled and ran her hand over his chest, Montel started working on her zipper. He could hardly wait to see her incredible body without the hindrance of clothes. And when she was finally standing before him naked as a jay bird, he was not disappointed.

Not by a long shot.

"Merry Christmas to me," he whispered, filling his hands with her beautiful breasts. His head dipped low and his tongue curled around a hard nipple. He listened to Candy's breathless sigh and then increased her pleasure by sucking one of her delicious tits into his mouth.

"Ooh." Candy's hand drifted lower until it found his hard dick bulging against the seams of jeans. "My. You're a big boy." Her fingers made quick work of his zipper.

Montel's ego inflated just as his cock sprung free into her silky hands. "I think he likes you."

"Mmm. The feeling is mutual." Without further ado, Candy sank to her knees and proceeded to torture him with small peppered kisses around the bulbous head of his cock. He ran his fingers through her thick hair while trying to nudge her to open her pretty mouth wider so he could just get straight to the program. But his ebony Venus made it clear that she was in control of the show and continued to rain those small kisses all along his shaft.

He unbuttoned his jeans and slid them down and pulled his boxers off his hips while he still waited for her to suction his dick into her warm mouth. Her tease continued until he was on the verge of begging. When she finally slid his straining cock into her warm mouth, he actually felt a tear of ecstasy threaten to slide down his face.

Within seconds, she had a good rhythm, deep-throating so good that he could hear "Here comes the bride" in the back of his head. He stopped her before he totally lost control and laid her down on the bed. "It's my turn to taste you," he said.

"Be my guest." Candy parted her legs and spread the lips of her pussy so that he could get a good look at her throbbing clit that was glazed to perfection with her body's natural honey.

"Hot damn, woman. Where have you been all my life?"

"Just waiting on you, boo." She lifted her hips as his mouth came down and his tongue started licking her rich dessert. *"Aww, yessss."* She tilted her head back and enjoyed every tingle, shiver and explosion he set off with his talented tongue. But that was nothing compared to what he set off when he climbed up her long, curvy body and hooked her legs over his shoulder.

He watched her face intensely as he eased the fat head of his cock into her tight walls. Her mouth stretched open at his seemingly endless length, but then those tingles, shivers and explosions were no longer tiny. They were big, huge and then massive while Monty ground and stroked until his body was slick with sweat. *"Oh, my God,"* he moaned over and over again. There was no doubt about it, she had complete control of her vaginal muscles. With each stroke, she squeezed his shaft tighter and tighter until he was talking in tongues and seeing white lightning bolts behind his closed eyelids.

Monty didn't want to be the first one to come, but that was starting to look like it was going to be out of his control. He started groaning loud and breathing fast.

"Oh, my God...oh, my God...oh my Gaaawwd!" Candy moaned and then started inching up the bed.

That was music to Monty's ears. Maybe he could hold out long enough so that they could come together. But it was looking like it was going to be a photo finish when he could feel his nut starting to rise. *"Jesus...Jesus...Jesus..."*

"Oh my God...oh, my God...oh, my Gaaawwd!"

Monty couldn't hold it any longer. He locked his hands around her hips, held her in place and sped up the tempo of his hammering hips. Candy's muscles clamped down on his cock as she cried out with her release. But Monty wasn't through with her just yet. He hopped up from the bed and positioned her in the "standing tiger, crouching dragon" *position. It was one of Candy's favorites, with her posed on all fours and her knees on the edge of the bed, with her tiger, Monty, standing behind her. Candace kept her knees together to narrow her vaginal canal and increase Monty's pleasure as he eased into her from behind.*

His every other breath came out in a long hiss and if that wasn't enough, Candace reached a hand down in between them and gave his balls a nice squeeze while they bounced hard against her ass. "Oh. Hot damn," he panted. He turned to the left and then to the right to make sure that he hit every wall in her pussy an equal number of times.

Minutes later, they were in the "couch canoodle." Monty eased back on one of the bungalow's chairs. Candy straddled his lap with her legs splayed apart and her knees bent up against his chest. Slowly, she leaned back with a smile until she was practically upside down with her arms stretched behind her to the floor. While he started slow grinding against the roof of her pussy, Candy thrust back and forth while opening and closing her legs.

Monty was hypnotized watching his cock thrust in and out of her while simultaneously watching her large breasts bounce and jiggle. Damn, she was beautiful. Hot, sweaty and just down right beautiful. A few grinds and deep strokes later, Monty pulled out of her creamy trenches and shot out a hot, sticky cum-load that sprayed across her flat belly and in between her heaving full breasts.

Smiling, he gazed down at his work of art and convinced himself that he was in love.

Chapter 5

"What do you mean you don't have a reservation for me?" Candace asked, barely holding onto her temper. "My assistant booked the room yesterday—or last night—or I don't know. The time difference is mixed up in my head. But I do know that she booked the room."

The petite black woman forced on a smile that didn't reach her eyes. But clearly she was trying her best to be professional. "I'll check again," she said.

"Thank you."

Montel waltzed up to the corner next to her and plopped his bags down. "Happy holidays, ladies."

"Happy holidays," the entire line of women behind the front desk chorused like grinning teenagers mooning the captain of the football team.

"Reservation for Starks. Montel Starks."

"Oh, Gawd." Candace rolled her eyes and then tapped a

nail in front of the woman who was supposed to be rechecking the system for her reservation.

"Oh, sorry, Ms. Lahane," the woman said, wiping the smile off her face as she returned her attention to the computer. "I do see your name, but we have you checking in on Saturday, not today."

Frustrated, Candace cursed under her breath.

"Here are your keys, Mr. Starks. The Presidential suite. I hope you enjoy your stay and happy holidays."

"Thank you…" Montel read the woman's name tag. "*Candy.* Well, what do you know." He elbowed Candace. "You two have the same name."

"My name is *Candace,* you ass."

True to form, Montel laughed.

She gritted her teeth. "Okay. I'd like a room, please." She reached over to her purse and pulled out her wallet. "I don't care what kind of room. Just a room—so I can shower, eat and go to sleep."

Teana, per *her* nametag, frowned. "I'm sorry ma'am, but we're all booked up."

"You don't have *any* rooms?"

Teana frowned again and gave her fake puppy dog eyes. "I'm sorry. We get a lot of tourists during the Christmas holidays."

Oh, what I'd give to be able to snap this bitch in half. "Fine. I'll find another hotel."

"You don't need to do that." Montel butted in and swung an arm around Candace's waist. "You can share a room with me."

Candace quickly scrambled out of his embrace and looked at him as if he'd just sprouted a second head. "You have seriously lost your mind. I wouldn't share a room with you if you were the last man on earth."

The women behind the counter all looked at her like *she* had lost her mind.

Montel pressed a hand against his chest. "You hurt me. Deeply." He curled his lips downward but his eyes danced with amusement.

"Oh, go to hell." She gathered her things and scuttled over to the lobby seating area.

Montel turned toward the women. "A lover's spat."

"Oooooh," they chorused.

Candace flopped down on a short, kidney-shaped upholstered sofa in the lobby and pulled out her BlackBerry. "C'mon, Mia, pick up." She glanced around as she listened to the phone ring and then spotted Montel walking toward her. "Oh, God, no. Make him go away."

No such luck.

"Who are you calling?" Montel asked.

"I really can't see how that's any of your business."

He leaned a hip against a stone pillar and folded his arms. "Well, I just wanted to remind you that it's two in the morning in New York. Mia is probably not in the office yet...or even conscious at this hour."

"I know that." Candace ended the call and jumped back onto her feet. "Not a problem. I'm just going to hop into a cab and go to another hotel. One of them is bound to have a room available."

"Probably one in a questionable part of town. You heard the woman at the front desk. Hotels are all booked up because of the holidays."

"As usual you're always eavesdropping on my conversations. That's probably why you're here in the first place—to spy on me. You know I'm meeting with...an important businessman."

"How vague."

"Anyway…if you think that you're going to snatch the rug from under me—"

"Oh?" Montel rocked on his heels. "Does this businessman have a name?"

"Like I'd tell you." She grabbed her bags. "I'm out of here."

"Whoa. Whoa." Montel rushed to block her exit out of the hotel. "What's the problem? You need a room. I have a room. You have to be just as exhausted as I am."

"And you're just sooo concerned." Candace rolled her eyes. "Get out of my way."

Montel tossed up his hands. "All right. Don't say I never offered you anything."

"Duly noted." She shoved past him, determined to put as much space between them as possible.

"In case you change your mind, I'll be in room 2623," he yelled after her.

"Don't hold your breath." Candace stopped and turned around. "Scratch that. Go ahead and hold your breath."

Montel laughed and watched her stumble around with her bags as she exited the hotel. He had a reason to start panicking right now since he had no idea where or how to get in contact with Walter Anderson. His and Georgine's sketchy plan was to stick to Candace like glue until he pried the information from her. Of course, prying was a nicer way to say steal, but who wanted to split hairs?

"All right. Time to retreat and come up with a plan B." He picked up his bags and headed to the elevator. A few minutes later he entered his suite, yawning. He was exhausted and the queen-sized bed was definitely calling his name.

The room was divided into two sections: a living room area and bedroom area. He dumped his things beside the television and warred with himself as to whether to jump in the shower or just dive face-first onto the bed and pass out.

The shower won out. However, when he did step out of the steamy bathroom wearing the hotel's robe, he gave in to the call of the fluffy-looking comforter and pristine sheets and dove in.

It felt like he'd just closed his eyes when a hard, persistent knocking invaded his dreams. "Go away," he mumbled into his pillow. The knocking didn't stop. He rolled out of bed, and, even though he could barely open his eyes, he sort of sleepwalked his way toward the door. "Who is it?"

No answer.

Frowning, he reached the door and then had to open one eye a little wider to see through the peephole. Who he saw there woke him like a full alarm fire. He jerked opened the door with a smile as wide as Texas. "Hello, Candy."

Chapter 6

The muscles along Candace's jawline twitched as she glared at Montel's smug-looking face. This was the last place she wanted to be, but she was cold, hungry and tired—not necessarily in that order. "One night," she said tightly.

"Excuse me?" he chuckled.

"Okay. Not a whole night—since it's not quite noon. Just a couple of hours so I can just take a nap."

Montel leaned against the doorframe. "All the hotels are booked up?"

Candace rolled her eyes. She had known that he would be an asshole about this. "Can I stay here or not?"

He pulled the door closed a bit and glanced over his shoulder. "Well, I don't know if that's such a good idea right now."

Candace's gaze narrowed as she seethed. "Do you have a woman in there? Already? Man, you don't waste any time, do you? What did you do—order a hotel massage?" she asked with air quotes. "Or maybe you asked one of those barely legal girls downstairs at the check-in counter. Typical."

Montel roared with laughter. "You're a pistol when you're jealous."

"I'm not—"

"I was just teasing you. There's nobody in here." He stepped back and swung the door open wide so she could see for herself. "I don't know what the rumor mill says about me at the j-o-b, but I'm not easy." He clutched the top of his robe close. "I'm a guy who likes to be wooed. You know, dinner—flowers."

"A bottle of Patrón."

Montel's smile stretched wider. "See. You do know the way to a man's heart."

"Oh, God. If I stay around you for any longer period of time, my eyes are going to be permanently rolled to the back of my head." She tugged her bags into the room.

"Let me help you with that."

Before he could touch her luggage, she pulled away. "I got it." She slowly crept into the room like she still expected a naked woman to jump out and flash her jiggle biddies at her.

Montel chuckled and closed the door behind her. "Well, make yourself comfortable. *Mi casa es su casa.*"

Candace sat her bags down over at the workstation in the living room. "There is only one bed."

"Good eye."

"I'll take the sofa."

"You're more than welcome to share the bed," he offered. "I promise I won't bite—hard."

"Not happening." She glanced around the room again. "All right. Let's go over a few ground rules."

Still amused, Montel crossed his arms. "Okay. This should be good."

"I'll sleep on the sofa."

"Okay."

Candace frowned. "You're not going to offer to take the sofa?"

"Oh, God, no. The bed is sooo comfortable. It's like sleeping on a cloud."

She stared at him, shaking her head. "Unbelievable."

"What? I said you were more than welcome to sleep in the bed. We're two mature adults. I'm sure that we're more than capable of being able to stay on opposite sides."

"Two?"

"Well, I was giving you the benefit of the doubt."

She tossed up her hands. "Whatever. You're giving me a headache."

"Are you finished with the rules?"

"You just…stay away from me. I don't trust you."

Montel shook his head as he headed back toward the bedroom area. "This is what happens when you try to help people. Sweet dreams, diva."

"I'm not…never mind." Why on earth did she keep allowing him to drag her into the most ridiculous arguments? Candace watched him as she slipped out of her coat. She removed her high, high heels and instantly her aching feet sang her praises. "Mind if I jump into the shower?"

"Uh, no. Go right ahead."

Candace grabbed her overnight bag and headed to the bathroom. Once inside, she made sure to lock the door. She didn't put it past Montel to creep inside the minute he heard the water come on, and frankly she didn't trust herself to turn him away if he did. The entire time that she was in the shower, she berated herself for being in this predicament. Mia's bonus just got a little smaller because she was not her favorite person at the moment. After she managed to get just a couple of hours of shut-eye she was definitely going to make sure that Mia got an earful.

Montel lay in bed with a hard-on listening to the shower. Just picturing Candy wet and covered in bubbles was doing a number on him. He could just imagine her long delicate fingers massaging the soap in small circles around her full, perky C-cup breasts, sliding down her firm tight abs and then gliding in between her thighs.

"Sweet baby Jesus." Swept up in the moment, he wrapped his hand around his cock, which was as straight as a flag post, and stroked it to relieve some pressure. However, the porno that was playing inside of his head had Candy bending her back low and twirling what her momma gave her while her soapy fingers caressed the back of her knees.

Then came her melodious humming that blended with the sound of the shower spray. Whatever relief he'd managed to find to soothe his throbbing cock was erased when the humming sound he heard from the bathroom transformed to moaning inside his head. Oh, what he wouldn't give to be able to just walk into that steamy bathroom and offer to scrub her back, her ass and any damn thing else he could think of. Montel tossed back the covers and tiptoed to the bathroom. When he twisted the knob, he nearly laughed out loud at discovering it was locked. *Some things never changed.*

He returned to the bed just as the water shut off. In his XXX fantasy this was the time she'd bust out the baby oil and take her time smoothing it into her skin. Drip. Drip. Drip. The oil rolls down the valley between her tits and then she'd smear it over that hypnotizing ass he'd loved to watch sway back and forth for the past year.

Montel was just about to reach for his hard-on again when suddenly the bathroom door jerked opened. He quickly rolled over and pretended to be sleeping. For whatever reason, he held his breath while he listened to her feet pad softly across the carpet.

Was he busted? Did she see him?

Montel added some fake snoring to sell his sleeping act. Yeah, it might've been overkill, but what the heck?

"Good God, I have to listen to that?" Candace complained as she zipped and unzipped bags.

Montel smiled. He absolutely loved this game he played with the anal-retentive—though sexy—ad executive. The proof was that his dick was still as hard as a rock while he listened to her move around the hotel suite in…what? What was she wearing right now? He had on the only robe that was in the bathroom. So what did that leave?

A towel?

Some sexy lingerie?

One of those cute, sexy nightshirts women loved to wear?

His mind ran wild with possibilities—all the while his dick was probably turning purple with the amount of blood that was rushing to its head. Playing it cool and slick, he moaned and staged a dramatic flop over to his other side so he could sneak a peek down toward the living room area.

Flannel.

What the hell? Couldn't a brother catch a break? He huffed out a long breath and went back to pretending to be asleep.

Candace was *not* about to ask Montel for either his comforter or a top sheet or even a pillow. The very idea of even walking toward that big bed made her light-headed. Montel Starks was a devastatingly handsome man in a suit, but when he had answered that door in just a white terry cloth robe, he had taken sexy to a whole other level. It had taken everything she had not to jump his bones and play rodeo until she passed out.

But he is who he is and hormones be damned. She wasn't going anywhere near that bed with him in it. She plopped down on the stiff upholstered sofa and crammed its tiny square-shaped pillows under her head. She just needed a quick nap and then she could go on a search for the elusive Walter Anderson.

Candace drew in a deep breath and then waited for sleep to come.

It didn't.

The sofa was so hard and uncomfortable, it felt like she was trying to sleep on a bed of rocks, and the pillows had absolutely no fluff whatsoever, and she was getting a crick in her neck. She tossed and turned but just couldn't get comfortable. Frustrated, she sat up and glanced over at the bed.

I'm not going over there. I'm not going over there.

She shifted her eyes over to the large window and thought it would be easier to catch some shut-eye if she closed the curtains and blocked out the sun. Once she did that, the room darkened, but sleep still eluded her when she returned to the sofa.

Montel's snoring stopped, and once again she found herself sitting up and staring at the vacant spot on the queen-sized bed. The pillows were huge and the comforter looked like one gigantic fluffy cloud.

It looks like there's enough room over there. I'll stay on my side and he'll stay on his side. She nibbled on her bottom lip while contemplating the situation. She was exhausted, and that bed was like the apple that tempted Adam in the Garden of Eden. Exhaustion won out, and Candace found herself tiptoeing toward the bed with bated breath. When she neared the foot, she wanted to make doubly sure that Montel was fast asleep, so she whispered, "Montel, are you awake?"

No answer.

"Montel," she said again. When only the soft sound of his steady breathing reached her ears, she took a deep breath and rushed to peel back the covers and then climbed inside. There was an instant sigh of euphoria as her body's muscles relaxed into the mattress's heavenly pillow top, but she made sure that she skooched her body along the edge to avoid any accidental touching of the giant sleeping beside her. A couple of seconds later, she was fast asleep.

However, Montel was wide awake.

Chapter 7

Mia strolled into the office of Nu4us, smiling and humming "Jingle Bells." If everything went according to plan, she was going to have one helluva Christmas. A big bonus and a sweeeeet haul from the office pool by the end of the month. "Morning, Wendi," she said, breezing past the receptionist's desk.

Wendi looked up and then excitedly covered the microphone on her headset with her hand. "Did you hear the news?"

Mia stopped and backtracked. "What news?"

Wendi glanced around the office lobby and then leaned forward to whisper. "Ms. Lahane and Mr. Starks went to Paris together. I wouldn't be counting on cashing in on that pool too soon if I were you."

Mia laughed. "The rumor mill got it wrong this time. Ms. Lahane is in Paris on business. She has a lead on a very important potential client. Trust me. I know. I booked the flight."

"And I booked Mr. Starks's," Georgine said, suddenly appearing behind her. "Six-fifteen to Paris. Sound familiar?"

Mia slowly turned around and stared at the pretty Latina with rising suspicion. Georgine must've been the one who placed the largest bet on Starks charming his way into Lahane's bed, which made this sudden monkey wrench in her plans highly suspect. "What are you up to?"

"The same thing you're up to—winning."

Candace didn't stay by the edge of the bed. Some time during her eight hour sleep-a-thon, she'd managed to roll over to Montel's side of the bed and curl up against his back. She didn't know when or how it happened, she just knew that Montel's familiar rich cologne scent was somehow seducing her in her sleep.

Montel lay as straight as a board, wondering what he should do with Candace's arms circling around his waist and her hands inching down toward his painful hard-on. Well, he knew what he wanted to do, but he certainly didn't want to be accused of trying to take advantage of someone while they were sleeping. But he wasn't made of stone and there was only so much a man could take.

"Candy?" he asked, quietly. "Are you awake?"

"Hmm?" She nuzzled kisses across his broad back.

"Candy, you're kissing me."

"Uh-huh." Her hand slipped into his silk boxers and latched around the base of his dick.

Montel sucked in a breath only to have his mind start spinning when she started stroking him. "Sweet baby Jesus, please say she's not asleep."

Candace pulled one of his shoulders back, but before he could say another word, she pressed a slender finger against his mouth. "Don't talk," she said, meeting his direct gaze. "I don't want you to say a damn thing."

His brows kicked up a notch, but he kept his damn mouth shut.

"Good boy." Candace removed her finger from his lips only to replace it with a searing, passionate kiss that nearly consumed them in an invisible ball of fire. While Montel's head spun, he was vaguely aware of her slender fingers slipping under the waistband of his boxers and then tugging them down.

"Oh, God, you smell so good," she moaned, abandoning his lips to start trailing kisses across his jawline, down the column of his neck and then down the center of his chiseled pecs. From there she flicked out her pink, glistening tongue and hypnotized him as he watched it descend lower and lower.

A muscle in his dick started twitching, causing it to rock up and down while he waited on pins and needles for that sweet mouth of hers to give him the relief that he'd been waiting for. Lower and lower she went. Her large breasts grazed each side of his cock, and for a few seconds, she rubbed each tit up and down the side of his shaft until pre-cum started oozing from its head.

"Sssss," he hissed.

"You like that, baby?"

Unsure he had permission to talk, Montel just bobbed his head and waited to see what she would do next. He didn't have long to wait. A wicked smile slanted across Candy's face as she continued rubbing her breasts against his cock and then rolling her tongue lazily across the head. "Mmmm," she moaned, sapping up his juices.

Montel's toes curled while he clenched his ass cheeks. But he was losing the battle, and he was going to come at any moment. "Can…Candy…"

"What, baby? Are you trying say something?"

Montel's eyes drifted closed as his mouth started to sag into a perfect circle.

"Oh, you're trying not to come." Her smile widened. "Here. Let me help you out." Candy dropped her head, swallowing him whole.

At the sudden feel of hitting the back of her throat, Montel's nut shot up from his toes and blasted out of him so hard and so strong that he could hardly catch his breath. Even then, Candy stayed locked in position until he could see his own creamy juices pour back down his still hard erection like erupting volcano.

"Goddamn, baby."

Candace's mouth bounced off his cock and she quickly began licking up the pretty mess she'd made. When she was finished, Montel grabbed her, folded her over like a taco and eased into her dripping trench in the same slow, torturous pace that she'd put him through. But the way she could work her inner muscles, he wasn't so clear who was torturing whom.

So they had a good rhythm going. Their bodies were smacking and popping just as loud as they were moaning and groaning. But nothing was as good as Candace taking the cowgirl position so she could wind her hips and bounce her ass as hard as she wanted. When she saw that he was getting ready to come a second time, she stopped and interrupted his flow. "This is the last time," she said.

"Wh-what?" He asked like a man suffering from a fever.

"This is the last time," she insisted. "We're not going to do this shit no more. Understand?"

He didn't answer.

"Understand."

"I understand this." He locked his hands around her waist, held her in place and hammered his hips so fast and hard that Candace's mind went completely numb. "You're _____ing this show, Candy," he panted. One. Two. Three orgasms popped off in quick succession and still his ramming dick showed no mercy. "This is my pussy. And I'll have it any time I want."

"Ah. Ah."

"Understand?"

"Ah." Fourth orgasm.

"Let me hear you say that you understand."

"I—I—I....understand."

Montel flipped her back over and delivered her fifth orgasm just as his own liquid candy gushed out in a hot spray across her belly.

Hours later, Candace woke up to an empty bed.

Damn. She glanced around until she found the red glowing numbers of the clock that told her that it was eight o'clock. "At night?" She snatched the sheets back and jumped out of bed. At the window, she jerked back the curtains and blinked stupidly at two things: the moon and the snow.

"What the hell?" Candace raked her hands through her hair and was very tempted to pull it out by its roots.

Shaking her head, she rushed over to her bags. On her phone, she was shocked to read she had fifty-three missed messages. She called Mia while she pulled clothes out of her bag and started getting dressed. "Hey, Mia. It's Candace. What on earth happened to my reservations at the Hotel Le Meurice? I got here and they said that you didn't book me until tomorrow."

"That's strange. I know I booked them."

Candace could hear her assistant shuffle paper around. "Doesn't matter. I need for you to book me somewhere else or I'll have to wait until tomorrow. As bad luck would have it, I had to crash in Starks's room for the day. By the way, what the hell is he doing here? You heard anything in the office about what business meeting he's supposed to have here?"

"Um, no—but I'll find out. Now, what do you mean that you had to *crash* with him?" Mia's voice lowered. "You don't mean that you two are sharing a room, do you?"

"Unfortunately, that's exactly what I mean. That's why I need you to find me another hotel room ASAP. The man is seriously working my nerves." She pulled her New York Jets T-shirt over her head. "I…"

The suite's door flew open and Montel breezed in with a smile and then froze. A shocked Candace stood in the center of the living room area naked. Long legs, nice ass, but it was her full breasts complete with chocolate-capped nipples that drew his eyes and caused his mouth to water.

"Candace? What's wrong? Are you still there?" Mia asked.

Finally snapping out her trance, Candace grabbed a pillow from the sofa and tried to cover herself. "You're just going to stand there and gawk at me? You see I'm naked!"

Montel slapped a hand over his eyes.

"Excuse me?" Mia shrieked.

"Not you, Mia. I'll call you back." Candace disconnected the call and tossed the phone on the sofa. When her gaze returned to Montel, she caught him peeking through his fingers. "What are you—five?"

Laughing, Montel finally turned around. "What do you expect when you go flashing those babies all willy-nilly? You can't just spring that on a man and not expect him to think it's his birthday."

"You have issues."

"But you knew that already." He listened as she shuffled through bags. "Can I turn around now?"

"I don't care what you do. I'm getting out of here." Candace headed to the bathroom and slammed and locked the door behind her. Ten minutes later, she emerged from the shower and raced back over to her clothes.

Montel turned, folding his arms. "Annnnd where do you think you're going?"

"I'm leaving," she said, cramming her legs into a pair of black slacks and then pulling her head through a red turtleneck.

"I don't think so. We're in the middle of a snowstorm. I just talked to the manager down at the front desk and they are urging people to stay put. I doubt you'd be able to even get a taxi."

"Just watch me." She heaved her bags onto her shoulders. "It's been real."

Montel had finally had enough of her antics and blocked the exit to the door. "Stop being stubborn, Candy. There's no way you're getting out of the hotel, just like you couldn't find another hotel earlier. You're stuck here. Deal with it. I'm sure that Walter Anderson isn't going anywhere in this weather."

Candace blinked. "What?"

"What?" Montel wanted to kick himself.

Candace cocked her head as her eyes narrowed to thin slits. "You said Walter Anderson."

"Did I?" His gaze cut away in a lame attempt to avoid scrutiny. "I don't remember."

Candace dropped her bags, crossed her arms and waited him out. He lasted thirty seconds.

"Would you believe it was a guess?" he tried.

"I knew it," she huffed and waved a finger at him. "You've been spying on me. I bet you had that nosy assistant of yours hiding in bathroom stalls again."

Montel's hands shot up. "Hey, I never question her methods."

"Unbelievable." She grabbed her things again. "You're not stealing this account from me."

"Stealing is a strong word, especially since you haven't nailed down this account yet." He flashed a confident smile.

"I prefer to think of this trip as providing you some friendly competition."

"The only thing you've ever provided me was amusement."

"Really?" He stepped closer and caused those alarm bells to start ringing in her head again. "You know there's a thin line between amusement and entertainment." His warm eyes danced as he tilted her chin up. "Remember the last Christmas we spent together?"

Candace drew in a shaky breath and then tried to smother those damn butterflies before they started fluttering around in her stomach. "No." Why she bothered pushing that lie out of her mouth, she didn't know.

Montel didn't bother calling her a liar. His eyes did that all on their own. "I know I'll never forget…"

Christmas Eve 2009…

Montel lay before a roaring fireplace in his cozy two floor cabin in New Hampshire's Bretton Hills. An avid skier, he'd always made sure to sneak at least one weekend away during the winter months. This year, he snuck away with his baby, Candy, determined for it to be a Christmas that they'd always remember.

With Godiva white chocolates, a bowl of strawberries and a bottle of champagne, Montel waited in a pair of black silk boxers and a Santa hat for his baby to come join him. Then at long last, Candy appeared at the top of the stairs wearing a sexy-as-hell red bra and panties set trimmed with white fur. When she started down the staircase, he took in the fishnet stockings, high-heeled pumps and her matching Santa hat. With each step she took, his cock inched higher and higher until it had actually pushed through the thin slit in the front and stood proud and tall.

Candy sashayed into the living room and then stopped before him for inspection. "Merry Christmas."

Montel released Candace's chin and started walking in a slow circle around her. "Am I starting to dust off any cobwebs on that memory of yours?"

Candace lifted her head higher and realized that those damn butterflies weren't going into that sweet night without a fight.

He continued…

"Merry Christmas to you, too," Montel said, drinking in every glorious inch of her. When he finally noticed her gaze was locked on his throbbing hard-on, he turned and grabbed a bow off one of the gifts spilling from beneath the Christmas tree and then plopped it on the head of his cock.

Candy laughed.

"What? You don't like your Christmas gift?"

Her laughter continued to dance around the room. "I love my gift. I plan on playing with it all night."

He hiked up a brow. "Really?"

"Really." She walked up until she stood over him and his straining cock. "The better question is whether you like your gift?"

In answer, Montel reached out and ran his hand up and down her firm legs. "I absolutely adore my gift. It's exactly what I asked Santa for." Their gazes locked and enough sparks flew between them to mistake Christmas for the Fourth of July.

"And have you been a good boy this year?" she asked, settling her hands on her hips.

With his hands roaming higher, he forced his smile to turn into a fake frown. "Actually, I've been very naughty." He sat up so that his head was eye level with her crotch. "But I think that you already know that." His fingers inched inside her thighs. "And if memory serves me correct, you've been a very, very bad girl yourself." Montel ended some of her anticipation by sliding his index finger through the crotch of her thin, silk panties. That mischievous smile she loved so much returned when he discovered the material was already damp.

"Mmm," she moaned, working her hips against his strong fingers.

"You like that, baby?" He kept stroking her.

"Absolutely," she whispered, breathlessly. Candy then took her hands off her hips to give her breasts a teasing squeeze. In doing so, she removed two tiny strips that exposed her chocolate-dipped nipples.

"Ah. You got tricks," he praised. "Well, let me show you what I can do." His eyes still watching her play with her nipples, Montel pressed his mouth against her damp panties and proceeded to lick and suck at her fat clit through the silk.

Candy's knees dipped. The heat from his mouth alone was enough for one mini orgasm to ripple up her body and tingle through her nipples. In no time at all his tongue moved her wet panties to the side and then glided along her pussy with one long, hard stroke. His reward was the trickle of the sweetest honey he'd ever known to drip into his open mouth and give him a sugar high like he'd never known.

She moaned and squeezed her tits harder while she waited for her lover to take her to paradise like he always did. Turned out that she didn't have long to wait once his tongue stopped gliding back and forth and instead start rotating like a mini tornado. Her head spun in sync with the rhythm he'd set.

"Jesssssusssss," she sighed. Her hand deserted her aching nipples, but only to glide across his low-cut hair until she was

*at the verge of coming—at which time she grabbed the back
of his head and held him firmly in place.*

"Give it to me, baby," he mumbled against her clit. "Spread
that pussy all over my face."

That was all he had to say because at the next flick of his
tongue, a galaxy of stars flashed behind her closed eyes. She
gasped. Her mouth rounded in an O. And still, Montel gulped
down her thick honey like it was the nectar of life. When it was
clear that she could no longer stand on her own, he wrapped
an arm around her waist and held her while she sank down
to the floor.

Candy was never the type of woman to let a man do all the
work, so she quickly slid out of her panties while sitting on his
chest and then flipped over into Montel's favorite position:
69. She smiled at the red bow that still decorated the head
of his cock and then sent that son-of-a-bitch sailing over
her shoulder. Next, while Montel and his magic tongue were
lost in the folds of her pussy, she wrapped her hand around
the thick base of his cock and sunk her mouth over its fat
mushroom head until she started gagging on it at the back
of her throat.

Montel's toes curled as his mouth popped off her pink pearl
and hissed, "Sssss."

Candy knew his ass was in heaven so she held still and
squeezed her throat muscles as long as she could. She gagged
a bit, but then took her time easing back up the shaft before
dropping back down for another go. After deep-throating him
for a few strokes, she pulled his cock under her chin and then
snaked her tongue down between his balls and played with
them as if they were a pair of dice.

"Oooh yeesss, baby. That's it." Montel moaned and lifted
his hips for a few strokes. Hands down, she was the best
and she damn well knew it. The sound of him gliding into
her mouth, hitting the back of her throat and occasionally

popping out of her full lips was an aural aphrodisiac, causing his hard cock to extend longer than it ever had. He luxuriated in the feel of her loving mouth while absently roaming his hands over the texture of her crotchless, fishnet stockings.

He reached over to the bowl of strawberries and selected a fat, juicy one. "Let's do something a little different, baby," he panted.

Candy didn't stop her groove, not even when she could feel him peeling her throbbing, bald lips open and pressing something cool into the center of her pussy.

"Squeeze your muscles, sweetheart."

A lover of Kegel exercises, Candy squeezed. Strawberry juice and honey squirted out between her thighs and splashed into Montel's mouth.

"Mmm, baby. You're fucking amazing." He lifted his head and proceeded to eat strawberry pussy cake. Twenty minutes later, Candy was turned back around and bouncing on his amazing dick as if she was a final contestant in a bronco-riding contest.

Montel moaned, hissed and promised that he would love her forever. And he meant it. What made the nasty things they did together so wonderful was the fact that there was this deep binding love for one another. That love had existed since the day they'd met. There were challenges—the main one that they still lived in two different cities. After this weekend, he hoped that all of that would change. He knew that she loved her career in New York, but surely she loved him more.

It was time to choose.

"Awww. Awww," Candy gasped as juice and honey continued to pour like an open faucet.

There was no point in asking whether she was about to come, the grip on his shaft was like a warm, silky vice, tightening with each bounce.

"Goddamn, baby. Hold up." Montel tried to catch his

breath, but the nice tingling in his balls signaled that his nut was rising—fast.

She leaned forward, placed her hands on both sides of his head and bounced her perfect brown breasts in his face. "I love you, Monty," she whispered and then asked, "Can I come? Huh? Can I come on your dick?"

"You better come." He sealed their lips and souls together with a kiss. With reserved energy, he locked an arm around her waist and then thrust his dick so hard and fast into her dripping pussy that she exploded with a double orgasm.

"Merry Christmas, Candy," he murmured against the curve of her neck. "I love you."

Candace shook her head to erase the memory she had spent the last year trying to forget. "Now that we're finished strolling down memory lane, I have to go."

Montel shook his head as he watched her snatch open the suite's door. "You can't keep running forever, Candy."

She stopped and glanced back over her shoulder. "Not forever. Just until you stop chasing me."

His gaze locked onto hers. "That won't happen."

"We'll see." With the threat of tears burning the backs of her eyes, she marched out of the room.

Chapter 8

Mia wasted no time rechecking the itinerary for Candace's Paris trip and just as she thought, she had booked her boss for an executive room. Armed with a confirmation number, she made a quick call to the Hotel Le Meurice, but then received a puzzling answer that someone had called and canceled that reservation. She then proceeded to argue with the woman until she caught a glimpse of Georgine, smiling as she sauntered down the cubicle aisles.

"That bitch," she hissed, narrowing her eyes.

"Excusez-moi?"

"Oh. Not you, ma'am. Thanks for your help." Mia quickly hung up the phone, jumped up from her seat and raced to catch up with Georgine. "You think your ass is slick, don't you?"

"Hmm?" Georgine turned with her smile still in place.

"How did you know which hotel I'd booked Candace with?"

She shrugged. "Lucky guess?"

Mia's eyes narrowed.

"Or I simply found out where Walter Anderson was having his company's annual Christmas party. You're not the only one here with contacts, you know." She shrugged. "What's the big deal? Paris has plenty of hotels. I'm sure that she can find a room somewhere."

"Or perhaps share a room with her colleague?"

Georgine's brow popped up. "Oh, did she now? You know I only booked a single bed for Montel. Any word on whether they—"

"No. You're barking up the wrong tree. Candace and Montel are like oil and water. They are never going to mix."

Georgine settled behind her desk. "You just keep telling yourself that. I know what I see. And I see two people fighting tooth and nail being in love."

"You're delusional."

"And you're going to lose your bet." She turned up her smile.

"We'll see about that." Mia whipped around and marched to her desk. She needed to get Candace another room fast.

In Paris, Candace was stunned at the amount of snow that was descending on the City of Light, and the blistering cold effortlessly penetrated her clothes and made her feel as if she was standing outside naked. She'd hoped to flag down a taxi as she'd done earlier that day, but now it appeared that she was one of only a few idiots trying to brave the icy weather.

When it became clear that she could quite possibly turn into a Popsicle, she tucked her tail—and her pride—between her legs and walked back into the hotel lobby.

"Welcome to the Hotel Le Meurice." The young valet greeted her with smiling eyes. Of course he knew that in fact she wasn't a new guest, and he seemed more tickled for having watched her stand outside for the past hour to no avail. "Will you need any help with your bags?"

Candace rolled her eyes and swiped snow off her hair and shoulders. "No. Thank you."

Across the lobby, the ding of the elevator caught Candace's attention. Montel lifted his head and strolled into the lobby in a pair of pressed casual khakis and white dress shirt that hung on his tall and broad frame to perfection. Once again, all female gazes shifted in his direction, including Candace's. Even though she was still angry and annoyed, she couldn't get herself to turn away.

Montel smiled but kept it moving toward the hotel's indoor restaurant.

She watched him go, feeling a rising tide of tears at life's injustice. The truth of the matter was that she did remember that beautiful time in New Hampshire last Christmas. How could she not? Montel had been all that she had hoped for in a lover…and even a best friend. But there were just some hurdles that were too big for them to leap over—or were they?

"Madame Lahane!" A woman from behind the front desk waved to her.

Candace sighed and dragged her bags over.

"We had a cancellation today. Are you still looking for a room?"

"Oh, thank God. Yes. I would love a room. Thank you."

"Excellent." The woman turned to her computer.

Candace happily dug through her purse and handed over her credit card. "You have no idea how much this means to me."

She smiled. "We're sorry for the inconvenience, Ms. Lahane. Here is your room key. Enjoy your stay."

"Thank you." She glanced down at her key holder and read the room number. "But this is…"

"Ah. Fancy seeing you here."

Candace turned and was equally surprised to see the kind Santa Claus-looking gentleman she had sat next to on the plane. "Oh. Hello." She glanced around. "You're staying here?"

"Seems I don't really have a choice, given the weather." He laughed with a curious "ho, ho, ho."

"Well, it looks like we're both stuck here." She expelled a long breath, thinking about her chance of doing an ambush proposal with the elusive Walter Anderson before Christmas. "I guess there are worse things than being stuck in a luxury hotel in the heart of Paris for Christmas," she said, grabbing her bags again.

"And what better place to make up with your boyfriend than in the City of Light and the City of Love?"

"He's not…"

He held up a hand. "I'm old—not blind." He winked.

Her gaze dropped from his twinkling ones. "No, I suppose not." She started toward the elevator bay.

Her fake Santa followed. "You know, I've been around the world many times and I've seen a whole lot. The one thing I know for sure is that love is a very rare and precious thing. Personally, I think it would be foolish for anyone in this day and age to just throw it away."

Contrite, Candace hung her head as she entered an empty elevator. "You don't understand."

"Oh, I understand," he said, stepping into the compartment behind her. "It's a conflict that is as old as time—a battle between your head and your heart. At the end of the day, you're going have to ask yourself one thing."

"What's that?"

"Do you love him?"

Candace opened her mouth to bark out an emphatic "no," but instead the words got caught in her throat, and she was reduced to having a choking fit. Lust was one thing. Love was another. Maybe it was time to figure out exactly which side of the fence her heart was really on.

The elevator arrived at her floor, and she flashed the older gentleman a brief smile and exited the compartment without answering his question. How could she explain her feelings to a stranger when she hardly understood them herself? She walked to her hotel suite that was two doors down from Montel's and quickly dragged her things inside.

The day was a bust—well, not completely when she considered that little sexcapade she'd had with Monty earlier. A smile swept across her face, and then just as quickly she scolded herself. "Stop it. Stop it. Stop it."

Candace walked over to the bed and fell backwards onto the plush pillowtop mattress. "I don't love him. I don't," she said, trying to convince herself. What she felt was lust. It just had to be. Lord knows that they couldn't be in a room for more than two minutes before they were ripping each other's clothes off.

Of course, they did have some fun outside the bedroom. Bora-Bora was fun. But then there were the extended weekend getaways to St. Lucia, Aspen, and even the week-long trip to Hawaii. They had managed to climb out of bed long enough to go dancing, surfing and skiing. And generally they tended to have a great time.

Then why are you fighting him so hard?

"Because it won't last," she argued with herself. The handful of boyfriends that she'd had in the past always had a problem with who she was outside of the bedroom. They couldn't take that she was an ambitious woman who worked long hours and oftentimes made more money than they did. It didn't matter whether they were professional businessmen themselves or not. At some point in the relationship, men always expected the woman to fall back and play some submissive role that wasn't in her playbook.

So when they realized that they couldn't control her—they left. *They always leave.*

Chapter 9

Mia dialed and redialed Candace's cell phone only to be transferred to her voice mail. After the twelfth time, she simply just e-mailed and texted the information for the new room she was able to book at the Castille Hotel. It was the best that she could do and she prayed that it would be enough.

"Merry Christmas, Mia," Vicki cheered as she stopped before her desk. "You ready to hit happy hour over at the Olivia? They are having a mistletoe and a karaoke contest. I figured that you, me and Sandra could get on stage and perform '"Santa Baby.'"

"Ooh. Count me in. But what is a mistletoe contest?" she asked, shutting down her computer.

"Heck if I know, but it sounds like a lot of fun."

Mia laughed and grabbed her purse from underneath her desk. When she went to stand up, she was surprised to see Mr. Carter making his way toward them. "Hello, ladies. Is Ms. Lahane in or has she already gone for the day?"

"I'm sorry, Ms. Lahane is out of town on a business trip. Is there anything I can help you with?"

"She's out of town, too?" He crossed his arms. "Hmm. Do you have a number I can reach her at? I had my secretary try to reach her on her cell phone, but we just kept reaching her voice mail."

Mia's antennae went up. "No. Not yet, but, um, I'm sure she'll get in contact with me soon. Would you like for me to deliver a message?"

"Well…" He looked around to see whether he was about to be overheard. "I wanted to be the one to tell her, but I'm about to take the family out to Texas for the holidays. My in-laws are there. Anyway, I wanted to be the one to tell her that the accounting department had recalculated the numbers and it seems that there was an error."

"An error?" Mia's heart leapt. "In Ms. Lahane's favor?" she asked, her eyes shining with hope.

"It appears so. Her numbers ending in November were actually 2.3 billion to Mr. Starks's 1.8 billion. She's clearly this year's winner for top ad executive for the year—and the company's next vice president of sales. When you talk to her, give her my congratulations."

Mia wanted to shout, "Hallelujah" but settled for just beaming at the president. "I will definitely tell her. Merry Christmas, Mr. Carter!"

"Merry Christmas, ladies." He tilted his head toward Vicki. "Good luck with the mistletoe contest." He winked.

Once he walked away, Mia did an odd sort of victory dance while Vicki rushed around and squealed with her in excitement.

"Now I know we're celebrating tonight!"

"You never miss a chance to celebrate."

"Damn right. So get your things and let's go."

The phone rang.

"Hold up." Mia picked up the phone. "Candace Lahane's office. Oh, Mr. Scarborough, Merry Christmas." She listened as he stated that he was missing a couple of pages on the final proposal numbers. "Let me just check if I can find those in Ms. Lahane's office and if so I'll fax those right over." She disconnected the call and held up a finger. "Give me one minute," she told Vicki and then rushed into Candace's office to see whether there was a backup file for the Scarborough proposal. She quickly rifled through the drawers, hoping for a quick find, but then had to sit down and take her time. But when she pulled open the bottom drawer, she got the shock of her life.

"Ohmygod!" Mia reached down, picked up a small frame and just stared.

"C'mon, girl. Are we going to hit the club or not?"

Mia didn't move.

"What's the matter, girl?" Vicki strolled over to the massive desk to see what had captured her friend's attention, only to look at the picture frame and gasp in shock herself. "Oh. My. God."

"I already said that," Mia croaked, shaking her head at a wedding photo. "I don't believe it. Candace and Montel…are married?"

Montel sat alone at a small table next to a window inside the hotel's restaurant, listening to Christmas carols sung in French. As he watched big flakes descend from the sky and blanket the beautiful landscape, a sadness that he'd been trying to suppress threatened to engulf him. Maybe it was finally time to give up, time to stop chasing after someone who didn't want to be caught—even if it was his wife. He closed his eyes and drew a deep breath. It wasn't in his nature to quit, but he definitely felt that his back was up against a wall and it was time to face the very real possibility that he and Candy had reached the end of the road.

When he thought about all the women in his past—and there were quite a few of them—he couldn't remember any of them giving him as hard a time as Candace Lahane had. Hell, he couldn't remember any of them holding his attention more than a couple of weeks, if he was going to be completely honest with himself.

He was a simple guy—at least that's what he liked to think. He came from a middle-of-the-road middle-class family. He had graduated at the top of his class at Morehouse and then had headed to Harvard Law. After passing the bar, he'd worked for a prestigious law firm and started rolling in some serious dollars. His sudden shift into advertising happened for one reason and one reason only: Candace Lahane.

He wanted her and he was willing to do and go anywhere to have her.

"Your drink, *monsieur*." His waiter sat a whiskey sour down on the table. "Your order will be up soon."

"Merci," he said and then cast his gaze back out of the window. He had done a lot of dumb things in his life—but marrying Candace Lahane just hours after meeting her in Bora-Bora was not one of them. He just wished that she could say the same thing….

Christmas Day 2009…

They had been secretly married for a full year and for the most part living separate lives—Candy in New York and he in Atlanta. At first he understood. They were, after all, two strangers who had done something really crazy by getting married after one wild night in Bora-Bora. She had a career and an image she had to preserve—at least that was what she kept telling him. To be honest, he didn't know how their impromptu marriage would work with his own family and friends, either, but he was convinced, beyond a shadow of a doubt, that he was in love. So he eventually worked up the nerve, sat his parents and siblings down and announced that he was married.

It would have been better if he'd actually had his wife by his side.

Sure, Candy would pencil him in for a hot weekend from time to time, and for a few days afterward, he'd forget about pressuring her to meld their two lives together. But after a while he started wondering whether she had any intentions of really becoming his wife. His mind ran wild with possibilities of their being another man in her life, but those accusations were met with laughs and assurances that that wasn't the case.

So this Christmas, their one-year anniversary, Montel was taking a leap of faith to force his so-called wife to make a choice. Christmas Eve had been another wild exotic ride with his playful use of strawberries. They had screwed each other's brains out and now that the sun was up, he was ready to make love again. He woke her up by nibbling on her lower earlobe and sliding his hands in between her creamy, chocolate thighs.

She moaned, smiling, and then turned over in his arms so that she could devour his Christmas morning kiss with equal passion. "Merry Christmas, lover," she said.

Normally that would've been a pleasant greeting, but on this morning, it touched a raw nerve. "Is that how you see me? As just your lover?"

Clearly the question surprised her because she pulled back from his kiss-swollen lips and stared questioningly into his eyes. "What do you mean?"

He wanted to buy into her innocent act, but a growing part

*of him was forcing himself to confront this situation head on.
"I mean...do you view me as your lover or your husband?"*

*There was a long pregnant pause that had Monty fearing
the answer.*

*Finally, she gave a half laugh and shook her head. "That's
a ridiculous question." She turned and climbed out of bed.*

He sat up. "Is it?"

*"Of course it is." She headed to the bathroom and shut
the door as if that meant it was the end of discussion.*

*Monty stared at the door, a bit shocked at her abrupt
behavior. The shower was turned on, and he climbed out
of bed with the thought of joining her—but was thrown a
monkey wrench when he discovered that she had locked the
door. "What the hell?" He knocked on the door and grew
frustrated when, instead of letting him in, she started singing
in the shower.*

*He walked down the hall to the guest room and used its
adjoining shower. The whole time he was in there he couldn't
fight the feeling that while he'd come to jump-start their
marriage, she had come to end it.*

*An hour later, she emerged from the bathroom fully dressed
and smiling as if she hadn't just walked out the moment they
were about to start arguing. He sat on the edge of the bed
with a small golden box, complete with a red bow, sitting on
his lap.*

*"What's that?" she asked, stopping in the center of the
room.*

*Monty, still a bit annoyed, looked up and locked gazes
with her. "It's one of your Christmas gifts."*

*Her smile lit up the room. "Are we exchanging those now?
I have yours down in the—"*

"Later. I really want you to open this one right now."

*She looked at him oddly. "Ooookay." She walked over to the
bed and sat next to him. He handed the box over and watched*

her hesitate before opening it. Finally, she took the plunge and ripped off the wrapping and lifted the top off the box. What she found inside caused her brows to dip with confusion. "A key?"

"A key to our future."

She cocked her head. "I don't understand."

He smiled. "Then maybe I should show you." Twenty minutes later, he pulled his black Mercedes up into the driveway of a stunning two million dollar estate.

He was incredibly nervous.

She was remarkably silent.

That is until he opened the door to their new house with the key from the golden box.

"You bought a house?"

"Surprise!"

But there was no squeal of excitement, hugs or even showers of kisses. Instead the woman he'd hoped to build his life with simply turned to him and said, "I want a divorce."

Monty stared at her. Either he couldn't or didn't want to believe he'd heard her correctly. Then again, hadn't he sort of expected this?

"Why?" he asked in a low whisper.

Candy slapped a hand against her forehead and started pacing in a small circle. "Do you really have to ask that question? I mean, we hardly know each other."

His groomed brows jumped up in amusement.

"I mean other than...sexually," she clarified.

Monty crossed his arms. "It certainly isn't because of my lack of trying."

"That's just it. Why are you trying sooo hard?"

"Excuse me?"

Candy huffed out an impatient breath. "I mean...what we did was really...really stupid. Hell, I'm not even sure that our marriage is even legal."

Monty stepped back. She was unloading an awful lot on him right now and he wasn't a man accustomed to rejection.

"I've been meaning to tell you," she said after a long beat of silence.

"And for a whole year you couldn't find the time?" He tried to keep his tone on an even keel despite the fact that he could feel his temperature rising by the second. He had never spent so much time trying to seduce, charm and romance a woman in all his life. What on earth did it take to win this woman's heart?

Candy drew a deep breath. "I was hoping you would…"

"What? Pick up on the hint?"

She dropped her head. "Something like that."

Monty took another step back and shook his head. "Well, maybe I did. And maybe I'm just a crazy, hopeless romantic who was hoping that I could convince you to change your mind."

She looked at him as if he was crazy.

"C'mon," he said, his confidence slowly returning. "Sure we met under unusual circumstances and maybe it was crazy to get married in Bora-Bora by, admittedly, a questionable pastor, but you can't tell me that you regret it. I won't believe you."

"I was drunk out of my mind," she insisted.

"And the weekend getaways since then? Hawaii, Aspen and St. Lucia?" She hesitated and he knew that he had his answer. His eyes fell to her long neck where he could see her fast heartbeat.

Buh-bump. Buh-bump.

Candy continued to shake her head. "Look. It will never work. I—I'm not even sure I believe in marriage."

"What?"

"You'll never understand."

He frowned. "Have you been married before?"

"No. But...you'd have to have been living under a rock for the past few decades not to know that marriages don't work anymore. Someone always leaves or cheats or just betrays the other person. And usually it's the man!"

"Excuse me?"

"It won't work—okay?" She glanced around the large home. "We should've just left it at sex. Anything outside of that gets too complicated."

"So you were just looking for a boy toy?"

"I didn't say that."

"You're not really saying that much," he charged back. His irritation started bubbling up again.

Tears started to glisten in Candy's eyes as if she was fighting some inner war with herself. "You shouldn't have bought this place like this. You should've consulted me." She sniffed and continued to shake her head. "I can't move here. Did you think I was just going to give up my life...my career and blindly move down here...and what—become a housewife?"

"Fine. I'll move to New York."

"No. I'm not asking you to do that."

"I'm offering."

"Just...stop." She held her hands up and stepped back as though his mere presence was making it difficult for her to think.

He decided right then and there that he liked it better when she wasn't thinking. He smiled. "Look, Candy. It doesn't matter how or where we met. The only thing that matters is how we feel about each other." Monty walked back over to her. "How we met wasn't an accident. It was destiny." He gathered her into his arms and waited until her watery gaze met his before he slowly lowered his head.

Encouraged that she didn't pull away, Monty dipped his tongue in between her cherry-flavored lips and slid his arms *around her curvy hips. She felt so good in his arms that nothing on earth would ever be able to convince him that she didn't belong there. His heart took flight when Candy's arm slid around his neck and pulled him even closer. The sparks that had always been there from the beginning were once again shooting all over the place. Once again they were swept into a passion that neither one of them could explain or could stop.*

In the empty foyer of their new house, they tore at each other's clothes. And in no time at all, Monty had his wife— legitimate or not—naked on their new hardwood floor in the "side wind-her" position. A wonderful pose that had Candy lying on her side with her left leg raised over Monty's shoulder while he straddled her bottom thigh and hugged her calf that lay across his chest as he entered her. Once he was in deep, he wound and whirled his hips.

With each thrust, he discovered a new pleasure zone that kept them both on the edge of ecstasy. He started kissing her calves and then behind her knees. She grew so wet, she felt like a giant water slide. But he continued to stroke slow and deep in between her smooth and warm walls.

Panting heavily, Candy got in on the act by dipping her fingers between her open legs and started twirling her fingers around her clit. Faster and faster her fingers whirled, causing her body to start trembling uncontrollably. Holding her steady gaze, Monty reached for her honey-coated hands and slipped them into his mouth where he proceeded to suck and lick them clean.

Candace's walls started tightening and Monty's eyes started to roll to the back of his head. He lowered her leg and turned her body into a straight missionary position. "You belong to me," he gasped against the shell of her ear. "We belong together." He was sure that he was getting through to her, if the tears that were sliding down the corners of her eyes were any indication.

Monty wasn't young or even naive. He knew that much of what Candy had said to him was the truth. And it wasn't as if there was any shortage of women that vied for his attention. And in the past he had definitely had had his fun. But there came a time in every man's life when he had to put away childish things and become a man. For him that time had come the night he met his wife. There was just something about the woman in his arms that monopolized his thoughts and kept his body in constant longing.

"Oh, Monty," she whispered, rolling her head back and thrusting her large breasts toward his hungry mouth. He sucked, nibbled and tugged on her dime-size nipples and then watched as she wiggled and squirmed. A few minutes later, he was entering her from behind. Candy released a long satisfying moan as his hands anchored on to her hips and he started hammering his way into her lower belly.

Monty hissed and moaned at the feel of her vaginal muscles tightening around him and then a few seconds later they started trembling violently. She could hardly catch her breath, and before they knew it they were calling out each other's names as a powerful orgasm overtook them and shook them to their core.

Spent and satisfied, they lay in each others arms with Monty peppering kisses across her collarbone and then down her shoulders. "We belong together."

It was a nice Christmas, but by New Year's, his elusive wife was gone—again.

But this time, Monty followed her...all the way to Nu4us.

"Your dinner, *monsieur*." His waiter placed his prime Angus rib eye in front of him with a smile. "Will there be anything else, sir?"

"No. Everything looks fine. *Merci.*"

The waiter bobbed his head and drifted off.

Just when Montel was about to turn his attention to his delicious-looking meal, he saw Candy stroll into the restaurant's door. As usual, she was stunning, even in a pair of basic black slacks and a red turtleneck. He was sure that he wasn't the only one who thought so either, judging by the number of men's heads that swiveled in her direction.

He waited, and eventually her gaze found his from across the room. For a long moment, they just stared at one another. And when the hostess approached, Candace surprised him by pointing toward him before heading his way.

"Mind if I join you?" she asked, gesturing to the empty seat across from him.

"Of course not."

She took a deep breath and then pulled out the chair. The moment her butt hit the chair, his waiter reappeared and asked for her drink order. "The pinot noir will be fine."

"But of course, *mademoiselle.*" He tilted his head and then drifted off again.

"It's nice of you to join me," Montel said, slicing a piece of his rib eye.

"Well, if I recall, neither one of us likes to eat alone."

One side of his lips kicked up. "Sure." He stabbed a piece of meat and then offered it up to her. "Would you like to try a bite?"

"No. I'm not that hungry." On cue, her stomach roared like a lion gaining ground on a wildebeest.

Montel's brows crashed together while he tried to hold back his laughter.

"All right," she said, exhaling. "Maybe I'll just have a little bite." She leaned forward and plucked the meat off the end of his fork with her teeth and proceeded to moan as she chewed.

"I take it it's good." He sawed off another slice and offered it to her again. This time, she didn't put up a fake protest and accepted the succulent strip of meat with another moan.

Montel smiled as he watched her eat. The last time he fed her like this was with strawberries and in front of a fireplace. "So are we going to call it a truce this evening?"

Her brown eyes fluttered up to him. "I guess I can put away my claws for one evening."

"Glad to hear it." He offered her another slice.

Candy accepted it with a smile. "It doesn't mean that you're off the hook. I still intend on landing this account tomorrow."

"I'm sure you do." He reached for his whiskey sour and stared at her over the rim of his glass.

"What?" she asked.

"Nothing."

"Now who's lying?" she challenged.

Their waiter returned. "Your wine, *mademoiselle?* Have you had a chance to look at our menu?"

"Uh, thank you, but I think I'll just order what he's having."

"Of course." The waiter disappeared again.

"Now, what were you thinking so hard about?" she tried again.

"Nothing you want to hear," he tried again. His gaze drifted from her eyes down to the column of her neck.

"Stop," she said. "Don't do that."

His smile returned. "As you wish."

Candace took a deep breath. "Look. It's no secret that I'm physically attracted to you."

"You don't say."

"But that's it, Monty. Outside of the bedroom we have very little in common."

He laughed. "You don't really believe that. We're both

competitive and ambitious. We both love to dance, gamble, ski, surf and even have a soft spot for strawberries."

She blinked at him.

"Should I continue?" When she continued to gape, he added, "Every morning you have to have a tall half-skinny, half-one percent extra hot split quad shot—two shots of espresso, two shots regular latte with whipped cream. You love your family, though you think they're dysfunctional. You've never forgiven your father for leaving, and every night you like to read a couple of chapters of the latest, greatest romance novel before falling asleep."

Candace still stared at him.

"What? Some men listen."

"Your dinner, *mademoiselle*." Her waiter reappeared and set her food down. "Is there anything else I can get for you?"

She shook her head and continued to stare at the man across from her.

"Aren't you going to say something?" he prodded.

"Yeah. You never cease to amaze me."

He licked his lips again. "That should be a good thing."

Chapter 10

Dinner was wonderful.

Candace and Montel fell into easy conversation and for a while it felt as if they were once again away on one of those many weekend getaways that they used to do in the first year of their dubious marriage. And after a couple glasses of wine, Candy's gaze warmed and she started regretting her declaration of never sleeping with him again. Hell, it was the Christmas holidays and technically they were approaching their second year anniversary of their legally uncertain marriage.

At least she thought it wasn't legit.

"So? This is your room?" Montel asked, stopping at her door while she searched for her key.

"Yes it is," she answered, smiling up at him.

"You know, you could invite me in for a nightcap. I won't tell anyone." He placed a hand against the door frame over her head and smiled down at her. "I'm really good at keeping a secret."

"*That,* Mr. Starks, you are. I have to hand it to you. You had me on pins and needles all year, wondering when you were going to tell everyone at Nu4us that we were married."

"Something tells me that wouldn't have gone over too well."

"You're right. I probably would've killed you."

He laughed. "Well, since I'm partial to breathing it's a good thing I kept my mouth shut." He brushed his hand under her chin. "But I'm still hoping that you'll come around."

Candace's heart squeezed at the hope shining in his eyes. And for a brief moment, it almost rubbed off on her. "Good night," she whispered.

Montel quirked up a brow. "Are you sure?"

No. "Yes." She bobbed her head, and to make sure that she didn't change her mind, she turned around and slipped her key into the lock.

"'Night," he said, backing away from the door as she hurried inside.

"Good night." With a final smile, she shut the door and then pressed her body against it. After several deep breaths, she tried to shake all thoughts of Montel out of her head and tried to get ready for bed.

"Do you love him?"

It was the last thing that drifted across her mind before she fell asleep and the first thing when she woke up the next morning. By the time she was getting ready for Anderson Vytex's Christmas party, she was sick of hearing the question. However, the answer had a hard time cresting her lips because it made no logical sense—why or how could she be in love? She had met a man during a wild time in Bora-Bora—a weekend where she'd let her hair down and acted like the complete opposite of the no-nonsense, take-charge woman that had kept her at the top of her profession. She'd gambled away a fortune, danced on top of tables and slept with someone she hardly knew on the first night and then hours later…married him.

So how in the hell could she truly be in love?

Sure, Christmas Day was technically their second anniversary and she had a whole year to make good on her promise to file for divorce. But the truth of the matter was that she couldn't bring herself to actually file the papers. And Montel knew it. He sensed it. That was the whole reason behind him dropping his life in Atlanta and following her to New York. Maybe she could have handled it if he'd stopped at just that. But to then take a job at her company and proceed to try and take away something that she had spent a lifetime trying to build? How could she ever forgive that?

And still I haven't filed for divorce.

Candace stared at her reflection again, hoping upon hope that the image staring back at her in the mirror would answer this complex question for her. The morning after their five-minute wedding ceremony on the beach of Bora-Bora, she had thought the simple fix would have been just to get their marriage annulled. But when Monty had awakened that morning smiling at her like she was the most beautiful and precious thing in the world—the words had just gotten stuck in her throat.

Candace's usual no-nonsense attitude had failed her. Days later, she had practically run to New York, telling Monty that she needed time to break the news to her family, friends and even business associates that she was a married woman. But once she'd arrived home, she'd fallen back into her old workaholic habits and couldn't admit to doing something that was so illogical and foolish to anyone. She had promised herself that the next time she talked to her *husband* that she would just tell him the real deal and request a divorce.

That was the plan.

Sticking to the plan was another story.

Every time Monty had called or tried to meet her, she had come up with excuses or exaggerated her work schedule. The times she had agreed to meet him for weekend getaways, she had fully intended to tell Monty that she wanted an annulment or a divorce. But each time she saw him and each time she was locked in his arms, reason and logic were no longer a part of her vocabulary or thinking.

Montel Starks had a way of bringing out another side of her that she wasn't so willing to let go. With him, she was uninhibited, wild and sexy.

But was she in love?

It was a hell of a question to be asking oneself after two years of marriage, but here she was—staring at herself in the mirror and wondering why, with such a desperate shortage of good men, was she trying her level best to get rid of the one she'd snagged by accident.

Because all men leave—maybe not today or tomorrow, but eventually they all do. Hadn't she witnessed that with her own father and the countless number of men in her and her girlfriends' past?

And yet…none of it felt true when it came to Montel Starks. The man was relentless and stubborn if nothing else. Their battle at Nu4us for the past year in some weird way showed her that he would stop at nothing to win her back. She kept running and he kept chasing.

But was she making the biggest mistake of her life by refusing to admit that maybe, just maybe, she couldn't control everything? While still staring at her reflection in the mirror, Candace pulled on the thin chain around her neck and pulled up the simple gold band that Monty had purchased at a casino shop in Bora-Bora. She remembered being giddy as a teenager when he had slipped it onto her finger. It was either that or one too many tequila sunrises.

It wasn't much—a simple band with a small cut diamond… but she kind of loved it. But did she love him?

Yes. Candace closed her eyes and mumbled under her breath, "Damn." She turned away from the mirror and marched out of the bathroom. She couldn't deal with any of this right now. She had a Christmas party to crash.

It was easier than she expected. Outside the main atrium of the hotel, employees and party guests were laughing and drinking in beautiful gowns and tuxedos. Christmas classics were being played on the piano by a handsome player in black tuxedo tails. Waiters and waitresses floated through the crowd with trays of hor d'oeuvres and tall flutes of champagne.

The mood was light and joyous. Candace put on her best smile and put her head into the game. The faster she cornered and gave her little pitch to Walter Anderson, the better. She glided through the crowd in a soft peach-colored gown with straps around her arms instead of her shoulder. The gentle draping flowed with soft waves from just below her breasts to around her curvy hips. Her long, firm legs were showcased by the long split on the side of her gown as she walked.

Men paused. Their heads and gazes tracked her while she moved through clusters of people to the open bar. Lord knew that she needed a drink. Bad. She ordered a Caipirinha in perfect French, smiled and then swept her gaze around the crowd.

"Bonsoir."

Candace turned toward the whiskey voice and saw that it belonged to a long-haired blonde with the most startling pair of blue eyes she'd ever seen. *"Bonsoir,"* she responded in kind.

They fell into easy, flirtatious conversation. The handsome Parisian praised her beauty and seemed downright fascinated by her smooth, *ebony* skin. She blushed and batted her eyes prettily before asking whether he'd seen Walter Anderson anywhere. It was sad to say that she didn't even know what the elusive and eccentric billionaire looked like. The man avoided having his picture taken like the plague.

"I don't see him around," the man said. "But I'm sure that he'll be along shortly."

Candace nodded and went back to flirting outrageously. That is until the energy in the room shifted and the hairs on the back of her neck stood up. She, like most of the women in the room, turned her head. Sure enough, Montel strolled into the crowd looking like a chocolate god in his black tuxedo. She watched him effortlessly turn on the charm and melt into the crowd.

She tried to pull her eyes away when a bevy of women started laughing around him.

"A friend of yours?" her whiskey-voiced friend asked.

"No. Not exactly," she said, finally returning her attention to the friendly Frenchman. "I'm sorry, Didier, what did you say you did at Anderson Vytex?"

"Actually, I'm the vice president," he boasted with a widening smile. "My father owns the company."

"Oh…is that right?" She eased up closer to him. "So you're Didier Anderson?"

"Yes, my father owns the company—for now. I believe that he'll be announcing his retirement this evening."

That news shocked her, and clearly it was written on her face.

"Don't worry. I promise not to run my father's company into the ground."

Candace couldn't believe her luck. "I'm sure you'll be great."

Didier inched closer himself. "I hope so. I have some rather big shoes to fill, but I think I'm ready to prove that I'm up for the job." He reached for his drink on the bar. "Now. About you. I don't recall ever meeting you before. Which department do you work in?"

"Oh, well...I don't exactly work for Vytex," she admitted.

Didier cocked his head. "Then you're here as someone's date? I should have known that someone as beautiful as you couldn't be here alone."

"No—"

"You would be right about that," Montel said, sliding up behind Candace and wrapping his arm around her waist.

Candace's smile melted off her face. She turned, but before she could scold or level an angry glare in Montel's direction, he pressed a kiss against her full lips.

"Hey, honey. Sorry, I'm late." He placed another kiss against the tip of her nose before shifting his attention to Didier and thrusting out a hand. "Thanks for keeping my *wife* company."

Didier's surprised gaze shot back to Candace. "Not a problem. It's been my pleasure. Excuse me, won't you?" With a final smile, he turned and drifted back into the crowd.

"Wait, Monsieur Anderson—" But he was gone. She whipped back around to her smiling husband. "Do you know who that was?"

"I gather Monsieur Anderson." He looked toward the bartender. "A whiskey sour, please."

"Right. *Walter Anderson's* son. I was just seconds away from—oh, never mind." She grabbed her own drink and tossed it back like a seasoned sailor. "If you think you're going to snatch this account out from under me, you have another thing coming."

One side of Montel's lips kicked up. "C'mon. You know the *real* reason I'm here." The bartender handed him his drink.

She stretched up a single brow.

"It's all about you, baby. It's always been all about you." He held up his glass in a silent toast before draining the contents in one long gulp. He seemed tense—edgy. Maybe he hadn't liked sleeping alone last night.

Her gaze narrowed as she picked up his somber tone. "Now what was that supposed to mean?"

"C'mon, Candy. Let's stop playing games. I'm practically at the end of my rope here. You say 'jump' and I say 'how high.' I honestly don't know how much more of this bullshit I can take."

"Finally, you've come to your senses." she quipped, but immediately regretted it after the look he shot her.

"Yeah, finally." He stood there for a moment longer, gazing into her eyes. "I'm sorry I've wasted your time." He surprised her by placing a kiss against the corner of her lips. "Goodbye, Candy." He pressed something into her hand.

Candace's brows crashed together as she watched Montel turn and thread back through the crowd. Unaccustomed to Montel retreating in the middle of a perfectly good argument, she actually stood there waiting for him to turn back around to finish what they'd started. However, the more distance he stretched between them, the more nervous she became. If he looked back, everything was going be okay, she told herself. She waited and waited. When he came close to disappearing from sight, she started mentally willing and then pleading for him to turn around.

He never did. She glanced down and opened her hand. Her vision blurred at seeing the simple gold band she'd given him on their wedding night.

"That didn't look like that went too well."

Candace jumped and then glanced to her right. Her Santa Claus look-alike stood next to her with a solemn smile. "Ah. It's you again."

His smile broadened. "Sorry to disappoint you."

"No. No. I didn't mean it like that." She flashed him a smile and then glanced back over her shoulder to see if she could still see Montel. When Candace realized he was gone, her heart dropped into the pit of her stomach and tears stung the back of her eyes.

He's just...testing you. She nodded at that logic. It was exactly something he would do: trick her into chasing after him—just so he could prove a point.

"Are you sure you're making the right decision?" her jolly friend asked.

"I'm not sure of anything anymore," she answered under her breath.

"Too bad. Because it's clear that man was definitely crazy about you."

Candace closed her eyes and shook her head. "It would've never worked out. I would've...messed it up somehow. I mean...more than I already have."

Her Santa Claus chuckled at her. "I knew that you loved him."

She closed her eyes and then turned to look at him. "And how did you know that?"

He reached up and touched her slender neck. "I can see your heart beating whenever you look at him."

Buh-bump. Buh-bump.

Those hot tears that she had been struggling to keep in check finally burst through the wall that she'd spent a lifetime building and rushed over her mascara-coated lashes. "Could you excuse me, um...I don't think I ever caught your name."

"Walter. Walter Anderson." He thrust out his hand. "Nice to officially meet you."

Candace blinked and then laughed at the situation. "It's nice to meet you, Walter. But...I really have to go."

Walter winked. "I completely understand. Good luck and Merry Christmas."

Candace kissed Walter's cheek. "Merry Christmas." She smiled and took off after her man.

She just hadn't planned on him already being checked out of the hotel.

Chapter 11

A giddy Georgine raced through the Christmas-decorated office of Nu4us in her favorite Prada heels and her staple tight pencil skirt. "He's back. He's back," she announced to the ladies in their cubicles.

In sync the women whipped out their compact mirrors, added swaths of lipstick, checked to make sure that their various hair-dos were picture perfect. Some even added a spritz of perfume, if need be. A split second later, a *ding* from the elevator bay had them all scrambling to put their mirrors and cosmetics away and then cast their eyes toward the opening elevator doors in time to see their early morning attraction.

Montel Starks lifted his head and strolled into the office dressed in a sharp royal blue suit that fit his frame to an absolutely perfect tee. The man's effortless sophistication still made head swirls, hearts flutter and moisten the panties of most of the supermajority female staff. But there was something different about him this time. Sure, he was still the definition of fine, but there was a melancholy air about him as walked down the aisle.

When it was clear that he wasn't about to offer his regular greeting, the women looked to each other and then chorused first, "Morning, Montel."

"Morning," he mumbled and kept moving toward his office.

"I wonder what's wrong with him?" Vicki asked, creeping out of her chair.

"I'd say that things didn't go so well with him and the missus in Paris."

"We don't know if they're still married," Mia said, appearing at her best friend's side. "I'm willing to bet that they're divorced or something. That's the only thing that makes sense."

"Uh-huh." Vicki rolled her eyes. "Is that a real bet?"

"I'll put five on that," Chanel said, from across the cubicle aisle.

"I got five," Sandy, a few cubicles over, piped up. Soon a group of about twenty were huddled around Vicki's desk as she took bets for the next office pool.

The elevator dinged again, and at first, the women didn't pay it any mind until Mia glanced up and started elbowing the women. "Morning, Ms. Lahane."

Candace glanced up as she rushed out of the small compartment. "Morning, Mia. Do you know whether Monty is in yet?"

"Monty? Um, er, you mean Mr. Starks? Yes, he just, um, walked toward his office."

"Great. Thanks." She rushed off toward Montel's office.

The group of women turned toward each other. *"Monty?"* Their gazes shifted among themselves for another half a second, and then they all took off running toward Starks's office so that they could see what was going on.

It was his last day, Montel had decided. No way could he keep working for Nu4us. It would be complete torture to see Candace day after day now that he'd made up his mind that it was time to let it go. He sat down at his desk, booted up the computer and started typing out his letter of resignation.

There a soft knock on his door, and he assumed that it was Georgine and didn't look up. "If it's not important right now, Georgine, could you come back a little later?"

"I'm afraid that it is important."

Montel's fingers stopped pecking away on the keyboard when he recognized the voice behind him. "What are you doing here?" he asked, still refusing to look up. "I thought you'd still be Paris."

"Well, I would've been if you hadn't pulled that little stunt."

Frowning, Montel finally looked up. "Stunt?"

"Running away…before I had the chance to push you away," she admitted, walking over to his desk. "It wasn't like our regularly scheduled program."

He sat there, staring at her.

Candace's small smile fluttered weakly. "You were supposed to laugh at that."

"Sorry."

"You're not going to make this easy, are you?"

He drew a deep breath while he thought it over. "No."

Candace's brows jumped in surprised, but then she seemed to realize that there was no reason for him to go easy on her, not after all she'd put him through in the last two years. "Fine." She drew a deep breath and pressed on. "During my flight back here, I really, really thought hard about what I was going to say to you. What words would really explain why I was so…scared of how I feel for you. And honestly and truly I don't think there are any."

Montel dropped his gaze. "Pity."

"I'm a realist. I have been all my life. *But* since I met you by accident or by destiny, I couldn't seem to fit this very square box into a round hole." She moved behind his desk, inching closer to him in his big leather chair. "Logically, we *don't* make sense. We don't. *But*…there's something. Some…"

"Spark?" he supplied.

Candace smiled and boldly sat down on his lap. "It's much bigger than a spark," she said and slid her arms around his neck. "I love you—and frankly I'm tired of fighting it."

Montel met her gaze, but made no move to return her affection. "I don't know, Candace."

Her heart skipped a beat. It was the first time he hadn't called her Candy. Maybe it was too late. Her gaze lowered, but then her smile slowly returned. "Do you want to know a little secret about how a woman can tell whether a man wants her?"

"This should be interesting," Montel said, folding his arms.

Candace lifted a finger and then tapped it against the side of his neck.

"This vein right here is connected to your heart muscles and whenever your heart starts racing, this little baby right here starts pulsing like crazy. And this sucker hasn't stopped jumping since I sat down."

"Is that right?"

"That's right. Buh-bump. Buh-bump."

He smiled and caressed her neck as well. "Buh-bump."

The women in the hallway startled Montel and Candace when they started clapping and chanting, *"Kiss! Kiss! Kiss!"*

Candace's face colored with embarrassment, but then she

turned back toward her smiling, not sure legal husband and felt she had to say one more thing. "I love you, *Monty*."

Montel's warm gaze swept over her. "I love you, too, Candy."

"Kiss! Kiss! Kiss," the women chanted.

"What do you say we get married—again?" he asked. "Make it stick this time."

"Kiss! Kiss! Kiss!"

Candace pulled at one of the small chains from her neck and lifted both of their wedding bands from Bora-Bora. "I'd love it."

"Kiss! Kiss! Kiss!"

There was a tap on the office window and Candace and Montel turned to see the window washer chanting, *"Kiss! Kiss! Kiss!"*

Candace leaned forward until their lips touched and then she fed from his mouth hungrily. Montel moaned and wrapped his arms around her.

A thunderous applause erupted from the hallway as the women then poured into the office.

Epilogue

Christmas Eve...

Montel and Candace's wedding was just as sweet the second time around. Candace was surprised that Montel was able to find someone to marry them in three days, but Montel boasted of calling in a few favors, and before she knew it, there they were at Mandarin Oriental standing before a preacher in front of family, friends and coworkers, exchanging vows and rings.

"I now pronounce you man and wife," their smiling preacher announced. "You may kiss the bride."

Monty leaned toward his wife in an amazing white Vera Wang gown that he had claimed he'd just happened to buy off the rack. It was just a coincidence that it fit her body perfectly. When they sealed their love with a kiss, the crowd erupted with cheers and applause.

At the reception, Candace was still answering questions about when and how she and Montel met and fell in love. Some of the women were clearly jealous and others were genuinely happy that she and Monty had found their way to love.

Mia, Vicki and Georgine were gathered around one of the reception tables, taking in the elegant décor of the room. "This place is absolutely beautiful," Vicki commented. "This man can pull off a miracle in three days."

"You're telling me," Mia said, sipping her champagne. She was actually looking forward to the newlywed's first dance. "Someone must've canceled at the last minute or something. No way can someone pull off something like this in Manhattan at the last minute."

Georgine smiled. "Well, I wouldn't exactly say it was all last minute."

Mia and Vicki's gaze shifted toward her. "What do you mean?"

Just then, Montel walked up to the table. "Is everyone enjoying themselves this evening?"

"Yes," Mia and Vicki said, grinning adoringly at the officially off-the-market handsome god.

Mia hastily added, "Wonderful wedding. We're so happy for both of you."

"Thank you." He turned toward Georgine. "I believe you have something for me?"

Georgine's smile widened. "I sure do." She reached for her purse and pulled out a thick envelope. "Here you go. Your pool winnings."

Mia's face dropped. "You mean that you...planned this wedding all along?"

"Never underestimate a man with a plan, ladies." Montel winked and then waltzed off with the sound of them laughing behind him.

Later that night, the renewed newlyweds wasted no time getting reacquainted with each other's bodies. Tears of joy leaked from the corners of Candy's eyes at the feel of Monty's mouth tasting every part of her. When that wasn't enough, he pressed his soft fingers through her wet, pink walls until her body's natural honey coated his fingers.

"Damn, baby....don't stop."

He had no intention of stopping. His warm tongue mopped up her honey, swishing against the base of her clit and causing her legs to tremble violently. She reached for his head and then grinded against his open mouth. When she came, fireworks exploded behind her closed eyelids and her body quaked deliciously.

Monty was willing to let her take a small break before they continued, but Candy pulled him upward until she had a firm hold of his thick cock and then slid it between her full cherry-red lips like she was sucking on the sweetest chocolate log ever made.

Monty's mouth sagged open at the pure pleasure that swept through him, plus the sound of her lips sucking and smacking was a heady aphrodisiac that made his toes curl. Candy turned her head and gave him a hard jawbreaker until a few drops of his salty cum started to ooze down her throat. He pulled back and kissed her lips. "Touch your pussy."

Candy obeyed, sliding her long fingers down in between her legs and spreading open her glistening brown lips and then twirled them inside.

"Are you nice and wet, baby?" he asked.

"Mmm-hmm," she moaned, reaching for his dick again.

"Yeah?" He reached down and got a good feel himself. "Ah. Yeah. That's what I'm talking about." He pulled his cock away before she could vacuum suck it back between her lips. A second later, Montel slid into his wife's warm, sticky honey pot while his eyes rolled to the back of his head. "Oh, baby. You have no idea how much I've missed us."

A wicked grin slanted Candy's face as she gave his cock a nice, hard squeeze with her inner muscles.

Monty hissed and threw his head back. "Awww. You're going to make me come too soon."

Squeeze. "I'm just showing you how much I missed you, too, baby," she panted. *Squeeze.*

Monty's eyes kept rolling to the point he doubted whether he could start stroking just yet. That didn't stop Candy's show. She rolled him over, happily taking the top position so she could bounce the ass he loved so much up and down his long shaft until he was the one writhing and thrashing beneath her.

Squeeze. "You know there's a new pool at the office, sweetie?"

"W-what?"

Squeeze. Squeeze. Squeeze.

His nut sack started to tingle.

Candy leaned forward and whispered in his ear. "I placed a bet that you'd give me a baby on our honeymoon."

Montel's heavy-lidded eyes opened wide. "W-what did you say?"

"I want us to make a baby."

A bright smile bloomed across his face. "Why didn't you say so?" He quickly tossed her onto her back, hooked her legs over his shoulders and finally got his deep stroking on until their bodies were dripping with sweat and Candy's body was filled to the brim with potential babies.

Monty collapsed next to Candy and pulled her close. "I love you."

"I love you, too."

Monty brushed a hand down the column of her neck and felt the steady beating of her heart.

Buh-bump. Buh-bump.

* * * * *

To my amazing daughter, who always motivates me to be the best that I can be.

CHOCOLATE TRUFFLES
Kimberly Kaye Terry

Chapter 1

Camille Jackson kept her composure until she stepped inside the elevator. Just barely.

She let out a loud "whoop!" and twirled around with her eyes shut tight as the elevator doors began to close.

"Hot damn!" She clapped her hands together and dropped it low…in her best video vixen imitation. "Who's the man? *I'm* the man!" Camille was on top of the world. Her career had taken an amazing turn in the past few hours.

She added an extra drop to her impromptu dance and laughed.

"I would agree. But you're much too pretty to be a man," a deep voice directly behind her replied.

Camille spun around as her hands covered her mouth in embarrassment. Her eyes widened as she gaped at the figure in the corner of the elevator.

Slowly her gaze followed the length of his dark gabardine slacks past a trim waist, over a broad chest and shoulders…

and up, to a face so fine it made her heartbeat speed up as heat flushed her face.

Dear god in heaven, she thought.

How in the world could she have missed seeing *him* casually leaning in the corner of the elevator, his chiseled arms crossed over his wide chest?

Camille smiled weakly and swallowed.

She tried to inconspicuously tug at the hem of her conservative navy blue suit while trying her best to ignore the heat steadily warming her skin.

He was tall, very tall, something that made her look at him even more closely.

He had a prominent, aquiline nose that seemed to dominate his angular face, which only added to his rugged masculinity. A deep cleft bisected his square chin, and a shallow dimple creased just one side of his face, which was punctuated with a well-defined mouth. Several sable-brown strands of hair lay over a thick brow, set above hazel-colored eyes that held a glint of amusement. He watched her watching him. She must have stared too long. But have mercy, the man was fine.

"I, uh, I...thought I was alone. I was...I was just celebrating," she stuttered. "I don't, uh, normally, you know...do that. Dance in elevators, that is." Camille clenched her mouth shut to stop herself from blurting out anything else and turned around, her face flaming. When she was nervous she had a bad habit of doing that—babbling.

She kept her eyes fixed straight ahead staring at the slow-moving numbers on the elevator panel, praying that they'd get to the lobby as quickly as possible.

"No problem. Actually, you just missed my own celebration." She heard the humor in his deep baritone. Did he have to have a voice that deep and sexy, *and* be that fine? The sound alone sent a shiver along her spine.

Camille glanced back over her shoulder hesitantly and caught the shy smile playing across his luscious lips.

"Oh?"

"Yeah. In fact I was just on my way down to the bar in the lobby to finish my celebration." He paused. "Don't suppose you'd like to join me?"

Before she could answer, the elevator stopped and three other occupants joined them.

As she made room for the new occupants, Camille eyed Mr. Tall, Dark and Fine from beneath lowered lashes, considering his offer.

She'd just received the promotion of a lifetime, which had included a fantastic raise. Although it meant moving from her native Seattle to the corporate office in Houston in a few months, she was *definitely* in the mood to celebrate.

Gideon hid his grin, not wanting to embarrass the gorgeous woman any more than he had. When she'd danced into the elevator, he'd been surprised and pleased to see her.

Thirty minutes earlier he'd returned to the offices of Silverman to sign one final document on the new contract to provide training for their upper management personnel. On his way to Matt Silverman's office, he'd passed a partially opened door. A sexy, husky laugh coming from within the office had stopped him dead in his tracks.

Slowly, he'd walked closer to the sound and the door.

The sexy laugh had accompanied a pair of long, bare, shapely brown legs casually propped up on a desk.

He had only been able to see her profile. Her shoulder-length, dark, curly hair and her cell phone cupped between her shoulder and ear had obscured much of her face. Cautiously, Gideon had stepped closer.

"Mom, I got it! I can't believe it, I got the promotion!" she'd said, twirling a strand of hair around her index finger as she spoke.

She'd paused, obviously listening to her mother on the other end before continuing. "I'll come by later tonight and tell you all about it!" She'd spoken a few moments longer, hung up the phone and happily spun around in her desk chair.

Unable to walk away, he'd continued to watch her, sliding closer behind the door so she wouldn't see him.

When she'd stopped spinning in the chair long enough for him to glimpse her entire face, his breath had caught in his throat.

She'd been breathtaking. Large eyes dominated her heart-shaped face; the corners slanted, slightly, and pouty pink-tinted lips had lifted in a wide smile. Her ear-to-ear grin, which emphasized the deep dimples in her cheeks, had completely captivated him.

And when she'd thrown her head back and laughed again, her face glowing in happiness, tilting her head to the side so that the long line of her neck showed…damn.

The phone clipped to his belt had buzzed, alerting Gideon to a call. The call had stopped him before he could have made a move toward her and made a complete and utter fool of himself, without a thought to what he would have said to the woman.

Uttering a mild curse he stepped away from the door. The call had been from Fred Silverman. After a moment of hesitation he'd turned and briskly headed toward the CFO's office. He'd hoped Fred wouldn't be long-winded and he could sign the contract quickly.

Although he hadn't known what in hell he'd say to the woman if she had been still there when he'd returned, Gideon had felt a keen sense of disappointment when her door was closed with no sign of her when he had made his way back to her door.

And now, here she was.

Today was *definitely* his day. Nice.

When the doors opened to the lobby, Camille eased past the woman next to her and quickly exited the elevator.

The ride down had seemed painfully slow and she could feel the man's eyes on her the *entire* time.

"So, will you join me?"

She swallowed the melon-ball-size butterflies fluttering in her stomach when she heard the voice behind her and turned to face him.

"Oh, uh, well…I thought I'd better go home. It's getting late and I kinda promised my mom I'd stop by, and, I, uh…" She stopped and wanted to kick herself in the butt for the rambling, something she did whenever she was nervous. "Thanks for the offer," she finally finished. "I'd better pass."

She forced an easy smile and ignored the way his intense stare was making her heart beat crazily in her chest.

"Are you sure I can't convince you? They have a bar right here in the lobby. Just one drink to celebrate?"

The seductive smile playing around his mouth coupled with her overall excitement made the decision for her. Why not? It was only one drink, after all. After that, she'd go her way and he'd go his. She gave a shrug of her shoulders.

Nothing wrong with accepting an offer for a drink with a good-looking man. And Lord only knew the last time she had gone out on a date, much less just shared a drink with a man.

With her nod of agreement, his smile grew. He grasped her elbow, leading her toward the lobby.

"So, what are *you* celebrating?" she asked as they made their way toward the bar. She glanced up at him as he adjusted his much longer stride to match hers.

They reached the entrance to the bar, and, although the

door was closed, Camille could hear the low rumble of music and voices from within. He opened the door, glancing down at her with a smile as he allowed her to enter before him.

Once inside, the music, that had been a low roar outside the heavy glass doors, bounced off the walls, the latest pop tune filling the crowded bar.

"Just got a great contract, one that I've been working to get for a while now!"

The faint scent of mint blew across her nose when he leaned down, speaking in her ear so she'd hear him over the music and voices.

"That's great!" she enthused, grinning up at him.

The bar was hopping. Happy hour was in full swing, packed with patrons forcing Camille into close contact with… She didn't even know his name.

She turned to ask when she was pushed from behind and forced into even closer contact with him. Their bodies brushed against each other, and he held her closer to avoid the loud, rambunctious patrons.

The hold he had on her arm was subtle, yet the way he positioned her closer to his body made Camille feel oddly protected as he guided her through the crowded throng. He walked them to the back of the bar where the noise was less grating, and they found a small empty table. Before Camille could pull out her chair, he was there, pulling it out for her.

"I don't even know your name," she said after a murmured thank-you, once they were both seated.

"Gideon, Gideon Taber."

He extended his hand, almost formally, and with a smile, she placed her hand in his. The instant their fingers touched a spark of electricity surged between them. The shock made her jump. Her eyes flew to his, and the lopsided grin tilting the corners of his mouth made her groaning heart speed up even more.

Yes. It had *definitely* been too long since she'd been out with a man.

"And yours?"

"It's Cami…pleasure to meet you, Gideon," she replied, giving only her nickname. Thankfully he didn't press her for her full name.

Camille turned away, scanning the crowded bar. "I'd heard this was the place to be during happy hour, especially on Friday, but I didn't know it was this popular!" Even though it was quieter in the area they were sitting, she had to speak much louder than normal in order for him to hear her.

"You've never been here before?"

"No, I usually work late. By the time my workday is done, happy hour is long over," she replied.

"Even on Fridays?"

"I work late most nights," she replied with a shrug. "Nothing special about Fridays."

"Doesn't leave a lot of room for play time."

"Play time?" Camille laughed lightly, smoothing her skirt down around her hips as she settled into the chair. "That is *so* not a problem. I don't know the last time I played or even had anyone to play with!" As soon as she made the remark, she groaned inwardly at the response.

A waitress came by to take their order, saving Camille from saying anything else revealing and avoiding further embarrassment.

"This beautiful lady and I are in the mood to celebrate… what would you suggest in the way of a nice vintage wine?" Gideon asked.

After giving Camille a cursory once-over, the waitress turned her attention to Gideon. All thirty-two of her pearly white, even teeth gleamed as she grinned at him and recommended a pinot grigio.

Gideon ordered their drinks, giving the woman a distracted smile before turning to Camille again.

"So, is that your normal way of celebrating?" he asked, a ghost of a smile flirting around the edges of his sensual mouth.

"I'm assuming you mean my dance in the elevator? No… that was a one-night-only performance," she said, laughing. "I just got promoted, that's all."

"That's all? From the way you looked in the elevator, I'd say it was a little more than a simple promotion," he said, grinning.

Camille groaned and laughed along with him. "Oh, God, *please* don't remind me!"

"Hey, like I told you, you had just missed my own celebratory dance!"

When she gave him a "yeah, right" look, he raised a brow. "Oh, you don't think I know how to dance?"

"I didn't say that, but since you asked…" She gave him an assessing once over, as though she was considering his talent.

"I'll have you know I can drop, lock and pop with the best of them…ask my niece. At her bat mitzvah I was the man. All the kids were standing and staring at me urging me on!" he proclaimed, proudly. A thoughtful look crossed his handsome features. "Hmm…then again, maybe they were laughing *at me,* instead of with me. Never thought of that."

Camille dissolved into giggles. When he put on a faux look of indignation, she raised her hands. "Well, you said it, not me!"

Her laugh died away when he continued to hold her gaze, the smile on his face fading. "Did I say something wrong?"

"No. It's just that you're really beautiful. And when you smile, well.…" He allowed the sentence to trail off, his gaze going to her mouth again before returning to meet her eyes.

Just like that it was as though there were only the two of them alone, the music and voices around them in the bar receding. Finally Camille broke the gaze and cleared her throat.

"Well, maybe you were showing them something new— something they'd never seen before." When he lifted a thick, sable brow, she laughed lightly, glad the intensity of the moment had eased. "Hey, I was just trying to be nice."

"You seem to doubt my prowess," he replied, humor in his deep voice. "Wanna give it a try?" he nodded toward the crowded dance floor.

Camille glanced over at the dance floor. Although the crowd seemed to be thinning, she wasn't up for jockeying on the small floor.

"I'll take your word for it," she finally answered, turning back to face him.

Again, the intensity in his eyes made her even more aware of him. God, the man looked good enough to eat.

And it seemed as though he felt the same way about her. It had been awhile for her, but he was looking at her as though she was a bowl of ice cream and he wanted to lick her until he scraped the bowl clean.

Her nipples constricted, pressing against her bra. Her mouth grew dry, and she felt a small bead of sweat trickle down the side of her face.

The longer he stared at her, that sexy little dimple flashing on the side of his mouth, the hotter she got.

Thankfully the waitress chose that moment to bring them their drinks. Camille brought the glass of wine to her lips and took a large swallow.

Although she hadn't gone out with anyone lately, having spent late hours and weekends hunched over quarterly reports—all of which had thrown a serious wet blanket on her love life—she'd had her fair share of attention from the opposite sex.

It had just been awhile, that's all.

And *that* was the reason for her over-the-top reactions to him. And nothing else.

At least that's how she mentally tried to convince herself.

But the intensity of his gaze was having one *hell* of an effect on her.

Camille gave a weak smile and again brought the glass to her mouth, taking a second fortifying drink.

"So, what are you celebrating?" she asked, once she placed the drink in front of her, diverting the conversation, and her mind, away from the two of them dancing on the floor together, bodies locked together.

Although he didn't say anything at first, she noted the way his eyes seemed to crinkle in the corner, as though he'd read her thoughts.

She recrossed her legs, clenching them tight together, and ignored her treacherous body's reaction to the sexy twinkle.

"I just got a major contract," Gideon said, after placing his own glass down.

He was having a hard enough time keeping his libido in check around her, and if she glided her tongue over her lips once more, he wasn't going to be accountable for his actions.

His focus shifted to the smooth, pretty curve of her neck where her hair brushed against her shoulders. Several pieces of hair lay near the decolletage of her breasts, at the V-neck of her silk blouse.

"What do you do?" she asked.

He resisted the urge to reach out and push the strands away, wondering if they would feel as soft as they looked.

Gideon moved his gaze away from the temptation, meeting her eyes.

"My company does training for upper management, mainly in human relations."

When she lifted her glass to her mouth, again his attention went to the full, sensual curve of her pouty lips as she sipped the drink.

"That's kind of a broad field, human relations. What type of training does your company do?"

"Yes, you're right, it's a broad term. And every day the field is becoming more wide open. In general, we train new management and other personnel issues related to their staff."

"Was it one of the companies in the Helmand Tower that you signed the contract with?" she asked. Gideon hesitated.

There were several companies in the building, and although the contract had been signed, it still had to be countersigned before it was official. He doubted there was any harm in sharing the information. "Yes. We provide on-site training as well as bring executives to our classroom facilities."

His answer seemed to be a good enough response, if her nodding head was any indication.

"So, you travel a bit then, I guess?"

"Yes, actually I just returned from Asia," he said, and filled her in on how he and two colleagues had trained a major Japan-based U.S. company on race relations and diversity in their workplace.

"I'd love to travel more. The one drawback is that the only traveling I do is limited to the U.S. and mostly local."

"Travel has its downside, but for the most part I enjoy it."

When the waitress returned to take their empty glasses, Gideon ordered them another round. Camille held up her hand, smiling.

"I think that's my limit. I didn't even realize how much

I'd drunk!" she laughed, and it was then that Gideon realized how quickly the time had gone by. Conversation with her just seemed to flow easily, and he hadn't noticed.

"How about just one more?" he cajoled her, not ready for their night to end. When she looked hesitant, he added, "We're celebrating, remember?"

"Okay, why not? It's been a while since I celebrated," she laughingly agreed.

"I've talked enough. Tell me more about you," he said, and she sighed.

"Hmm, let's see. Not sure there's much to tell. I work for a major retailer. I've been there since I graduated from college. Actually, I started when I was in college, in the mail room." She stopped and gave a shrug of her shoulders. "It's not very exciting to someone outside of retail, I suppose," she finished.

"I'm fascinated."

When she gave him a look, he laughed lightly, "Seriously, Cami, I'm finding that the least little thing you tell me about yourself is…interesting," he said, surprised at his candor.

But it was the truth.

Maybe it had been too long since he'd been in the company of a beautiful, intelligent woman. Lately, his dates had left him feeling wanting, as though something was missing. He dismissed the thought as soon as it entered his mind. He had no time, nor was he interested in anything more than a casual affair.

"Is it me, or has it gotten quieter in here?"

Her question brought him out of his mental fog, and he looked around. Since they'd been talking, he hadn't noticed, but the crowd had died down significantly.

"I was enjoying your company so much, I hadn't even noticed." In the dim light, her golden brown complexion seemed to glow.

When a classic R & B song drifted from the sound system in the bar, her fingers tapped lightly against the table.

"Would you like to dance with me now? No excuses… there's no one on the dance floor."

The request had another meaning besides the obvious. One that sent a wave of goose bumps to her flesh.

She didn't know if it was her promotion, the effects of the wine…or the man holding his arms out to her that made her feel so bold, but whatever it was, she gave in to it, relaxing into his embrace as he swayed with her in time to the music.

Their bodies melded together in perfect synchronicity, like magnets drawn to each other. Camille bit back a groan when he wrapped his arms tight around her waist and pulled her close. The smell of his aftershave mixed with his natural masculine scent wafted across her nose, tantalizing her senses.

He was tall—at least several inches over six feet—and as he held her, even with three-inch heels, Camille had to reach to place her arms around his neck, something she rarely had to do, given her own above-average height.

When her breasts brushed against his wide chest and her thighs met his thick hard ones, her nipples constricted. Again Camille felt an intense throbbing between her legs and subtly clenched her legs together before pushing away from him slightly.

Yet each time she pulled away, he pulled her back to him until their bodies were again in close alignment, and Camille could feel every long…*hard* inch of him against her. A deep breath of air escaped her partially opened mouth.

When she felt a tug on the back of her hair, nudging her to look up, she dragged her eyes to meet his.

The look of desire and lust in his eyes mirrored her own need provoking a startled gasp from her. The intensity of his gaze wrapped around her sex, making it pulse and contract, matching the rhythm of her pounding heart. The air around them seemed to grow thick, moist. When she tried to look away he hooked a finger under her chin, turning her back to face him.

"No," he murmured. "Look at me."

His gaze drifted to her lips and seconds later his head descended, his lips capturing hers.

With a helpless-sounding moan, she tugged his head down closer and gave in to his kiss, his guttural response meeting hers. His hand circled her waist and traveled down her body until he cupped her, molding one round, firm globe with his large hand, pressing her tight against him, his erection pressed against the front of her skirt.

Her breath was coming out in shuddering gasps when he finally released her.

The image of the two of them filled her mind. As though she were viewing a movie, she saw his big, hard body covering hers…could *feel* his hands on her body, his fingers digging into the flesh of her hips as he stroked inside her.

The images were so real, so unexpected, she gasped. Embarrassed at the pool of wetness saturating her panties, she turned away from him, but before she could move away he lifted her face to his.

Camille saw her own desire sharply reflected in his eyes.

His eyes swept over her face, down her throat and stopped at her heaving chest. When his eyes met hers again, his nostrils flared, lust and desire burning bright in his amber gaze.

He turned, keeping her body close to his, and walked toward the exit, saying, "Let's go."

Chapter 2

"It's nice. Your room, I mean." Camille entered farther inside Gideon's hotel room and looked everywhere but *at* Gideon. Her glance fell to the king-size bed in the center of the room and quickly moved away.

"Really spacious…" Camille's rambling was cut short when she felt his broad chest brush against her back and his arms wrap around her waist.

"There's nothing to be nervous about." The words were whispered hotly against the nape of her neck, and Camille shivered.

He eased her blazer off her shoulders and ran his hands down her bare arms that were exposed in the sleeveless silk blouse. Hypersensitive, she acutely felt the brush of fabric on her skin as he slid the blazer off, exposing her arms to the air-conditioned room.

A rash of goose bumps peppered her skin, both from the cool air and nervous anticipation churning inside her. When he placed soft kisses along her shoulder, her body bowed, and a cry tumbled from her lips.

Gideon turned her around to face him. Her eyes trailed up his body, past his broad chest, the strong line of his neck, and stopped for a fraction of a second at the hollow of his throat. His pulse beat strongly, under his V-necked shirt.

He ran a finger down the line of her cheek, past her chin and down the line of her throat and stopped at the valley between her breasts. Gently he cupped one of her breasts in his big hand, his thumb caressing her nipple through her blouse.

Her eyes feathered shut again when his head bent down toward her, capturing her lips. He dragged her full bottom lip into his mouth, suckled it languidly before slowly releasing it.

"I won't do anything to you that you don't want," he promised against her mouth and ran his slick tongue over lips.

The promise, although meant to ease, instead heightened her need.

"God, you taste so damn sweet," he murmured, running the rough pad of his thumb over her lips. "But we don't have to take this any further. We can stop now…just say the word."

"No…I want this," she whispered, looking up at him.

"Are you sure, Cami?" he asked, and she nodded her head, unable to speak because of the constriction in her throat.

With his eyes locked on hers, he began to slowly free the buttons on her blouse. Once the last button was undone, he tugged the blouse from her body. His eyes fell to her breasts, watching them rise and fall under the lacy demibra, before coming back to meet her gaze.

In what felt like slow motion, he dragged her closer, pressing her into his hot, hard body. The look in his eyes and the feel of his cock pressing intimately against her stoked the flames of her arousal even more.

Camille wasn't worried that he'd do something she didn't want. Her fear instead was she was game for *anything* he had in store for her.

She ran her tongue over the rim of her bottom lip and kept her eyes on his, her heartbeat slamming against her chest in heady anticipation for what he would do next.

Lifting her arms, she placed them around his neck, bringing his head down to hers, this time initiating the kiss.

With a rough-sounding moan, he lifted her high, his strong arms wrapping securely around her. Without breaking contact with her lips, he briskly strode across the room until he reached the large, four-poster bed in the center. He followed her body down to the bed, his mouth still locked with hers.

Lifting her skirt, he shoved his hands inside and nudged her thighs apart, centering himself between her legs.

Camille whimpered when he placed his hands under her bottom and pulled her tight against him, grinding her softly against the hard ridge under his zipper.

He finally lifted his head, breathing heavily, his hazel eyes wild with carnal lust and need.

"Stay right there," he demanded huskily, and Camille bobbed her head up and down, her heart beating erratically against her chest.

With rough impatience he removed his shirt before his hands quickly went to the top of his slacks and he shoved them, along with his briefs, down the length of his legs, in one quick movement that freed his erection.

Long…impossibly thick—her eyes widened in fascination as it grew longer, lying heavy against the tight, muscled ridge of his abdomen.

Although it had been longer than she wanted to remember, Camille didn't know the last time—if ever—she'd seen a cock as beautiful as Gideon's.

Perfectly sculpted, it lay against his stomach, the same

smooth color as the rest of his body; no lines of demarcation marred its flawless masculine beauty.

Without thinking she rose, reached a hand out and grasped him lightly in her palm. She ran shaky fingers over his length, from the base that jutted out thickly from the swirl of curls surrounding his groin, to the mushroom-capped head. She ran her fingers lightly over the tip, brushing away the dew of pre-cum that beaded in the tiny opening.

When he groaned, her eyes flew to his.

A smile of female appreciation curved her lips upward at the look in his eyes.

"If you keep touching me like that…this won't last long," he promised, his voice low and rough.

"I'm sorry, I just…" Her sentence trailed off, words escaping her. With a tight laugh, he pressed her down and blanketed her body, covering her mouth with his in one move.

"We have plenty of time for that," he said, sliding between her legs. "Later," he promised.

"Later," Camille whispered in agreement before their mouths touched.

He silently urged her to lift her lower body, before removing her skirt. Hooking his thumbs under the lacy band at the top of her panties he tore them, along with her skirt, away, allowing her clothes to float to the floor beside them.

Her skin grew moist, sensitive, on fire, lust and need surrounding her in scalding waves. The feel of his naked, hot skin, his thick cock positioned against her mound, was nearly unbearable. It felt so good against her heated flesh.

The smell of her arousal, sweet and pungent, wafted to Gideon's nose, fueling his desire and stroking the flames of his desire higher.

He broke contact with her mouth and nosed the crook of her

neck, inhaling her scent deeply into his lungs, before licking the soft skin just beneath the lobe of her ear.

"And if you keep grinding on me like that...no doubt about it, this *won't* last long," he murmured against her neck.

She hooked one long, supple leg around his waist, pressing his cock into the direct path of the place he wanted to be in so damn badly. His cock throbbed, aching to fill her.

"So what are you waiting for?" She issued the invitation in a low voice.

That was all Gideon needed to hear. The time for slow, careful lovemaking was over. He had to get inside of her.

He deftly unclasped the snap on her bra, freeing her breasts, allowing them to tumble out. There was a slight tremor in his fingers when he cupped one, running the pad of his thumb over her chocolate-colored nipple. In lustful fascination he watched it spike hard against his finger.

He licked a rough caress over the extended nub and opened his mouth wide and took as much of her breast inside his mouth as he could, hollowing out his tongue and tugging on her long, hard nipple. Her head tossed back and forth on the pillow in feminine distress, her body arching up from the bed, her arms tightening around his neck, silently urging him.

With broad strokes of his tongue, he licked...ate, suckled her breast. Made love to her breast. Her taste was driving him wild.

"Just like chocolate, sweet, creamy chocolate," he murmured and felt her body react, the cream of her arousal trickling down her inner thigh, moistening his leg.

When they faced each other, she ran a hand between their bodies until she wrapped her slim fingers around his cock.

"Oh," she breathed. "You're so thick...I...I don't think I can take it all."

She groaned when her hand was unable to fully circle him.

Gideon pushed himself fully into her soft hands, her words heightening his desire.

"You can...I'll go easy. We'll take this slow. I want this to be good for you."

His body was humming in pleasure, his very skin on fire as she stroked her fingers over his shaft while he tugged and sucked on her plump, perfect breasts.

"Oh, God, I need this. I need you," she whispered when he bit down on her nipple. Her breathy words made his erection go rock hard. His love bite wasn't hard enough to hurt, but enough that he knew she felt the stinging caress deep inside her body.

Camille felt him reach across her body and seconds later heard the rip of foil and waited to feel him finally inside of her body.

To her surprise, he didn't cover her again. Instead he moved toward the end of the bed, pushed her legs up and settled between her thighs.

Her heart was beating so wildly she thought it would explode from her chest when she felt his face brush back and forth across the tiny thatch of hair covering her vagina.

"Is there anyplace on you that *doesn't* smell good?"

Before she could answer, he stroked his tongue against her wet folds. She held her breath and released it in a long whoosh of air when she felt the slick stab of his tongue slice into the very core of her.

"Oh god, oh god...wha-what are you doing?" She cried out when a thick finger separated her and pressed inside while his slick tongue continued to dart over and around her clit, suckling it deep within his mouth.

Camille's head fell back against the pillow. Her body no longer hers, she gave in to the mind-blowing pleasure he was giving her. She pulled at the sheets, grabbing them in both hands tightly as he ministered to her body.

When he stabbed his tongue in and out of her in easy glides, she ground against him, the pleasure so intense it bordered on pain, stars steaming behind her closed lids. When she thought the pleasure too overwhelming, he moved away, bringing his body up until he covered hers again.

"Are you ready for me, Cami?"

Camille swallowed hard, her throat gone dry, the strum of pleasure making her weak.

"Yes…" The word was torn from her just as he began to slide inside her body.

"Oh, God, oh, God…wait, Gideon—" she panted, and Gideon's hands tightened on her hips for a fraction before he forced them to relax, fighting his need to rush into her sweet, clinging sheath.

Her soft hands came up to rest on his shoulders, holding on to him tightly, and he stared down into her face. The almost fearful look on her face made him relax and not give in to the need to spread her legs and drive deeper.

"We'll take it slow, Cami, I promise."

Slowly, he fed her more of his shaft in careful inches, gritting his teeth as her walls clamped down on him, tight. With every inch he gave of himself, her soft mewling sounds of feminine distress were having a hell of an effect on him.

He wanted to go slow, make it special for her. He'd picked up on the cues she'd given throughout the night, knew she wasn't the kind of woman who went home with every guy she met. But, damn, he didn't know how much longer he could hold out before driving deep into her.

Her tightness and the way her walls clamped down on him as he tried to delve deep told him it had been a while since she'd made love.

So he simply held on to her hips, feeding her his shaft slowly until he was all the way in.

He leaned down and captured her lips, stroking his tongue across her teeth, until she opened for him. After stroking his tongue inside hers, and exchanging languid, drugging kisses, Gideon couldn't hold off any longer.

"I need to move soon, baby. I don't know how much longer…"

"It's okay…I'm ready."

He released his hold on her hips and in one deft movement, flipped them so that she straddled him.

"Why don't you control the ride?" he said, and she gave him a half smile, shyly nodding her head.

"It's, uh, been a while since I've done this…." She didn't finish her sentence before she began to ride him.

"Damn." He bit out the expletive as she began to move.

As she rode him, her eyes were tightly shut, her hands held within his, her big pretty breasts dangling close to his face, jostling with every bounce and stroke.

He closed his eyes against the sight, afraid he'd come too fast if he continued to look at her.

He grasped her by the waist and lifted her slightly, angling her so his shaft hit her clit and brought her back down, grinding her against him, both of them groaning so loudly, Gideon was sure they could be heard in the room next door.

When she rotated her hips against him, he lost the threadbare control he'd had. With a growl, Gideon pulled out, ignoring her cry of protests and flipped her until she was face down on the bed.

He grinned despite the painful throb of his cock, despite the sweat pouring down his face, as he stared at the picture she presented—soft, pretty brown bottom high in the air and the lips of her pussy pouting, begging to be filled. With one long stroke he obliged and went so deep, he felt the tip of his cock press the back of her womb.

Holding on to her hips with one hand, the other reached around and sought out her clit, fondling it as he continued his plunging strokes.

She moaned out her pleasure, her head hung low as his thrusts grew wilder, harder. He felt her orgasm, felt the violent trembling begin to rock her body before she screamed out her release, rolling her hips against him, and, grinding on his shaft, she took her pleasure. The sight of her giving in to her orgasm sent Gideon over the edge.

He raised her hips higher, threw back his head, the muscles in his neck straining. His thrusts became short, controlled, and with one final push into clenching heat, his release exploded from his body.

Chapter 3

As her head lay pillowed on his chest and his heartbeat had returned to a *semblance* of normalcy, Gideon stared down at Cami.

Damn. Hell. *Shit*.

He drew in a deep breath.

What he'd just experienced was like something out of his wildest erotic dreams. The type of dreams he'd had as a kid that had him waking up with a hard-on and his sheets wet, sticky with his own cum. The kind that he'd outgrown a long damn time ago.

And like a kid after he'd gotten his first taste of a woman, his head was spinning, limbs shaking from the mind-blowing release… He felt his dick stir when she shifted her body along his. His body, *still* aroused, obviously wasn't satiated; he needed to feel her again, needed to be deep in her body. He shifted their bodies, and she turned to face him.

Her eyes, drowsy, with lids low and sexy, held a question in their deep brown depths.

He placed a hand at the nape of her neck and drew her nearer, captured her lips and flipped their bodies so that she lay sprawled on top of him.

Without any words exchanged, Gideon sampled her lips with small biting nips and made love to her mouth until he ran out of breath. His breathing was labored when he was forced to break the kiss, staring at her in the dark room.

She opened her mouth to speak but closed it. There was a question in her eyes that he didn't know the answer to, or maybe it was that he didn't want to think too hard about it, didn't want to examine what he was feeling.

He reached over her toward the nightstand and grabbed another condom before sheathing himself. Their eyes never lost contact with the other in the dark room; no words spoken from either of them. None were needed. Not now. Later in the morning, they could talk about what happened and decide where to go from there.

Later.

He lifted her so that she straddled him, grasped her hands in his and stroked back inside her wet, warm, welcoming heat.

When Gideon awoke, he reached over, blindly searching for Cami, only to find the place where she'd slept empty.

He sat up in bed, and looked toward the alarm clock on the bedside table. It was ten minutes after five in the morning. He listened for the shower, and when there was no sound from the bathroom, he called out her name.

He ran a hand through his disheveled hair and cursed the silence.

Shit.

She'd gone before he'd even had the chance to find out

her full name, and he had a plane to catch in less than three hours.

He looked down at his cock.

The damn thing was hard as a rock, with no outlet save his hand to relieve it. But he didn't want to do the job himself. He wanted to bury himself in Cami until neither one of them knew where their bodies began or ended.

With a curse in anger, at her for leaving without saying goodbye and himself for having sex—incredible, don't-ever-wake-me-if-I'm-dreaming kind of sex—without at least finding out her last name, he angrily strode toward the bathroom to take the longest, coldest shower of his life.

Chapter 4

The sound of her high heels hitting the tile floor as Camille hurried toward the classroom was the only echo in the deserted hallway.

She couldn't believe she'd actually overslept of all things, and here she was late for the first day of her management-training class.

But that fact shouldn't have surprised her considering her fractured sleep the past week, interrupted by nightly dreams so vividly erotic she'd woken up with her hands buried in her panties, and a moan on her lips.

Preparing for her sudden trip, making sure she had cleared her schedule, and the stress related to her upcoming move to a new city hadn't helped either, all of which finally had taken its toll on her.

As soon as she'd gotten settled in her hotel, she'd glanced down at her watch, noting the time after she realized the clock radio near the bed had been unplugged. She'd had enough time to lie down and try to get some rest before her class started.

Three hours later she had wakened with a start, realizing she'd overslept. Unlike the past week, her sleep had been uninterrupted, no vivid, erotic dreams invaded it. But her mind and libido had chosen a hell of a time to finally calm down, she thought, hurriedly striding down the hall.

She glanced at the number on the slip of paper before eyeing several doors and spotting the one that corresponded with the one on the note.

"God, *please* don't let this be the front of the room, please oh, please…" she mumbled as she opened the door.

She sighed in relief when the door opened into the back of the room. Biting down on the corner of her mouth, she hunched her shoulders and crept inside as though that would somehow diminish the sound and her appearance.

Camille blew out a relieved sigh when she noticed the room was dark, the small light from the overhead projector the only illumination as she walked inside as inconspicuously as possible. At that moment a raucous roar of laughter erupted from the occupants and again Camille sent up another silent thank you—someone upstairs had her back—comfortable that the dark, coupled with the roar of laughter, was sure to disguise her entrance.

Quickly she found an available seat at the back of the auditorium and eased into the swivel-backed chair. Placing her bag beside her, she glanced around the room, surprised at the number of students in the class.

She'd only had a week to prepare herself to travel after being informed that the class was mandatory, before Silverman would promote her to her new position. She'd rearranged her schedule, worked long hours to make sure her work was done and she wouldn't be behind when she returned, all to accommodate taking the two-week class. So, in less than a week she'd packed, arranged for her mother to take care of her mail and plants, and had only had time to give a cursory glance through the course packet she'd been given.

She crooked her neck and squinted her eyes in an attempt to see the instructor, as he bent over the overhead projector.

"Okay, and on that note, how about we end early tonight! We'll pick it up tomorrow…break into some small groups, maybe do a little role-playing."

Her eyes widened and she glanced again at her watch. Yes, she was late, but she wasn't that late! It was only six-thirty and the class was scheduled to end at eight. Realization hit and with it, she groaned. With every thing going on in her mind, she'd completely forgotten to set her watch.

Could this night get any worse, she thought with a groan.

Camille gathered her briefcase, slung the strap over her shoulder and stood as the other students started filing out of the room.

There were several female students as well as a few males gathered around the instructor's desk, so Camille took her time walking down the isle, her intent to go and apologize for her tardiness.

As she walked toward the front, she finally got a good view of the instructor as he smiled down at the student in front of him. Camille stumbled, her eyes widening, a startled gasp forming a perfect *O* of surprise around her mouth.

Although there was no way he could have heard her—the noise from the departing students had to have hidden the sound—he turned and stared directly at her.

The look of surprise that flickered across his face gradually changed, his eyes narrowing as he stared at her. Camille's heart jackhammered in her chest, her steps slowing. Like a deer caught in headlights, she was unable to move, no matter how hard she willed her feet to run in the opposite direction away from him.

His eyes raked over her face and down the length of her body, and Camille felt the familiar sensation race through her body, as though it was his hands, his fingers, running over her instead.

When he finally broke the connection and returned his attention to the student in front of him, Camille felt so dizzy she nearly fell down in the seat near her.

Not thinking, and unsure what to do, she did the first thing she could think of and spun around, her intent to get away from him and the unexpectedness of the situation.

"Miss…" Before she could make her dash, his deep baritone called out to her, stopping her in her tracks. Camille closed her eyes, exhaling a deep breath. "Please stay. I'll be with you shortly." Camille felt her stomach drop to her feet.

Taking a fortifying breath, she counted to five and mentally squared her shoulders.

Where did she think she was going anyway, she wondered glumly, as she slowly turned back around and faced her instructor—Gideon Taber.

Gideon felt like he'd been hit by a semi.

It was her, Cami. The woman he hadn't been able to get out of his mind, no matter how hard he tried, over the past week. The woman who'd managed to—after spending one night with her…just one damn night—reduce him to a horny teenager.

Nightly, he'd awakened in the morning fisting his cock, dreaming it was her gloving him so tightly, pissed off when he'd realized it wasn't, his anger growing when he remembered waking up in the hotel, only to find her gone. She'd left before he'd had a chance to find out if what had happened to them the night before had meant as much to her as it had to him.

The entire flight back from Seattle, Gideon had been unable to get her out of his head. His first thought had been that once he got back home he'd find out who she was, how to reach her....

The only thing he knew was that she worked for Silverman, the same company he'd received his training contract with, but how in the hell was he supposed to ask who she was when he didn't even know her full name?

Frustrated, he'd been in an aggravating state of fluctuating anger and arousal.

No matter how many times he'd told himself she was a one-night fling, that she was no different than any of the ones he'd had before, it hadn't mattered. No one else had ever reduced him to the current state he was in.

Frustrated, his mood fluctuated between anger that she'd left without telling him her name and arousal, remembering how good she'd felt wrapped around him, how beautiful, how sensual she'd looked when he'd pushed inside her...

"Dr. Taber. Would you be able to...help me?"

Gideon dragged his gaze away from Cami. He absently glanced at the student in front of him, forcing a smile on his face while trying to remember what they'd been discussing before Cami had walked into his classroom and back into his life.

"Uh, yes, that would be fine, Amanda," he said, hoping he hadn't just agreed to something he would regret later. "And please, it's Gideon."

She smiled widely, giving a short toss of her long blond hair over her shoulder. "Okay, Gideon—so, um, what would be a good time? After class I'm free. I'm staying at the Hilton. We can meet anytime—"

The student's words brought Gideon completely back to the present. He'd been so caught up with Cami, he'd obviously missed a vital piece of the conversation. From the look on Amanda's face she was asking for help that had nothing to do with human relations, that went beyond what he provided in the class curriculum.

"I'm sorry, Amanda, I'm afraid I have other plans. But, I heard a few of the others are planning to get together tonight and start a study group. I'm sure they wouldn't mind if you joined them." He decided it was best to pretend he didn't know what kind of help she was seeking.

Even as he spoke to the student, Gideon kept Cami firmly in his peripheral vision, not trusting her to not pull another David Copperfield and disappear on him.

"Well, I, uh, guess. Although I thought a little one-on-one would be more beneficial," she said, her smile faltering. Boldly this time, she touched his arm in a casual but obvious move to let him know exactly what kind of help she was looking for, just in case he hadn't caught her meaning the first time.

"Know what I mean?" she asked. Gideon gently, but firmly, removed her hand.

"I think it would better if you met with the group, Amanda. Like I said, I have other plans." Although he kept his attention on her, the student turned, glancing over her shoulder at Camille, before turning back to Gideon.

The smile on her face was noticeably cooler.

"I see. Well, I guess I'll see you tomorrow night then, Dr. Taber," she replied stiffly. Gideon didn't bother to repeat the invitation to call him by his first name.

No sooner had the door closed behind her than he was striding toward Cami, not in the mood to wait for her to come to him.

The easygoing, funny, sexy man Camille had met less than a week ago in no way resembled the one quickly approaching her.

The one striding toward her, his long steps eating up the

distance, looked pissed off—sexy as *hell,* but still, really, *really* pissed off.

A shiver ran through her body.

She sucked in a calm, steadying breath. Okay, okay…she could handle this. She could handle *him*.

Besides, it had only been one night. Yes, it had been the best sex she'd had in a month of Sundays, but it hadn't been meant to be more than that. It had been a release, one night of pleasure between two strangers who'd never see each other again. Something to temporarily fill the void and growing loneliness she'd been feeling for longer than she wanted to admit.

But she didn't regret what she'd done and neither was she going to cower away. Nope. She was a grown, independent woman.

And the fact that fate had decided to throw them together again? Well, they were both mature adults. They could handle the situation. All they had to do was—

Right in the middle of her mental ramblings, Gideon grabbed her. Wrapping one, big arm around her waist, he unceremoniously pulled her tight against his body until her feet dangled from the floor.

With a whimper, Camille allowed the strap of her bag to slip from her shoulders and leaned into his embrace.

One hand cupped the globe of one of her round butt cheeks before impatiently tugging her shirt from the waistband of her skirt.

As his fingers sunk into the soft, fleshy skin of her waist, he wrapped the other around her head, his fingers stroking down the length until he reached the ends of her hair and wrapped them around his hand, fisting them.

He tugged on the strands, forcing her to meet his gaze. The anger in his eyes made her heart stutter against her chest, the desire made her nipples tighten into achy little nubs.

She stroked her tongue over her lips, her eyes riveted to his, her mouth grown dry. He leaned down and without saying a word, stroked his tongue over the seam of her lips.

"Open for me." He breathed the words against her mouth.

With a will of their own her arms ran up his chest, her fingers caressing the corded muscles before wrapping around his neck.

Completely unexpectedly and so fast her head spun, the kiss changed, morphed into something so intense her body instantly went up in flames.

He didn't just kiss her. He consumed her.

Licking the seam of her lips with the edge of his tongue, he pushed past her token resistance, stroked deep inside her mouth, and devoured her.

And heaven help her, she wanted him to.

She pressed into him, her breasts brushing against his hard chest, her nipples now rock hard, her body clenched, folding in on itself as he delivered hot, hungry, open-mouthed decadent kisses.

Camille whimpered against the sensual assault deep in the back of her throat, a wordless plea for him to touch her.

When she arched her back, pressing herself closer to his hot, hard strength, he released her hair and cupped her breasts in both hands, molding them in his big hands before shoving his hands beneath her blouse.

Camille moaned, her body on fire, pressing closer, desperate for his touch.

He released her mouth, his lips trailing around to nip the lobe of her ear, before licking down the length of her neck. His tongue dipped into the hollow of her throat, his other hand went to the base of her throat, to lightly circle it.

It wasn't enough. Her head rolled to the side, to give him better access…she needed more, more of what he'd given her a week ago; images of their bodies wrapped around each other slammed into her mind, making her dizzy with desire and need.

When he mouthed her breasts, tugging her nipple through the silk of her blouse, she nearly came.

With a harsh grunt he broke contact, pushing her away from him, his breathing labored.

"What's your full name?" he demanded. His voice was a rough, scratchy rumble, his gaze sliding over her face.

Camille could barely think straight after his sensual assault, much less remember her own name. Her body was on fire and aching, the essence of her own arousal pooling in the seat of her panties while her mind screamed at her that this was crazy—the two warring for dominance in her sanity.

"Um, my name—Camille. My name is Camille Jackson," she finally replied, in a breathy murmur.

He nipped at the corner of her mouth, the sensation startling as much as it was instantly arousing. Camille involuntarily squeezed her legs together and dragged her eyes up to meet his hot, steady, regard.

"Don't be late for class tomorrow, Camille."

And just like that, with the same suddenness of his kiss, he turned, his back stiff, and left the room. Dazed from their kiss, and confused about what had just happened, her body slumped back against the desk.

On the heels of that thought came another—what would he do to her if she were late again…

An unexpected curl of carnal anticipation swept through her at the thought.

Chapter 5

When Camille awakened the next morning, she set up her laptop and worked on a report, determined she wouldn't think of Gideon and just as determined not to spend the day wondering what would happen later that night when she saw him in class.

Finally giving up on both, she spent the rest of the day checking out the real estate section of the newspaper. Thinking of her upcoming move to Houston and the hundreds of things she still had to do to get ready for the big move managed to keep thoughts of Gideon at bay. Mostly.

Dragging her mind back to the here and now, Camille glanced at the clock she'd made sure was plugged in last night.

Now she had less than an hour to get her act together and make it to class on time, and she had no intention of even being a minute late. She suppressed her body's reaction as she remembered the look in Gideon's eyes.

She wasn't about to test him to see if he'd make good on the threat in his eyes if she were late again. Camille ignored the irritating little voice in the back of her mind mocking her for the bald-faced lie. She went into the bathroom for a quick shower to clear her mind, but her thoughts drifted back to Gideon.

After the devastation on her senses the evening before, Camille had stayed rooted to the spot long after Gideon had left, her mind and body a chaotic mass of whirling nerves, before she'd finally gotten the strength to leave the classroom and make it back to her hotel room.

Even as he'd kissed her, she'd *felt* his anger. It had radiated off his broad frame in scalding waves while he'd held and kissed her, making love to her mouth and breasts.

Deep inside she'd known the reason for his anger.

Everything they'd done was etched in her mind. In vivid, erotic detail, she'd remembered every touch, every caress. The way he'd paid attention to her body each time they'd made love throughout their night together…the way he'd brought her to climax so many times she'd lost count.

After she'd woken early the next morning after that night, she'd eased out of bed, careful not to waken him. She hadn't known what to say to him. She'd felt raw, exposed. And afraid.

Afraid of the feelings he'd ignited after only one night. How special he'd make her feel. Afraid to see his withdrawal, or worse, pity in his eyes when he told her it had only been a one-time thing for him, nothing more, nothing less.

Camille sighed, turned off the shower and looked at her reflection in the bathroom mirror, wrinkling her nose. She ran her tongue over her lips, turning her face one way and then the other, critically examining her image.

She knew she was reasonably attractive. Her face was clear

and blemish-free, and she'd always considered her eyes her best features: large and slightly tilted in the corner, they were dark, nearly black, and her lashes were so dark and thick she rarely needed mascara to enhance them.

She glanced at her breasts in the mirror. Fresh from the shower, her skin was slick from the oils she'd rubbed into her skin.

Thoughts of Gideon filtered into her mind, the way he'd kissed her, held her…the way he'd taken her from zero to one hundred miles per hour in two-point-two seconds.

Carefully she ran one hand over a breast, her fingers flickering over her nipple until it spiked. Biting her lip, she palmed her breast firmly, just as he'd done when they'd made love, allowing her finger to continue to glide over the tightening nub, imagining it was his hand cupping her, his finger pinching and releasing her nipple.

Her other hand trailed down her body, stopping at the juncture of her thighs, and hesitated.

She cupped her mound, now warm, felt the sticky moisture dampen her hands, and allowed her eyes to close as she slipped a finger inside. It wasn't her hands fingering her plump clit and toying with her breast, it was his….

Her eyes flew open and she pulled her hands away from her body, feeling oddly ashamed at what she was about to do.

Not because she had any problem with self-pleasure, but because it was Gideon's face and hands she had been picturing as she touched herself. Wanting it to be his hands instead of hers.

Angrily she snatched out the pins she'd just placed in her hair and allowed it to tumble back to her shoulders.

Rolling her eyes at her reflection, she went to the closet where she removed her dress from the hanger and slid it over her head and down her body. With a final look in the mirror, she left the room.

* * *

"This will be the first time in a long time that the entire family will be together. Which is why I want to make sure you're going to be here, Gideon. It won't be the same without you." There was a short pause, and Gideon barely checked his irritation.

"You will be here, won't you, Gideon?" The warning implied in her voice told him what he'd have to face if he wasn't.

Gideon's thoughts had been preoccupied with Camille Jackson while talking to his mother. His patience had been wearing thin in direct relationship to his desire to get back to the hotel he knew Camille was staying at and force her to see him.

But he was stuck. Thinking he'd brush his mother off, he'd tried to hang up the phone and opened the door to his office to her smiling face instead.

She'd caught him. With a sigh of resignation, he motioned her inside his office and sat down, knowing the conversation wouldn't end any time soon.

After he'd missed the dinner his mother had hosted for the Jewish high holidays—Rosh Hashanah and Yom Kippur—Rebekkah Taber had been in a bad mood.

After his grandmother had passed away, his mother was the self-proclaimed matriarch of the Taber clan, and she took her duties seriously.

When Gideon hadn't shown up for the dinner she'd given for their large extended family, she'd first sent his sisters out to guilt-trip him into coming home. When that hadn't worked, she'd then sent his father. When no one had managed to coerce Gideon into celebrating the holidays at home with the family, she'd been forced to bring her prodigal son in herself.

It wasn't that he didn't want to spend time with his family, but because the new contract with Silverman had been so important, Gideon had decided to teach the workshop himself. But lucrative contracts didn't mean anything to his mother. She just wanted him home for the holidays.

Although Gideon didn't attend temple on a regular basis, he always tried his best to get home for the holy days. He knew his mother well. She wouldn't stop.

With a defeated sigh he'd given in, promising her he'd attend and, with a kiss on her forehead, ushered her out to her car.

By the time she'd left, it had been too late for him to go by the hotel, and he'd gone home instead.

After throwing his keys and wallet on the bar in the kitchen, he went to the fridge, grabbed a bottle of Dos Equis and flopped down on the sofa. Lifting the remote control from the chair, he absentmindedly flipped through the channels, his mind on Camille as it had been for the entire day. Hell, since the moment he'd met her she'd seemed to take up permanent residence there.

One of his instructors had been unable to teach the workshop, and he'd been the only one who knew the material well enough to pitch hit for him. The class was taught in a facility on the north side of town and by the time he'd made it back to the office, it was close to midnight.

Instead of seeking her out, he'd headed home to his loft, an old firehouse he'd bought two years ago and had painstakingly renovated, using every spare moment he had. With pride, he'd done most of the work himself and lately found more satisfaction in his DIY labor than he did on the social scene.

But not tonight.

Tonight, as he had every night for more than a week now, his mind inevitably went to Camille Jackson.

Restlessly he stood, beer in hand, and wandered over to his briefcase that he'd tossed on the counter. Maybe doing some work would get his mind off the beautiful, curvy little manager, he thought irritably.

After twenty minutes of staring at the lesson plan for the next day, he gave up and tossed the papers aside. He rummaged through his briefcase until he found her bio. The corner was dog-eared from the number of times he'd read and reread it after realizing who she was.

Taking his beer, he walked back to the sofa and sat, perusing the bio.

Not that he didn't already know it by heart.

She was twenty-eight years old, had graduated from college in three years and had immediately enrolled in graduate school. In college and graduate school, she'd interned at Silverman's department store, and in graduate school had begun their management program. Before completing her master's degree, she'd already been promoted to floor manager.

He scanned the rest, rereading how she'd quickly risen in management and now was one of the youngest junior executives in the company with her latest promotion.

Taking a swig of beer, his brow furrowed, he read between the lines. Unlike most of the other students' biographies, Camille's didn't list any interests outside of work, and neither did her bio have a picture attached.

All work and no play.

She was dedicated, spent long hours at work and, if his hunch was right, didn't have a man in her life. Until now.

Gideon glanced at the time. Resigning himself to the inevitable, determined to settle what was between them once and for all, he grabbed his keys, heading toward the Hilton.

Chapter 6

Camille had not only been on time, she had arrived ten minutes early. Her smug satisfaction was cut short when a female entered the classroom and informed the class she was substituting for Dr. Taber.

When one of the others asked if he'd be returning, the relief she felt was as immediate as it was unwelcome, when the woman assured them he would, that a personal obligation prevented him from teaching tonight.

Camille wondered what the personal obligation was, but relegated it, as well as thoughts of Gideon, to the back of her mind, forcing herself to pay attention.

After class she began to gather her things, preparing to go, and overheard some of the students making plans to go to the bar in the hotel where most of the out-of-town students, including herself, were staying.

Preparing to leave, she paused when she felt a hesitant tap on the back of her shoulder.

"Hi…you're Camille, right?"

Camille turned as a voice spoke directly behind her, startling her as her thoughts had been preoccupied with Gideon.

She'd noticed him—Carl—last night after class. She'd caught him several times eyeing her throughout the night and again tonight. Each time she'd looked up he was staring a hole right through her.

When she'd caught him staring, she'd smiled slightly, and he would duck his head shyly. She gave him the once over.

Like Gideon, he was tall, but where Gideon was athletically built, his physique similar to a runner's, Carl was solid, with the body any defensive linebacker in the NFL would envy.

"Yes, it's Camille. And you're Carl?"

"Yes, Carl. You know my name," he said, grinning ear-to-ear, his glance casually raking over Camille. Unusually high, his voice had a nasal quality that was completely at odds with his large frame.

He extended a hand, and when she placed it in his, he held it a fraction longer than necessary. Casually, Camille withdrew her hand, subtly wiping the moisture she'd gotten from his away, running her hands down the sides of her skirt.

He was good-looking in a cuddly bear kind of way. His dark brown eyes were wide and direct, and he had a set of deep-set dimples that would flash every time he spoke. Despite the oddly high-pitched voice, he was probably the type of guy who picked up women with the ease that other men used to change their shorts, Camille thought.

What she found disconcerting about him, more than anything, was that he seemed too…eager.

"Some of us are headed to the bar in the hotel we're staying to have a few drinks. They all are from the study group… wanna come?" he asked casually. His piercing gaze made Camille feel the slightest bit uncomfortable.

"I think I'll pass tonight, but thanks. I've got a lot of work to do…"

"Oh, come on, we won't stay long, it'll be fun! We can all get to know each other better," he pleaded, and despite the fact she suspected his intentions had nothing to do with forming a study group, thoughts of Gideon brought a halt to her automatic refusal.

What better way to get him and the way he'd kissed her, made love to her and mooning over him than having a little fun? Carl's eagerness to be with her was appealing in a puppy dog sort of way.

"Sure, why not," she said forcing a smile as she looked up at him.

A big grin split across his face. When he placed his large, damp hand at the back of her waist, the warmth and moisture seeping through her silk blouse made Camille instantly want to retract her agreement.

A little too eager was putting it mildly.

She should have paid more attention to her earlier warning bells, that red flag that went up, the one that every woman had that alerted her that she may or may not be dealing with a bugaboo.

After telling Carl she'd meet him and the others at the bar, she'd gone to her room and changed out of her high heels and exchanged them for flats before heading back down.

She'd stepped inside the bar and eyed the rambunctious group of students. Just as she'd suspected, none of the so-called "study group" members had any intention of going over the course material.

Despite the fact that she'd noted several of them wearing wedding rings, it didn't stop them from coupling up the moment they met in the bar. And judging by the amount of empty glasses that littered the table, the night had already begun.

Eyeing the group from the doorway, she would have turned and walked away had Carl not spotted her before she could escape.

Not giving her time to place her purse on the table, he eagerly grabbed her and pulled her on to the postage stamp-sized dance floor, hauling her tightly against his big, sweaty body before swinging her away.

Camille's eyes widened, her mouth forming an *O* when he started dancing by himself, swinging his big arms and legs, thrusting his hips in time to the rap song being played.

When he went old school on her—real old school, his body becoming stiff as he did the robot before falling to the floor and spinning around—she was done.

She turned and with her head held high, started for the exit.

He ran to meet her before she could leave, his face flushed, sweat pouring down his face.

"Hey, what's wrong? I thought we were having fun!" he said and started doing that weird robot move again.

She shook her head. "No, I wasn't having fun, Carl. You were. Look, I'm going to head back to the room. It's been a long day."

"Oh, okay, I understand, that's cool. This isn't exactly your scene, huh?" he asked and Camille frowned at him. "Tell you what, why don't I come up with you?" he asked, a sly look crossing his face. Camille barely checked an *are you serious* look from crossing hers. "Let me just tell the others…"

"No!" she said, loudly. "Seriously, go on and have fun with the others. I'll see you in class tomorrow," she said, lowering her voice. "It's been a long week. I just want to go chill out in my room—"

"Hey, that's cool, Camille. I like the sound of that, a little alone time." He grinned wide. The calculating, slick look on his face made her wonder why she ever thought he was the least bit shy. Obviously she needed the course she was taking more than she thought. Reading people correctly was not her strong point.

"Alone," she stated firmly.

Before he could protest further, and to prevent an ugly scene she saw coming, Camille turned, murmured a good-night and nearly ran from the bar.

The ten o'clock news provided background noise as Camille sat propped on pillows in bed, her hair tied up in a scarf, a bag of flaming hot Cheetos next to her laptop. Scanning the Excel spreadsheet on her monitor, she paused when she heard a noise outside the small bedroom of her suite.

She grabbed the remote and turned the volume down, her brows scrunching, and tilted her head to the side to listen, and again heard the rat-a-tat sound of knuckles pounding on the door.

"Who in the *world*…" she mumbled, glancing at the alarm clock.

After coming to her room an hour ago, she'd quickly showered, powered up her laptop and flipped on the television, ready to get some work in.

She pushed both her snacks and laptop to the side and stood. Grabbing her robe on the way out and sliding into her flip-flops, she strode toward the door.

Through the peephole she saw a tall, broad figure standing on the other side.

"I thought you might like a little company…can I come in?" Carl begged.

Camille was so not in the mood to deal with him again and turned to tiptoe away, hoping he'd think she wasn't there, when she bumped her foot against the door, cursing mildly at the small injury.

"I hear you in there, Camille. Come on…can't I come in?" he asked, his voice slightly slurred.

"Doesn't that guy get it?" she mumbled, rubbing her sore toe and counting to ten before answering him. "Look, Carl, I already told you I'm beat. I'll see you tomorrow, okay?" she asked, trying to inject a pleasant tone into her voice.

She leaned against the door and waited for a response. There was no way on earth she had any intention of opening the door. No telling what he would do if she did, bogarting his way inside. And if he thought she'd be his booty call for the night, he seriously had it twisted.

"I thought maybe we could go over the assignment for tomorrow's class," he continued to wheedle.

Again Camille noticed how high and nasal his voice was, and that alone skyrocketed her irritation with him. A man that big should not have a voice that high. Period.

"Just go, Carl." Camille eyed the phone near the door. If he didn't go away soon, she would be forced to call security. She sighed.

"Okay. I can take a hint."

She breathed easier.

"But if you change your mind, I'm just one floor down. I…"

"I won't," she broke in, her voice clipped.

After a few minutes of silence, she leaned down and peered though the hole again. When she saw his broad, retreating back she slumped against the door. Thank God, he finally gave up.

With a shake of her head, she turned, heading back to her bed, where her flaming hot Cheetos and laptop awaited her. Removing her robe, she was poised to jump back in bed when he knocked again.

"Okay, you know what?" she said aloud to herself and the room at large. "That is *it!* I tried to be nice. This is ridiculous!" She stomped back angrily to the door fully prepared to let him have it.

Grabbing the doorknob, she yanked the door wide open and said, "I told you I'm not interested! Why don't you just take your boogy nights and—" She stopped midsentence, her eyes widening as she stared up into the face of Gideon Taber.

Chapter 7

"Expecting someone?" Gideon asked, racking a glance over Camille from the top of her scarf-covered head, to the tiny T-shirt that molded her round, firm breasts to perfection, over skimpy matching shorts and down to her coral-painted toenails as she stood in the doorway.

She bit at the corner of her mouth and shook her head. "No, I…I thought you were someone else, but no. I'm not expecting anyone."

Gideon frowned, jealously wondering who she had been expecting.

"Well, if you're not expecting anyone, can I come in?"

She gave him a pensive look and finally nodded her head. "Yes. Sure, I suppose."

As he followed her inside her suite, he gaze again fell to her shorts that just barely covered her bottom. With each step she took, the globes of her perfect ass swayed, and he bit back a groan.

"So, um…why are you here?" she asked over her shoulder, casually lifting her robe from the bed and drawing it over her body before turning back to face him.

Gideon hadn't given much thought to what he would actually say to her, his need to see her driving him to come to her hotel room. He was glad for her directness.

"Come on, Camille, don't play games. You know why I'm here," he said, eyeing the robe that covered her.

"Can I get you anything? I have some Diet Coke in the fridge…?" she asked, her voice formal as she walked to the small kitchenette area.

"No, I'm fine." He slowly strode toward her. When she backed up, putting distance between them, his jaw tightened.

"I don't bite, Cami…unless you want me to."

"Camille. Please call me Camille," she said and looked away.

"Okay, I don't get it. When we first met you were Cami. In fact, according to my recollection that was the only name you'd give me. Now you're Camille? Seems a bit ass-backwards, if you ask me."

"Camille is the name most people call me. Friends and family call me Cami," she shot back.

"So, you were Cami when you shared your body with me, and now you're Camille since I'm not a…friend?" he asked and saw her creamy brown face flush dark red.

She turned away from him, walking over to a chair in the sitting area. Picking up a T-shirt that had been laying over the arm, she folded and refolded it, the nervous reaction telling.

"Look, I think we need to talk."

Her hands stilled. She sighed, asking, "What do we need to talk about?"

"Cami—Camille," he corrected himself. "Let's not play

games. You know what we need to talk about. What happened between us back in Seattle…"

At that, she placed the T-shirt back over the chair and stood facing him.

"What I did—"

"What *we* did," he interrupted, correcting her.

"What *we* did…was a one-time thing. It wasn't meant to be more than that. The fact that we are thrown together again doesn't change anything."

"And why can't it? What happened that night was special… the way we made love, the way you responded to me—"

She held up a hand, forestalling what he would say next. "It was a one-time thing. Something that shouldn't have happened. But it did, and I don't regret it. I was feeling good, had too many drinks, and well…" Her sentence trailed off.

The look of fury on Gideon's face stopped Camille from continuing. She swallowed, taking a step back.

He pushed away from the wall, advancing toward her. With every step he took, she backed up further, until her back was pressed to the wall and his body was a hair's breadth away from hers.

"If it makes you feel better, you can blame it on the alcohol. But we both know that didn't have a damn thing to do with why you moaned and cried when I made love to you, when you begged for me to make love to you," he said coarsely, his face flushed in anger, his eyes boring into hers. "All through the night."

When he trailed a finger down the line of her face, Camille didn't flinch and defiantly stared up at him, refusing to look away.

He braced his hands on either side of the wall, trapping her, his unique scent making her breath catch in her throat.

Bringing his face close to hers, he rubbed the side of his cheek against hers and nudged his nose under her earlobe.

"We both know it didn't have a damn thing to do with how well we fit together, as though we were made for each other," he murmured, his tongue coming out to lick the sensitive spot behind her ear. "Like perfect pieces to a puzzle."

Camille held herself still, trying hard not to respond to his voice, his scent…his nearness.

"Didn't have a damn thing to do with why you ran out on me before I could wake up and start all over again." When his tongue bathed the hollow of her throat, a small whimper escaped.

"And it didn't have a damn thing to do with why you're so scared about how we made each other feel that you can't be in the same room with me for two minutes and your panties aren't wet."

The truth of his words sliced into her swift and deadly, deep into the heart of her femininity.

Before she realized his intent, he'd loosened the ties of her robe, one big hand lifting her T-shirt and deftly slipping down inside the waistband of her shorts.

She gasped when a finger went to her vagina and separated her slick folds.

Unable to look away from him, she squirmed around his finger when he withdrew the dewy moisture. Helpless, caught in his sensual web, she watched him bring his finger to his mouth. Her wet lips went dry when he licked his finger clean of her cream.

Camille's body was trembling hard when he rested his forehead against hers briefly.

"If you want to find out if there was more to this…us, than a one-night fuck, let me know. Otherwise, I won't bother you again," he promised.

When she heard the door to her suite slam shut, Camille

allowed her body to slide down the wall until she sat on the floor, covering her arms over her face and leaning her forehead against the tops of her knees.

For the next two days Camille did her best to focus all of her attention on the class and not think about what Gideon had said to her…what he had done to her. In fact it took a considerable amount of willpower to simply not think of him at all. Not so easy to do when she was in the same room with him for three hours every night.

Whenever she'd catch his eyes on her in class, she'd find herself unable to look away.

Just as in the bar the first night, everything and everyone around them faded away as though they alone shared that space.

She felt completely out of control around him, an unfamiliar feeling and one she didn't like.

She forced the memory of them together, as well as the curiosity of what they could have, from her mind.

She had to. She had to concentrate on the reason she was here, had to focus on the one thing she *knew* she had some control over. She had come to Houston for her career and wouldn't allow anyone or anything to distract her from that.

No matter how many times she recited the mantras designed to remind herself she had no time for love, remind her what her goals were and the reason she was even taking the workshop, in the end it hadn't mattered. He was right.

She couldn't be in the same room with him and *not* be turned on. Not imagine what if…

Once, she'd caught his eyes on hers, a knowing look on his face as his eyes fixed on her breasts. Her nipples reacted as though on cue, growing tight and achy, straining against the confines of her bra. Embarrassed, she'd cast a furtive glance around, sure every student in the room had to have noticed what was going on between them.

Not wanting to deal with him, her confusing feelings or the words he'd flung at her, Camille went out of her way to escape him as soon as he ended the class for the night. But her gut told her it was only a matter of time before her day of reckoning would come.

Her day of reckoning came on Friday.

Relieved when the workshop ended and he didn't try and detain her, Camille prepared to leave the classroom.

When he wished all of them a fun, restful weekend in the casual smile he gave the class, she pushed away the disappointing feeling.

Shaking her head at her conflicting feelings, she walked toward the door, and hesitated, waiting for him to stop her. When he didn't, she squared her shoulders, pulled the strap to her bag closer to her body and walked out.

It was what she wanted, she reminded herself.

Chapter 8

The last two days had been hell on Gideon.

When Camille had walked out of class, he'd seen her hesitate, and for the first time in two days, he felt a smile, a real smile, lift the corners of his mouth in satisfaction. Just as badly as he wanted her, she wanted him. She was just too damn stubborn to admit it.

After Camille had told him she had no interest in furthering the relationship, that it had been a one-night stand *only* for her, he'd seen red.

Despite the fact that he'd said the same words more times than he wanted to remember to others, it was all he could do to not pick her sweet little body up and throw her on the sofa and do her so good she forgot her own damn name and the lie that had tumbled from her lips effortlessly. And it *was* a lie.

Gideon smoothed his hand over his hair, sighing in frustration.

The way she'd responded to him from the first moment they'd met to the first time they'd made love, he knew the wild attraction was mutual. She wasn't the type of woman who shared her body easily, engaged in casual sex, despite her attempt make him think otherwise.

He also knew she had a defensive wall a mile high around her, a wall Gideon was hell-bent on breaching. Glimpses into the woman she kept hidden had fueled his determination to get past her walls.

To get past the woman who worked long hours and sacrificed for her successes, the one who wore Brooks Brothers suits during the day, yet wore Tinker Bell pajamas to bed.

The one who, after a night spent together and days after where he couldn't get her out of his mind, all but made it impossible for him to think of another woman.

Not to mention her laugh, Gideon thought. When he'd told a joke in class, he'd been able to single out her laugh above all the other students. It had reached out and grabbed him, pulled him in, made his heart pound, his gaze seeking hers. As it had when they'd danced, everything and everyone had faded away, and it was as though no one else shared their space.

He *had* to get to know her better.

Really know her, beyond the sex, as good as it had been. Scratch that, as mind-blowing as it had been.

But he was hemmed in by his own words, telling her she'd have to come to him if she wanted to further what they had.

He laughed ruefully at himself. He'd given her space the last two days. She was running scared, he knew it. Hell, there was a part of him that was just as scared. This was unchartered territory for him, as well.

But his gut told him she was worth it.

His mother would be clapping her hands together in glee if she knew he'd finally found a woman who'd captured his attention as much as Camille had. Not that he had any intention of that happening.

His main focus was to get her to open up to him. Hell, he had to get her to agree to see him first, and time was running short. The class ended midweek, next week, which gave him little time to get her to realize that it was more than great sex between them, to get her to admit that there could be something more.

Camille had spent most of the early part of Friday evening rambling out loud to no one but her empty room and herself at the absent Gideon she couldn't stop thinking of.

At one point she'd stopped and grabbed the handout he'd given the class, where he'd given his cell phone number in case of emergency. Plopping down on the arm of a chair, she'd chewed at her bottom lip, worrying it between her teeth, thinking.

She needed to get him out of her system, one way or another. She'd thought of calling, but each time she'd dialed the number, she'd pressed the End Call button on her phone, disconnecting before the call could go through.

She'd called her mother instead, hoping she'd give her perspective on the situation. She and her mother were close, more like sisters than mother and daughter, and talked about everything.

However, their conversations had been brief since she'd been in Houston. The two times she'd phoned, her mother had within minutes hurriedly gotten off.

When her father had passed, it had been hard, financially and emotionally, for both her and her mother. Yet, together, they'd survived, leaning on each other for support. Because of their close relationship, Camille worried when she would have to move to Houston in three months, permanently. She didn't know what her mother would do without her.

"Sweetheart," her mother broke in, before Camille had been able to spill everything on her mind. "I love you, you know that. I've always wanted the best for you. After your father died, it was just you and me, and you've always been there for me….you're a good girl."

Camille smiled, already feeling better with just the few words. Her mother continued, "But, baby, now it's time for you to have some fun. It's time for both of us to, sweetie!"

It was then that Camille heard a *very* masculine voice murmur in the background before she heard the receiver on the phone muffled. But not so well that she didn't hear her mother giggle.

When her mother returned to the phone, she said, "Look, baby, mama's gotta go. Uh, some of the ladies from the church auxiliary are here to discuss the fundraiser…." She stopped, and again Camille heard a male voice and her mother's responding giggle before she said a quick, "I love you, and it'll all be okay, baby!" and hung up the phone, leaving Camille with a dial tone humming in her ear, her mouth gaping open in confusion.

After an hour of staring at the TV, Camille tried hard not to analyze what was really going on at her mother's house. She gave up and started getting ready for bed, when the hotel phone rang.

Camille sat on the edge of the bed, hesitant to answer the phone, knowing it was Gideon. She drew in a deep breath and answered.

"Can we start over, again?"

She sat back on the bed, crossed her legs underneath her, twirling the cord between her fingers.

"My name is Gideon Taber, and I would love to take you out," he said simply. A smile, a real one, tugged her lips, before blossoming into a full grin. She scooted her body until her back bumped the pillows against the headboard.

"Hi. My name is Camille Jackson." She paused before continuing. "But you can call me Cami," she said, almost shyly.

When she heard the smile come through his voice when he spoke next, she relaxed fully, stretching her legs out on the bed.

When he asked her if she'd spend the day with him tomorrow, like an adolescent being asked out on her first date, Camille's grin grew even wider as she snuggled down into the plush comforter and agreed.

"What do you have planned?"

"Why don't we play it by ear?"

Normally Camille balked at playing anything by ear. She was a planner, down to the bone, an "if I don't have it on my day planner it ain't happening," type of planner.

So when she heard herself respond with a "sounds great," she didn't know who was more surprised, she or Gideon.

"Great! Dress casually. I'll pick you at 11:00 a.m. And we'll see where the day takes us," he said, and after saying goodbye, they hung up.

As Camille waited for Gideon to arrive, she was a mass of nerves, wondering if what she wore was okay, unsure where he was taking her. To say she was out of her comfort zone was putting it mildly.

In the end she'd chosen a halter-back yellow sundress, topped with a cropped, cream-colored, crochet-styled sweater. Both the style and color complimented her figure. Tapering in the waist, the skirt flared and fell just above knee level.

She'd thrown on a few accessories, a delicate silver bracelet and matching necklace, diamond studs in her ears, and light makeup, hoping what she'd chosen would work no matter where they went.

The appreciative gleam in his eyes when she opened the door assured her she had.

"Wow…you look beautiful," he said, running his gaze over her.

"You don't look too bad yourself," she said, smiling up at him.

She'd only seen him in business casual clothes—dress slacks and shirt—but today he looked as though he could have stepped out of any Gap ad, wearing relaxed fit jeans, slightly worn, a thin, long-sleeved, gray T-shirt, the sleeves pushed up to the elbows, and a pair of loafers. The overall look was casual and sexy.

"I thought we could go on a picnic. I know the perfect place."

It was then that Camille noticed the basket he was carrying, and as her stomach growled, she laughed. "Sounds perfect. What's in the basket?" she asked, walking to his side. "Um, I can smell it! Can I have a peek?" she asked, reaching out to lift the lid. "I'm starving!"

"Me, too," he murmured, his voice slightly husky, and Camille glanced up at him. "But what I'm hungry for isn't in the basket."

When he pulled her into his arms, she eagerly went, opening her mouth, hungry for him.

His tongue snaked out to deliver a swipe across the entire length of her mouth, before he grabbed her bottom lip with his mouth and suckled it, slowly allowing it to pop back out.

"Hmm…delicious," he murmured against her mouth.

Camille wrapped her arms around his neck and heard the thud of the basket as it hit the floor at the same time he placed his arms around her waist and hauled her tight against his hard body. Their bodies flush, Camille could feel every hard ridge of him against her.

With a low growl he ground against her. The kiss took on

a life of its own as their bodies merged against each other. Lifting her until her feet left the floor, he allowed her body to glide back down, their tongues performing a sensual duet mimicking the action of their bodies.

When he finally pulled away, freeing her lips, he trailed his tongue to her ear, biting down on the lobe, and suckled it into his mouth. "God I missed your mouth," he said in a raspy voice against her mouth.

"I hope you like strawberries. I thought we could have them topped with cream…and you…for dessert."

"Oh," she said, her eyes widening as he gently pulled away from her.

On wobbly legs she walked to the counter and grabbed her purse and allowed him to lead her out of the room, not sure she could walk steady by herself.

A short kiss and a few well-chosen words, and once again Gideon had sent her body into a lust-filled overdrive.

Chapter 9

"This looks like a good place to land. What do you think?" Gideon asked, hunching down and placing the basket on the soft grass.

He'd brought her to the Buffalo Bayou Park, and as they'd strolled along the winding paths, he'd put on his "tourist guide" hat, pointing out the various sites as they walked, including the art park where local artists had their work displayed.

"Yeah, it's perfect," she said, smiling down at him. With a grin he withdrew the blanket and spread it on the grass, patting it, inviting her to sit down.

Along their walk, they'd stopped at a vendor's cart and he'd bought them hotdogs and drinks, but once he lifted the lid, the aromatic smell hit her, reminding Camille how hungry she was.

Rubbing her hands together, she asked, "What do you have for us…besides the strawberries?" she asked, and immediately blushed.

He laughed. "Maybe we can skip the main course and go straight for dessert? I'm game, if you are," he said, his mouth stretching into a lecherous grin. Before she could react, he'd reached out for her hand and tugged her down onto the blanket. She tumbled into his lap, laughing as she righted herself.

Camille's stomach growled loudly. "As tempting as that sounds—the whole dessert thing first—I think I'll go for what's in the basket. For now," she qualified and again blushed.

He gave her a wink. "Later," he promised.

She ducked her head and waited for him to open the basket. When he didn't, she glanced at him. His attention was on her hair. Self-consciously, she brought a hand up, and he stopped her.

"I like your hair like this." He moved her hand away and fingered several of the curly strands that had escaped her ponytail. "You should wear it like this more often. It suits you."

Camille had forgone flat-ironing her hair that morning. Instead, after showering, she'd used her favorite hair butter and allowed her kinky curls to do their own thing, something she rarely did at the workplace.

"Thank you," Camille said simply, yet Gideon saw the faint blush warm her skin and hid a grin. For all the confidence she displayed in the corporate world, there was a side of her that he could make blush at the slightest compliment or whenever he kissed her.

Gideon broke their gaze, resisting the urge to pull her into his lap to do just that—kiss her. Kiss her until she blushed all over her body, something he'd wanted to do the entire morning.

He reluctantly allowed her hair to slip from his fingers and withdrew the food he'd packed.

"I wasn't sure what you liked, so I may have gone a bit overboard. One thing I did pack that I think you'll like are these," he said, and smiled when her pretty face lit up and she clapped her hands together, grinning from ear to ear as he withdrew the bag of Cheetos.

"Ooooh! You even got the flaming hot ones! I think I'm in love! How did you know those are my favorites?" Although she said it light-heartedly, Gideon felt as though he'd been punched in the gut.

He stared at her, wondering when, how, it had happened. When had he started falling in love with her…?

"Hey…are you okay?" she asked, a puzzled look on her face when he didn't respond.

"Yeah, yeah, I'm fine." He forced a smile. "The Cheetos? I saw them the night I came to your hotel room. You were eating them in bed."

He didn't realize until now how he'd made mental notes about everything to do with her from the moment they'd met. He noticed everything, nothing escaping his attention. From the way she bit at her bottom lip when she was nervous, to the fact that she ate flaming hot Cheetos in bed at midnight.

God, he had it bad. How had he *not* seen it coming?

"Well, that seals it. I'm going to have to keep you around," she quipped and opened the bag as Gideon smiled weakly.

He wanted to grab her, take her far away and tell her how he felt, tell her he wanted more, much more with her, than the rest of the week they had together. He wanted more…

As she placed the food on the blanket, telling him how she'd first discovered her love for flaming hot Cheetos, he sat staring at her, wondering how he could tell her how he felt.

He'd had a hard enough time convincing her to go out with him this time. How in the hell could he tell her he was falling in love with her?

Earlier in the morning she'd been on guard and stiff with

him. But within a short time she'd loosened up, so much so that when he'd pulled her hand into his as he'd played tour guide, she'd allowed the casual intimacy. When he'd wrapped an arm around her waist, she'd even leaned into his embrace and in turn wrapped an arm around him.

He'd kept the conversation light, finding out small things about her. He learned her likes and dislikes from her favorite type of music—the two of them shared a love for jazz—to her favorite junk food, flaming hot Cheetos, which he already knew, and yet another thing they shared in common.

As they ate, he told her he was Jewish and the youngest of five children—and the only boy—and groaned at her laughter. He regaled her with tales of his life growing up, while he found out that she was an only child and that her father had died when she was in her teens.

"I've always wanted to know what it was like to be a part of a large family."

"Being the only son and youngest in a Jewish family has its challenges. You ought to see the pains my mother has gone through trying to set me up with a 'nice Jewish girl who'll give my *bubeleh* lots of fat grandbabies'," he replied, lifting his voice mimicking his mother as they began to eat.

"Her *bubeleh?*" she asked, trying to keep her face straight as she pulled a muffin from the basket.

He rubbed the back of his neck, his face reddening, "It's a, uh, Yiddish word for child...one I've never heard anyone actually use. Except my mother."

When she laughed outright, the dimples in her cheeks creasing, he pulled her into his lap. Taking the muffin from her hand, he fed it to her instead.

"You think that's funny, do you?" he said, lifting a brow.

"Yep. I think it's absolutely hilarious!" she laughed swallowing the food in her mouth.

"Well, wait until she meets you. We'll see who's laughing

when she starts asking you when you plan to give her *bubeleh* those healthy grandbabies!"

At his retort, the laughter died from her eyes and she quickly swallowed the last bit of muffin. Easing herself from his lap, she dusted the muffin crumbs from her hands and stood.

"Well, uh, since I'm not a nice Jewish girl, I don't see that as a problem."

"Mom doesn't care about that. She just wants to see me married, and happy…and of course the babies," he said, and immediately the image of Camille's stomach heavy with his baby came to his mind.

He stood, reaching out a hand to her, pulling her around to face him.

In her eyes he saw a glimmer of something that made his heart slam in his chest, a look that told him she might have had the same thought, the same image he'd had, in her mind as well.

They stood staring at each other, neither one able to look away, until finally Camille turned away, looking at the remnants of the picnic.

"Well, me meeting your family won't happen for a long time. For now, we'd better get ready to go. It's getting late," she said with a tight smile, looking at the sky and the dwindling sun.

Although she tried ignoring his mentioning meeting his family, the fact that she didn't completely dismiss the idea outright was a step in the right direction and gave him hope that she would eventually admit her feelings for him were growing as strong as his were for her.

After the picnic, he'd taken her on a short tour of Houston, ending at Bojangles Blues Bar for a light dinner and drinks as they listened to a live blues band perform. After the tense moment at the picnic, the rest of the day had been relaxed, and they returned to the lighthearted banter they'd had earlier in the day. By evening, Camille hadn't wanted the day to come to an end.

When he'd told her about the renovations he'd done on his loft and invited her to come and see it, she knew the visit was more than a desire to show off his carpentry skills.

The love he had for his family and how hard he'd worked to achieve his success in his business were all things she admired. Overall, Gideon was someone she knew she wanted to get to know better, someone she could actually see herself having a future with.

She shied away from the thought, even as she remembered his remarks at the picnic, sure he hadn't meant it the way it sounded.

And she'd been right.

Face-down on his large, king-size bed, her naked skin caressed the silk sheets, his hard body blanketing her body.

Camille felt a slight tremor run through her body when he ran the tips of his fingers down her bare back along the length of her spine until he reached one round cheek.

Her eyes feathered closed and blew out a soft sigh when his breath whispered against the back of her neck, quickly followed by his lips and tongue.

She allowed her head to tilt to the side when he pressed his mouth to the side of her throat, his hands coming up to slide under her dress, fingers trailing up her thighs, until he reached the waistband of her panties.

"May I?" he asked, eliciting a small laugh from her. With her nod, he slipped a finger inside her panties, his finger brushing over her mound, stroking her slick opening.

A strangled gasp tore from her throat, and her body arched, her breasts pressing against the silk sheets, when his wicked tongue mimicked the trail of his fingers, ending at the indentation of her waist.

"I didn't notice this the first time we made love." She felt his smile against her skin, referring to the tattoo she'd gotten in college when she was in a band. Her one, private rebellion, the small tattoo rested at the base of her spine and featured a set of drums below a pair of drum sticks.

"I think I will," he said, in response to the words scrolled over the drums, *"tap this."*

A breathy laugh escaped from Camille, followed by a moan when he outlined the tattoo with the tip of his tongue.

"Yesss…" she hissed, her breath rushing out with a sigh of pleasure when his tongue lapped against her skin.

He continued with his tongue, stroking down her leg, repositioning her so he could reach her inner thighs. With his hot, wicked tongue, he swirled over the cream that had eased down her leg making, her squirm beneath his touch on the sensitive skin.

When he flipped her over, gazing at her, she unconsciously placed a hand over her mound, covering herself.

He grasped both of her hands and shackled them within one of his, before pulling them up and over her head. "Don't hide your sweet, beautiful body from me," he admonished, before his tongue swept over the crest of her breast, making her nipple spike and her body arch sharply off the bed.

Gideon ached for her to feel at ease enough with him to have no inhibitions about her body, ached for her to feel as comfortable with sharing her body with him as he was with her. He knew that he gave her pleasure—her sweet moans and helpless cries told him that. But he wanted more. He wanted all of her. Body and mind.

He shifted his body so that he lay crosswise over her, retrieving his pants from the floor.

Camille heard the rustle and then slide of his belt being removed from his trousers. When he returned, a smile of pure mischief lit his face.

"So you don't try and get away this time," he said, bringing her wrists together and wrapping the makeshift bond around them.

"I'm not…I'm not going anywhere," she promised, her words barely audible as he snaked his body along hers, rubbing his face against the springy hairs that covered her mound.

"I plan to make sure you that you don't. No more vanishing acts from you," he admonished and pushed her legs up, his hands grasping her by the ankles, anchoring her feet to the bed.

Two fingers separated the lips of her vagina, exposing her clit. Camille gasped with pleasure when his lips covered her, his tongue swirling around her tight, throbbing nub, dragging it deep within his mouth.

Her chest rose and fell in panting breaths as she widened her legs, peering down at him as he lay between them. The sight of his dark head between her thighs and the feel of his tongue licking and stroking her made her body tremble.

"You like that, Cami," he stated, when he finally released her.

"Yes," she breathed and whimpered when he moved away.

"Shh, it's okay, baby. I'll make sure you like the rest just as much."

He brought his face to her stomach, trailed his tongue over and around her belly button, dipping his tongue inside, swirling around the small indentation. The sensation startled her. Surprised at how good it felt, she threw back her head, grinding her body against his face.

His laugh was a pure masculine purr against her skin. "If not more."

With careful attention he licked and suckled her, using lips, tongue and fingers to bring her to a screaming release, her body arching so sharply from the bed that had she not been bound she would have bucked him off her.

When her body began to calm and her limbs stopped trembling, Gideon deftly removed the belt from her wrists, his cock hard, throbbing, his own breathing as labored as hers as he witnessed the way she gave into her release. She was devastating when she came.

Quickly he sheathed his erection, centered himself between her legs and plunged deep in one long stroke.

When her tight, warm sheath gripped him like a glove, he had to clench his teeth to prevent himself from slamming into her. He was close to orgasm from simply watching her.

"Are you ready for me, baby?" he asked in a tight, controlled whisper against her temple.

When she moved beneath him, not responding, he asked again, his control all but gone.

"Yes…yes, please, Gideon…"

He groaned, opened his mouth and clamped it over her breasts, pumping deep inside her. Wanting to heighten her climax, he gathered her closer and scraped her clit against his groin with every downward stroke. He held her tightly, his fingers digging into her hips, while his body plundered hers, his mouth on her breast greedy, sucking her with a frenzy of need and wild desire.

When her orgasm began to unfurl, she inhaled a swift, desperate breath of air and clutched his neck as he continued to plunge and retreat. As her orgasm hit its pinnacle, she screamed out his name, her walls milking him until he could no longer hold out. Rearing his head back, he felt his seed burst from his body as they both yelled each other's name in unison, until their voices died down to a hoarse cry.

"That was…incredible. Thank you, Camille." The words were inadequate, but Gideon couldn't find the ones that would convey what he felt after what they'd shared.

When she nodded her head in response, her lids droopy and her body still trembling, he pulled out of her, arranging their bodies so that he could rest his head against the top of her head, his mind busy.

Although they'd been together a short time, his instincts told him that she was the one for him. Now he had to convince her of that.

Chapter 10

A few months later...

"Mama, Mama, where are you?" Camille called, after entering her childhood home and throwing her purse on the sofa.

"I saw your car in the garage...." she said distractedly, heading toward the kitchen. Opening the door to the fridge, she snooped around, hunting for something to eat. It was close to the Christmas season, so eagerly she searched for the sweets her mother had promised she'd make, Camille's favorite—chocolate truffles.

Her face fell when her search came up empty. Grumbling, she grabbed a can of Coke from the side shelf instead.

"Hey, Annie, baby, I found the oiiiilll," a man sang. "Where are you hiding from big daddy?"

Camille dropped the can of Coke and spun around. Shocked to the point she was nearly speechless, Camille stared at the older man standing naked as a jay bird in the middle of her mother's living room. She quickly recovered and yelled, "Who the hell are you and *what* in the hell are you doing in my mama's house naked? And dear god in heaven, what are you doing with that oil in your hand?!"

The naked man's eyes grew round, and, a millisecond later, he hastily grabbed her mother's crocheted blanket from the sofa and wrapped it tight around his waist.

"Oh, God, I'm so sorry! I...I thought you were Annie Mae!" he stuttered.

"Who says I'm hiding, big boy?"

Feeling like Alice after falling in the rabbit's hole, Camille spun around to see her mother, clad in a long, *sheer* gown, come strolling into the living room.

Confused and shocked, Camille didn't know whether to laugh at the look that crossed her mother's face when she saw Camille in the kitchen or go screaming from the room in horrified denial because her mother was wearing a *sheer* gown and had a naked, oil-toting man in her living room.

She opted for the latter. Spinning around, she ran from the room and heard her mother's friend speak. "Annie, baby...why don't I, uh, give you and your daughter some time alone? I'll uh, go to the bedroom and get dressed."

"Camille, wait."

Camille stopped and slowly faced her mother. "Baby, I don't know what to say. I, uh, wasn't expecting you to visit."

"Well, that much is obvious. I hope to *hell* you weren't, what with your...friend and the oil and all." Camille fought the tears threatening to overcome her.

Tears she didn't understand.

The past few months of uncertainty about her move to Houston, the career change, leaving home and Gideon all caught up with her, and the tears started falling down her face, slowly at first, before the flood gate opened as she rushed toward the front door, her mother on her heels.

"Baby, I can explain," she started and Camille stopped walking and held up a hand.

"Mama, you don't owe me an explanation." She laughed, the sound unnaturally high. "You're a grown woman. And like you said, it's time for you to have some fun."

Tears were streaming down her face so hard her face she could barely see the floor in front of her.

She'd made it to the door when her mother's hand covered hers on the doorknob. "Camille…" she said and stopped, as much at a loss for words as Camille was. An uneasy moment of silence stretched out between them. Hearing her mother sigh, she turned to face her.

"Let's talk," she said. Camille spun around and stared at her mother.

"Forget it, Mama. Go back to your new man." She spit the words angrily, wiping at the tears in her eyes. "Now I know why you kept rushing off the phone when I was in Houston. You're too busy *getting* busy to talk to me!"

As soon as she flung the words at her mother she knew she'd gone too far. Camille instantly regretted them and felt like a spoiled child, instead of the nearly thirty-year-old grown woman she was.

"Camille Antoinette Jackson!"

"When your friend leaves, maybe you'll have time for me," Camille said, rushing out the door before her mother could stop her.

"Done acting like a brat, now, Cami? Think we can we talk?"

Camille rose from her sofa, startled out of sleep when she heard her mother speak.

She looked around, glancing out of her living room window, surprised to see it dark outside.

Her mother had turned on the corner lamp, bathing the dark room in a soft amber glow.

She perched on the side of the bed and Camille glanced at her with wary eyes as she sat up.

"About what happened…" she began, only to have her mother hush her.

"It's okay, baby. I guess I kinda had it coming." She laughed, softly, reaching out to brush the hair away from Camille's eyes. "I think I got so caught up in my own life, I neglected you for a while. I'm sorry,"

"No, Mama. I owe you an apology. I guess I was just…surprised. That's all. It's no excuse for how I acted, though."

"How about we both agree we could have handled the situation better, from both of our ends, and start over, hmm, baby?" her mother asked and opened her arms.

Camille hugged her mother tightly, laughing with her.

Her mother pulled away, reaching over to get a Kleenex for both of them, and said, "Now, tell me all about this Gideon, and don't leave anything out."

"I'll tell you all about him. But don't think you can get out of telling me about…the oil man," Camille quipped, and both she and her mother laughed.

"Deal. I'll tell you all about him. After you fill me in on what's going on with you!"

Camille grinned, feeling lighter than she had in months, setting back into her mother's familiar embrace as she began to tell her mother about Gideon.

As Camille strode through the Houston terminal, pulling her carry-on bag behind her, her nerves were as taut as the strings on an antique violin. And like the fragile strings on the old violin, the wrong touch would make her snap.

One minute she was up, confident; the next minute down and confused, uncertain about her future with Gideon.

Luckily, over the last two months, her roller-coaster ride of emotions hadn't affected her job performance. Surprisingly, she'd accomplished not only the task of training her successor but had also completed the training for her new position.

After her childish breakdown with her mother, the two had talked...talked in a way they never had. Her mother had told Camille that she'd been lonely for a long time and had gotten used to being alone. But she didn't want to be alone anymore.

Camille had felt a smile tug the corners of her lips when her mother had told her about the new love in her life.

Initially Camille hadn't wanted to really know anything about the man—the first man in her mother's life since her father died. Then she'd felt awful for feeling that way. Her mother deserved to be happy. As much as she'd thought her mother needed her to be near her, Camille realized that it was she who needed to be around her mother.

Her mother deserved happiness—of the male variety. And the man she'd found seemed to make her mother happy. She'd delicately avoided the subject of her mother wearing the costume and her boyfriend chasing her around the house with a bottle of Johnson & Johnson baby oil.

Some things a mother and daughter didn't need to discuss.

She laughed, thinking about it in retrospect.

Who would have ever thought her Bible schoolteacher mother would have it in her?

Gideon...that was a different matter.

When she'd gotten home they'd both been busy—Camille with catching up on the mountain of paperwork that had accumulated since her two-week absence and Gideon with two classes he had to teach back-to-back—and the two had only spoken briefly over the phone.

After her routine had normalized, although still busy, she would find herself smiling throughout the day, thinking of him. Often they'd talk on the phone long into the night until both of their voices were drowsy, and they were forced to end the conversation.

Not a day had gone by that Camille hadn't heard from him. No matter how busy he was, he'd made time to call her. The few times he hadn't, he'd texted her and asked about her day. Camille had blushed when he'd asked her to text him a picture of herself wearing only a smile for him and nothing else.

Camera phone in hand, she'd obliged and blushed even harder when he'd returned the favor.

She stepped outside the Houston terminal, knotting the ties of her knee-length black leather jacket, looking for the nearest taxi stand.

Even with all the work, she'd managed to find a place to live, thanks to Gideon.

As promised, he'd given her the lead to a great place to live, and two weeks prior to the move she'd flown out to Houston to look it over and had signed the lease. Because of an out-of-town workshop he was conducting, he hadn't been able to be there when she'd arrived.

She hadn't known if she should have been happy or disappointed.

Maybe it was a good thing she had a few days to get it together before she faced him, again. Some of their late-night conversations had gone from garden variety, "I miss you, and wish you were here, baby" to straight-out get her panties wet, I need you now, phone sex.

When he'd told her he wouldn't be able to pick her up at the airport, since he was out of town at a workshop in Denver and his flight had been canceled due to the weather, she'd been disappointed.

"Oh, well, okay. I guess that can't be helped," she'd said, missing him so badly that she ached.

"Which is too bad, really. I had plans for us," he'd murmured.

"Oh, yeah? Like what?" she'd asked, pushing the disappointment aside, as she packed the last of her clothes in her travel bag. A crease had formed between her brows as she'd surveyed the near empty room, making sure she hadn't left anything.

"I think you know what kind of plans I'm talking about," he'd said and she'd stopped packing, holding the shirt tight in her hands.

"Yeah, I think I have a general idea," she'd said softly, her body reacting to the meaning of his words.

"What are you wearing?" he'd asked, his deep voice scraping against her skin in a rough caress.

"What am I wearing? Now?" she'd glanced down at the oversized T-shirt, the corner of her mouth lifting in a small smile. "Just a T-shirt."

"Is it mine?"

"Yeah…" she'd replied, her voice gone soft.

"Are you wearing any panties?"

A strangled gasp had torn from her throat, and she'd croaked out a "no."

"Take your hands, pretend their mine."

"Gideon…" her words had barely been above a whisper.

She'd placed the T-shirt inside her bag and sat back against the headboard. Hesitantly at first, she'd done what he'd instructed. In a low voice, his words a smooth caress along her body, he'd told her what to do, each word whispered along her body, up her legs, stroking into her until she'd gasped, her body trembling as the orgasm had washed over her, leaving her as shaky as though he had been the one to make her climax.

Hundreds of miles away and he'd given her one of the best orgasms she'd ever had in her life, except for the times when she'd been in his arms.

She had it bad for him.

But *do I do for him what he does for me?* The disturbing thought filtered into her mind as it had with increasing frequency over the past few weeks before she'd left Seattle.

"Did you want to share my taxi with me?"

Startled, Camille was pulled from her thoughts.

"Would you like to share a taxi?" the man asked again. She recognized him as the one she'd sat next to on her flight to Houston.

He'd tried several times during the flight to engage her in conversation until eventually she'd had to put on earphones, keeping the cord in her purse, pretending to listen to music she didn't have, in order to avoid him.

She'd been too on edge, her mind on her uncertain future with Gideon, to be able to engage in idle chitchat.

"Uh, no, that's okay. I—"

"No, the lady is already taken care of," a deep voice interrupted.

Camille spun around, a surprised look on her face when she saw Gideon smiling at her, standing near a black SUV behind the taxi.

"Gideon!" She ran the few feet that separated them, and as he grabbed her, she jumped into his arms. "I thought you were snowed in!"

"I managed to get a flight out. Thought I'd surprise you, baby."

Over Gideon's shoulder she saw the man give her a shrug and climb inside the taxi and speed off.

Once Gideon had released her, she asked, "Hey…how did

you know that guy was asking me to share his taxi? You were too far away to hear him!" she laughed.

He looked her over, grinning. "I'm sure that's not all he wanted to share with you," he said with a mock scowl.

"Oh, please, I look a mess! I've been traveling all day!"

"You always look good and you know it."

"I'm serious!" she said, but couldn't stop smiling. Seeing him again made the uncertainty she'd felt slowly fade.

"Me too…look, baby, as good as you look, as good as you always look, what sane man wouldn't ask you to share his taxi, or anything else?" he said, and she smiled, her cheeks dimpling at the compliment.

"God, I missed you," he said and pulled her into his arms to kiss her.

Their lips had barely touched when a shrill whistle interrupted it. "Hey, buddy, move the car or get a ticket," a uniformed officer yelled. Gideon released her and took her bag from her.

After putting it in the trunk, he opened her door before jogging over to the driver's seat and hopping in. After putting on their seat belts, he turned to her. The expression on his face, the look in his eyes as he stared at her, made butterflies settle in her stomach. He wrapped his big hand gently around the nape of her neck, tugging her toward him.

His mouth slanted over hers, covering her lips with his. A shrill whistle broke into their private party, and he broke away.

"We'll pick up where we left off when we get home," he promised, his voice hoarse.

The promise in his hazel eyes sent butterflies racing to her stomach.

Chapter 11

"Camille…what would you think about coming to dinner to meet my family?"

Gideon's question brought Camille fully awake. Coming home from the airport, he'd taken her directly to his house and within five minutes had had her naked under him.

After allowing their bodies to calm, he asked the question he desperately wanted her to say yes to.

Raising her body, she stared down at him.

"Meet your family? Uh…for what?"

"Oh, I don't know, for the usual thing…to eat," he said lightly.

When she looked as though she would decline, he said, "It's not a big deal. I just thought it would be nice for you to get to meet them and for them to meet you. I've told my mom about you and she invited you over to meet the family. Like I said, it's not a big deal." He mentally crossed his fingers. "Just a small family gathering."

She looked down at him, chewing her bottom lip, considering. "Just a small gathering?"

"Yep, not a big deal at all."

When she nodded her head, he breathed a sigh of relief, pulling her back down to lay on his chest.

Gideon's mother had called last week, reminding him of the dinner she had planned for the family during Hanukkah, one he'd completely forgotten about. Hearing the hesitation in his voice, his mother had reminded him of his promise to come, and Gideon had mentally cursed, realizing the day fell on the same one that Camille would be returning to Houston.

When he'd asked her if she could change the date, he'd had to pull the phone from his ear as his mother had gone on a diatribe about how long she'd been planning the meal, the inconvenience it would be to change the date…her rant coming to a halt when he'd said it was because he wanted to bring someone special home for her to meet.

The change that had come over her had been as immediate as it had been laughable. After a slight pause, where Gideon could have heard the proverbial pin drop, she'd quickly switched gears, assuring him she'd take care of everything, and the change in dates would not be a problem *at all*.

Now all he had to do was get Camille to agree to meet his family. Telling one small white lie wouldn't hurt….

Staring out of the window as Gideon exited the highway, Camille frowned as she nervously bit her lower lip.

"Stop it."

"Stop what?"

"Stop biting your lip."

"How did you know I was biting my lip?" she asked distractedly, thinking more about the fact that she was about to meet Gideon's family in less than thirty minutes than about his uncanny abilities to see her without looking.

She bit down harder on her lip.

"You always do that when you're nervous," he rebuked lightly. "Besides, you have nothing to be afraid of. So stop."

Ignoring his reprimand, Camille continued to chew on her lip. She heard him sigh loudly.

After taking the next exit, he came to a stoplight and turned to face her, turning her around until she was forced to look at him.

"And the way you're going at it, you're gonna gnaw your lip completely off. Which would not make me happy seeing as how much I love your mouth." Pulling her across the console, he kissed her. When the light turned green, he reluctantly moved away.

"I can't help it," she said, but his kiss had managed to ease some of the building tension.

After driving less than a mile, he turned into a gated subdivision. He pressed a button on a remote above his windshield visor, and the wrought-iron gate opened, allowing them to enter.

"Well, as much as I love you, I'm not sure that would be a cute look for you. The whole missing mouth thing, I mean. Maybe the right lipstick would help…so as not to draw attention to the missing part. Of course there's reconstructive surgery."

"You nut! I'm not that bad! Okay, okay…maybe I *do* bite my lip when I'm nervous," she admitted when he lifted a brow, "But it's not every day I meet your family. I mean, what if they don't like me?"

"That's really lame, Cami…of course they'll like you are we, teenagers? " He laughed, and she punched h on the arm.

"I'm serious, Gideon! I'm nervous!"   you as much as

"I'm sorry, baby. Don't worry. They'l I do, I promise. What's not to love?"

Camille paused, ready to rebut his claim, when the fact that he'd told her he loved her—not once, but *twice* in less than ten minutes—finally penetrated her mind.

"What? Wait a minute, Gideon, back up...did you just tell me you love me for the first time, while chewing me out over me biting my lip?"

He brought his Land Rover to a stop in front of a large, sprawling two-story brick home, cut the engine and turned to face her.

"Uh, yeah. Well, I meant to tell you, but I was waiting for the right time."

"And you think *now* is the right time?" Camille asked, her voice rising as she turned to see an older-looking couple approaching, the woman waving her hands and smiling as they quickly made their way over.

"Looks like my parents are coming. We'll have to discuss this later."

"Discuss this later! Gideon, you don't tell a woman you love her and expect her to..."

Before she could say more, Gideon had hastily turned away from her, rolling down the window as his father approached.

"Hey, what are you two doing out here? Come on in. Everyone's inside!"

Camille turned to see Gideon's mother outside her door, waiting for her to open. Reluctantly, Camille opened the door and stepped outside.

"So, this is Camille," she said, her lips lifting in a ghost of a smile. "So glad you could make it, dear. Gideon's told us a about you."

son, then turned to Gideon and placed her hands out in "Now, and he grasped them. She ran a glance over her soming. *"Boker tov Eliyahu...bubeleh."*

don't embarrass him. Give the boy a

break. Of course he remembered to show up. And not only that, he's brought a…friend, along with him," Gideon's father said, coming up behind them.

"And that is the reason I'm allowing this rascal to come inside and celebrate…because he brought such a lovely young lady with him."

Camille cast a confused glance at Gideon and he shrugged.

"She's just chewing me out for not being around lately," he said, giving a rough translation of the Hebrew his mother had spoken.

Camille remembered the gift she'd brought along and handed a small box to Gideon's mother.

"They're chocolate truffles. My mom's specialty. She makes them every Christmas and asked me to bring them tonight when I told her I was coming."

"Well, tell your mother I said thank you. Maybe one day soon, I'll be able to meet her and we can exchange recipes. I make them myself around the season. I'd love to compare recipes with her," she said, the smile she gave Camille made her more relaxed.

"Well, now that the two of you are here, let's go inside. Everyone's waiting," she said, grasping Camille beneath the elbow.

Camille put a determined smile on her face and allowed the woman to usher her to the door, shooting darts at Gideon over her shoulder, mouthing the word, *"everyone?"*

Chapter 12

Camille had met so many of Gideon's family members that, by the time they sat around the dinner table, her head was spinning trying to remember them all, wishing they wore name tags so that she could keep them straight.

At first she'd been nervous. Not only about meeting his family, but because of their differences—although she hadn't given a thought to it before. She'd always been open to dating men outside her race and religion, so it had been a non-issue for her.

But then again, she'd never gotten serious enough with any of her previous boyfriends to ever *meet* their families.

After Gideon's mother had said the prayer in Hebrew, which of course Camille didn't understand, and they'd gone around the table and everyone had given thanks, it was Camille's turn.

She swallowed the lump in her throat, feeling on the spot, as all eyes turned to her.

As she glanced around the table over the sea of expectant faces, she had a surreal moment, as though there were a neon flashing marquis above her head scrolling the words "clueless black girl."

She felt like she was in a real life version of the classic movie, *Guess Who's Coming to Dinner.*

Although his family had made her feel welcome, this was all new to her. She didn't want to say something wrong.

Sitting next to her, Gideon leaned down and whispered in her ear, "Anything you want to say is fine, baby. There is no right or wrong answer."

"Guess this is a lot different than what you're used to, Camille, isn't it?"

Camille, as well as everyone at the table turned to the man who spoke. Camille frowned, trying to remember who he was and what was his name.

"I'm not sure what you mean…Evan is it?" she asked, perplexed.

"I mean you're probably used to celebrating that Kawanzaa your people celebrate. This must be foreign to you since it's a lot different than what your people do."

A collective gasp went around the table, and Camille felt her indignation rise.

"My people?"

"Actually, Evan, Kwanzaa and Hanukkah have more in common than you think."

Camille turned surprised eyes toward Gideon's mother as she broke in. Rebekkah caught her glance and winked, before turning back to Evan.

"In fact, like Hanukkah, Kwanzaa is a week-long celebration that honors heritage. Although differing in the amount of days the candles are lit, in the celebration of Kwanzaa there is also lighting of candles."

To Camille's surprise and growing admiration, she

continued to "educate" Evan on the similarities between the two celebrations, and by the time Rebekkah Taber finished speaking, Camille knew more about Kwanzaa than she ever had before. To say she was impressed was putting it mildly.

"And Evan, for the record, not every black person celebrates Kwanzaa, which is a cultural holiday not a religious holiday like Christmas. Just like not every Jewish person celebrates Hanukkah." Camille was trying hard to keep her laughter at bay, as she glanced over at Gideon and saw the same strained expression on his face, trying to hold back his laughter.

"In fact, when was the last time *you* went to Temple?" Rebekkah asked pointedly.

When Evan turned five shades of red and proceeded to profusely apologize to Camille if he'd offended her, the ice had truly been broken and Camille relaxed, at ease with his family and able to enjoy the remainder of the evening after Gideon's mother had put a classy smackdown on cousin Evan.

As the evening came to a close, Camille was truly sorry to see it end. When it was time to go, his parents followed them to the door. After Gideon had hugged both his parents, Rebekkah turned to Camille and surprised her when she leaned down to give her a short, tight hug.

"Thank you for what you did during dinner," she said, smiling at the taller woman.

"Oh, that?" she waved a dismissive hand. "Don't take what he said personally, sweetheart. Whenever Evan drinks a little wine, the man gets a severe case of Foot in Mouth disease," she said, and Camille laughed along with her. "And besides, I have always found it preferable to focus on the similarities in cultures rather than the differences."

At that, Gideon brought his arm around Camille's waist. She glanced up at him and exchanged a secret smile. He brought his head down to hers and gave her a soft kiss, breaking it when his mother coughed.

"Okay, you two, looks like you're ready to be alone," Rebekkah said, her mouth twitching. "Now, be careful out there…it's getting cold outside," she said, surprising Camille further when she fastened the buttons on her jacket, much as her own mother would, forgetting Camille's age. Gideon had a smile on his face and lifted one shoulder, shrugging, when Camille's startled glance met his.

She then turned to Gideon. "And as for you, make sure I see you at Temple this weekend, young man. And bring Camille with you. I want to introduce her to the rabbi. I have a feeling he'll be meeting with you two soon, anyway," she said, running a sly glance over the arm Gideon had wrapped around Camille.

Hastily, Gideon rushed Camille out the door before his mother could make any more covert demands.

After leaving his parents home, Gideon brought Camille back to his loft. Suddenly nervous around him, Camille went into her normal M.O.…chattering about any and everything except the very thing on her mind.

The two of them.

She eyed the king-size bed in his bedroom and jumped when she heard him approach her from behind after storing her bag in the closet.

He placed his hands on her shoulders, turning her to face him. "It won't bite, you know."

"What won't bite?"

He nodded his head toward the bed. "You're looking at it as though it's going to come to life any minute, when you're not looking."

She shook her head, fighting away the smile. "Sorry. I guess I was just thinking…."

He ran a finger down her face, his expression sobering. "About?"

She shrugged a shoulder. "Me. You. Us…"

He grasped her hand and led her to the bed and sat her there. He stood and hunched down near her feet.

Taking off one shoe and then the other, he rolled her socks off her feet.

"Gideon, what are you doing?" she asked, but he ignored her.

He rose and lifted her bottom to slide her slacks down her legs, along with her panties, and then motioned for her to raise her arms, quickly divesting her of her sweater before going back down to her feet.

"Gideon…" she moaned when he lifted her foot, his tongue darting out to tease her instep. An unexpected giggle erupted when he swirled a path around her foot, which quickly turned into a purr of delight when he captured it in his mouth and sucked.

"Oh, God, Gideon…what are you doing?"

"Taking care of you," he said. "Something I'd like to do for the rest of your life, if you let me." His eyes met hers, and Camille stared at him, her heart thudding against her chest.

Giving her foot one final kiss, he placed it down on the floor and stood, ridding himself of his clothing.

As he laid her down on the bed, he kissed a path slowly up her body. He took both sides of her face in his hands and peered deeply into her eyes before placing small kisses over her face, down her throat and back up.

"You're beautiful, Camille," he murmured huskily.

A shiver ran over Camille when Gideon peeled the straps from her bra down her arms.

"Inside and out," he said, before cupping a breast and bringing it into his mouth.

She'd never had a man make love to her as Gideon did. With one look…one touch, he did it for her unlike any other ever had. As he kissed her breasts, lapping and tugging on them, she felt his body shift before centering himself between her, the tip of his shaft poised at her entry.

She tugged on his head to draw him away from her breasts. As much as she loved the way he kissed her, she wanted... needed to look in his eyes as he made love to her this time.

The look in his eyes made her gasp. Raw, open emotion blazed in them, so much emotion she closed her eyes against the sight, afraid to believe what she saw.

"No...open your eyes. Look at me," he demanded, his voice gruff.

He lifted her thighs and pushed her legs up until they were planted near her waist. This time it was he who shut his eyes as he slowly pressed deep inside her body.

Once fully seated, they released moaning sighs before he slowly moved his hips.

The easy glide of his shaft stroking deep into her core soon gave way to an increase in tempo, becoming short, slick and lethal until Camille cried out, "Yes, yes...oh. God, Gideon... oh, God, oh, God," her cries blending into one long cry of passion.

He spread her legs impossibly further apart as he dug into her body, grinding his groin against her clit until Camille was mindless with pleasure.

"Gideon!" she screamed, feeling the orgasm begin to unfurl deep inside her body.

He released her legs and grasped her wrists, bringing them above her head, and paused.

Her eyes flew open, a cry on her lips, as she tried to get closer to him, tried to make him move.

"Why did you stop?" she panted, her chest heaving.

"Tell me how you feel about me, Camille," he demanded, the ends of his nostrils flaring, sweat running down the side of his face.

"Wha-what are you—"

He leaned down, flicked her nipple with his tongue, and she whimpered.

"Tell me."

Camille glanced into his eyes, trying to read him, trying to figure out what he was demanding of her.

"Tell me, Cami…"

"Tell you what," she cried, not wanting to say what his eyes were demanding.

"Tell me you know we belong together. That what we have is special. That you love me as much as I love you."

The break in his voice and honesty in his eyes forced the admission from her.

"Yes, God, yes…I love you, Gideon!"

As soon as the words left her mouth, he claimed her mouth with his and resumed making love to her. Lifting her legs high, he stroked inside her, over and over, until she felt stars ricochet behind her tightly clenched lids.

Before her orgasm hit, she felt him grip her legs, rear away from her and, after two more plunging strokes, felt him come deep inside her body, bathing her womb with his seed.

"Wake up, sleepyhead. It's Christmas."

Camille came awake with a start and then smiled drowsily when she felt Gideon slide between her legs, nuzzling the side of her neck with his nose.

"Hmm," she moaned in delight, wrapping her arms around his neck when she felt his mouth, warm and wet, touch her breast, lapping at the spiking nipple. She stretched languidly.

Coming fully awake, she remembered their last lovemaking. "Gideon…"

"Yes?" he mumbled around her breast.

"Baby…when we made love last night, that last time, you, uh, didn't use a condom."

"And?"

"And, well, I'm not on the Pill."

"And?"

She grabbed his hair from the back and yanked hard, forcing him to look into her eyes.

"Hey, that hurt," he said, frowning down at her.

"Sorry. But you weren't paying attention. I'm not on the Pill and we didn't use protection," she said again, worrying her lip with her teeth.

"I told you to stop doing that."

Instantly, she released her lip.

"So, what's the problem?" he asked, still frowning.

"The problem is…we could be, you know…pregnant."

"And that would be bad, why?" he asked, scrunching his brows as though confused.

"I'm serious, Gideon."

He laughed and gave her another swift kiss before bounding from the bed. "You worry too much. If we are, well let's see… it's December, so that means this time next year we'll just be giving my mother an early Hanukkah gift," he said, giving her a swift kiss on her gaping mouth.

"Glad you can be so flippant about it!"

"On that thought, I have a surprise for you."

Camille rotated her body until she was lying on her side and propped her chin in the palm of her hand. Although he had completely ignored what she was trying to say, she still appreciated the view of his tight muscled cheeks flexing with each step he took.

He knelt down once he reached the far corner of the bedroom, and Camille's mouth formed a perfect *O* in surprise when she noticed what was set up there.

A small tree, no more than three feet tall, was festively

decorated. Although unlit, the little tree sparkled with the myriad of bright ornaments that adorned it.

A broad smile began to lift the corners of her lips, "Gideon...you got me a tree!" she said, clapping her hands together, sitting up in bed.

"That's not all I got you," he said, laughing. He walked back to the bed, and her eyes went to the small, white box he held in his hand.

Her heart began to beat faster. "Gideon?" she asked, instinctively knowing what was in the little box before he opened it.

He smiled, yet Camille sensed his nervousness as he sat on the bed, drawing both of her hands within his.

"We've only known each other a few months..." she said in denial of what lay inside the box he held clutched in his hands.

He lifted the lid and withdrew the ring. Taking her left hand in his, he slid the ring onto her finger.

The morning light hit it at an angle that made the diamond sparkle brightly.

"It's beautiful," she breathed. She tore her eyes away from the dazzling ring. "Can this be real, Gideon? The way we feel? It's happened so fast..." she said, swallowing down the tears clogging her throat.

"It can and it is." He took both of her hands in his, brought them to his mouth and kissed the finger that wore his ring.

"But, you know what?" he asked, pulling her back down on the bed, bringing her body on top of his.

"No, what?" she asked past the tears and big silly grin she felt, trying to break free.

He lifted her and eased her down over his straining shaft, continuing to speak as though he hadn't just completely turned her world upside down.

"Neither one of us was looking for love. We were both

focused on our careers and had grown used to being alone." As he spoke, he shifted her, and they began the familiar, achingly sweet glide of their bodies against the other. "So, when love found us, we knew it immediately."

"Just like that?" she asked, trying hard to continue to talk, the task becoming near impossible.

"Just like that." He tugged on her until she fell forward, capturing her mouth as he made love to her. "I don't want to go it alone anymore," he said, emotion roughening his voice. "I've found what has been missing in my life. You. Please say yes…please tell me you feel the same way, that you'll marry me."

Camille had worked hard for her success, had been so focused on work she'd left no room in her life for love. When love came she'd been afraid and had almost thrown it away.

Tears fell from her eyes as he moved inside her.

In his face…his eyes, she saw the love he had for her was real. She also read the challenge he had thrown out with the proposal, a challenge that she believe in them, that what they had was real. Or would she give in to fear and doubt?

She made her decision.

"I don't want to go it alone anymore, either," she said before completely surrendering to him, mind, body and soul.

* * * * *

REQUEST YOUR FREE BOOKS!

2 FREE NOVELS
PLUS 2 FREE GIFTS!

KIMANI ™
ROMANCE

Love's ultimate destination!